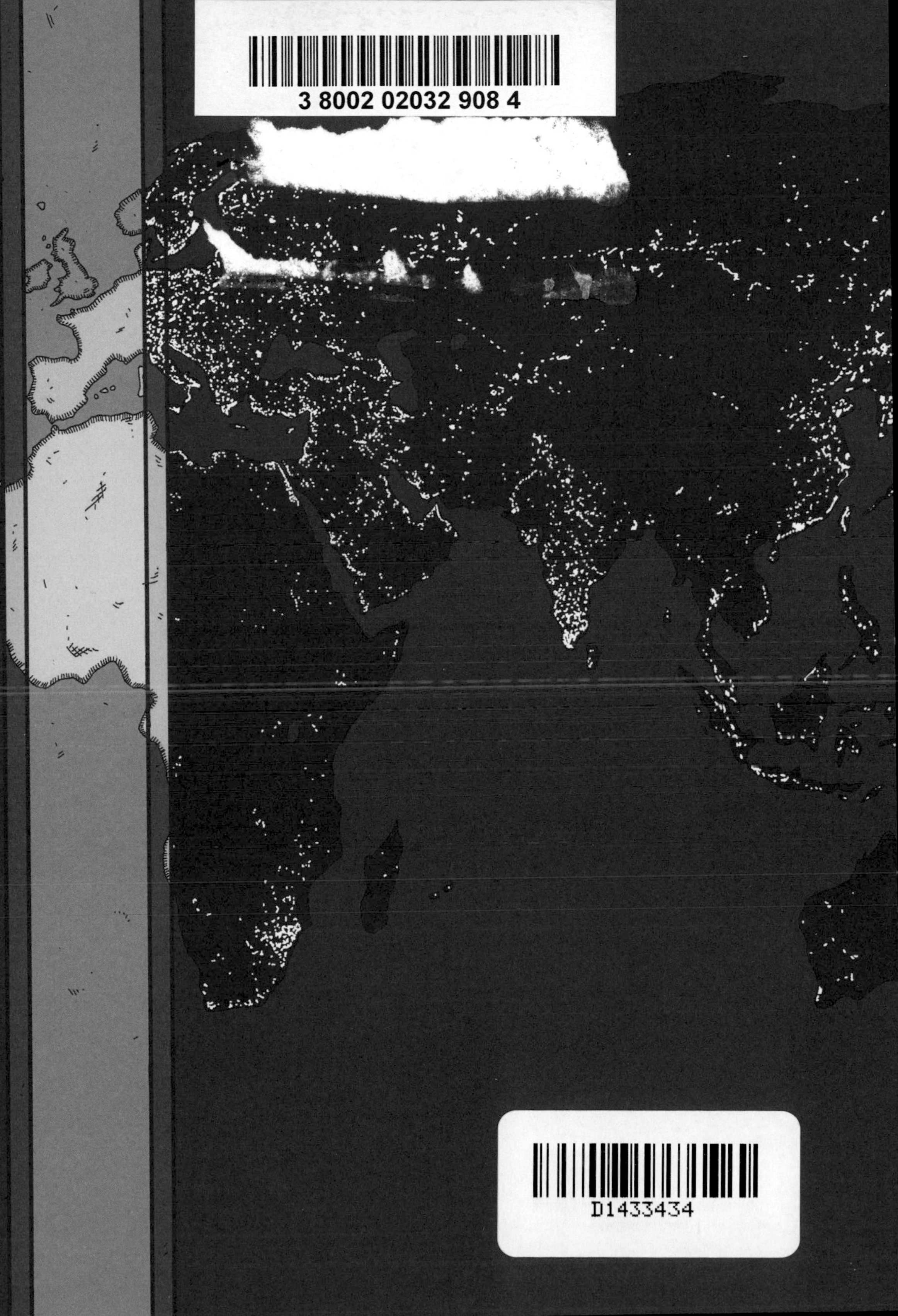

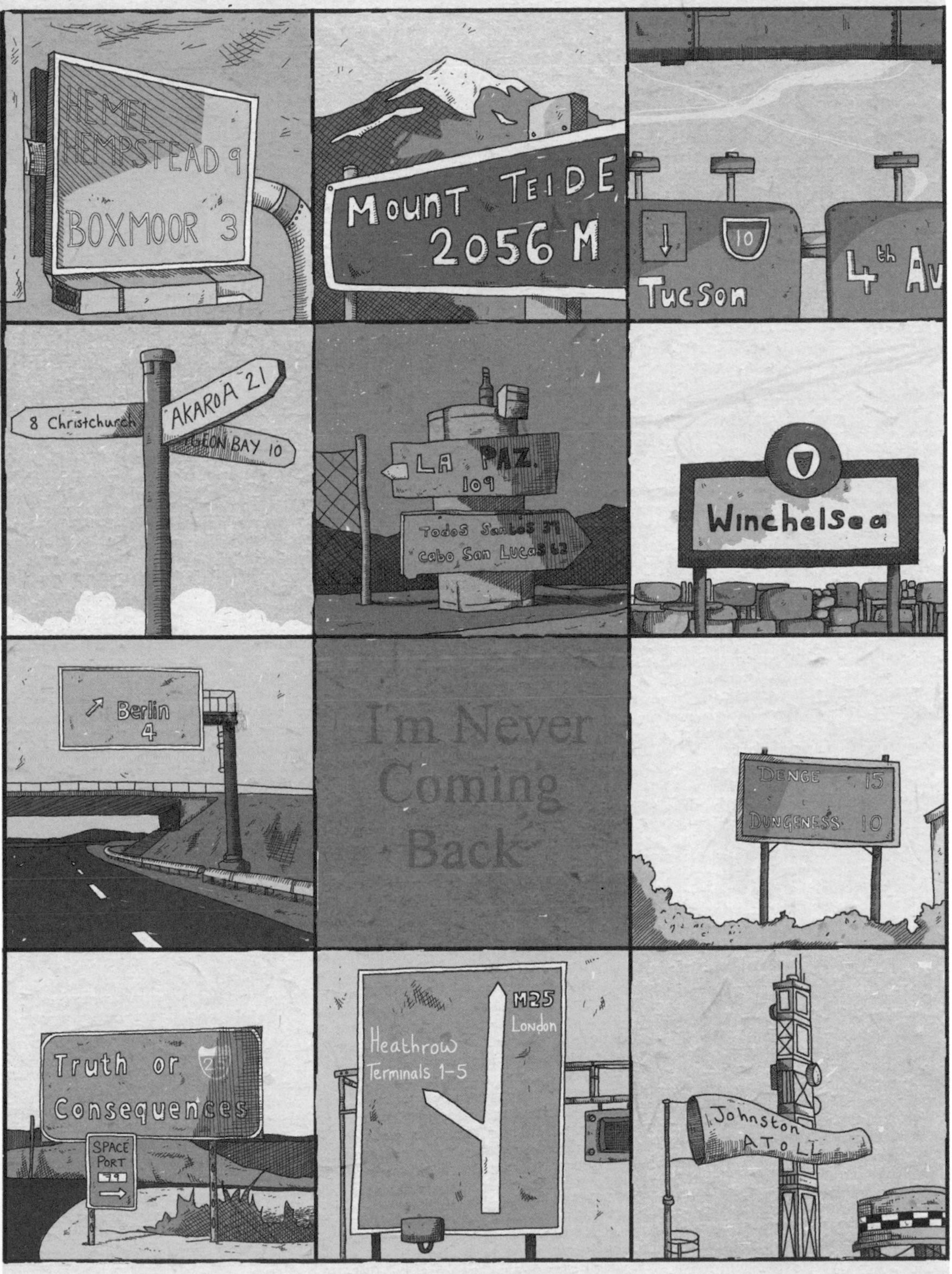
HEMEL HEMPSTEAD 9
BOXMOOR 3
MOUNT TEIDE
2056 M
Tucson
10
4th Av
8 Christchurch
AKAROA 21
GEON BAY 10
LA PAZ.
109
Todos Santos 37
Cabo San Lucas 62
Winchelsea
Berlin
4
I'm Never Coming Back
DENGE 15
DUNGENESS 10
Truth or Consequences
25
SPACE PORT
M25
London
Heathrow
Terminals 1-5
Johnston
ATOLL

I'm Never Coming Back

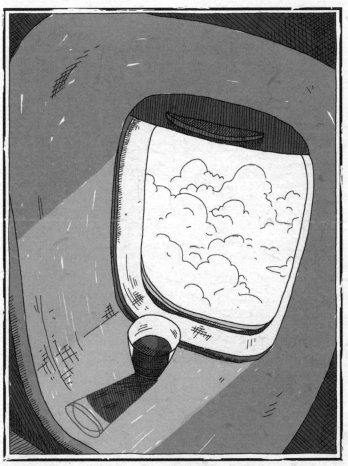

JULIAN HANSHAW

Jonathan Cape
London

AUTHOR'S NOTE

The short stories collected in this book were
drawn between 2008 and 2010.

It started with 'Sand Dunes and Sonic Booms' after a visit
to the 'Sound Mirrors' just along the coast from where I live.
After it won an award I began to slowly pull together an idea
of a collection of short stories that were interconnected.

As with my first book *The Art Of Pho* I enjoy depicting places
that I have travelled to and this collection is no different.
From Tucson to Berlin these landscapes offered a backdrop
for events that occured during that two-year period.

It all happened in some way and at some time. And *Test
Match Special* is still the greatest use of radio. Fact.

Julian Hanshaw. East Sussex. January 2012.

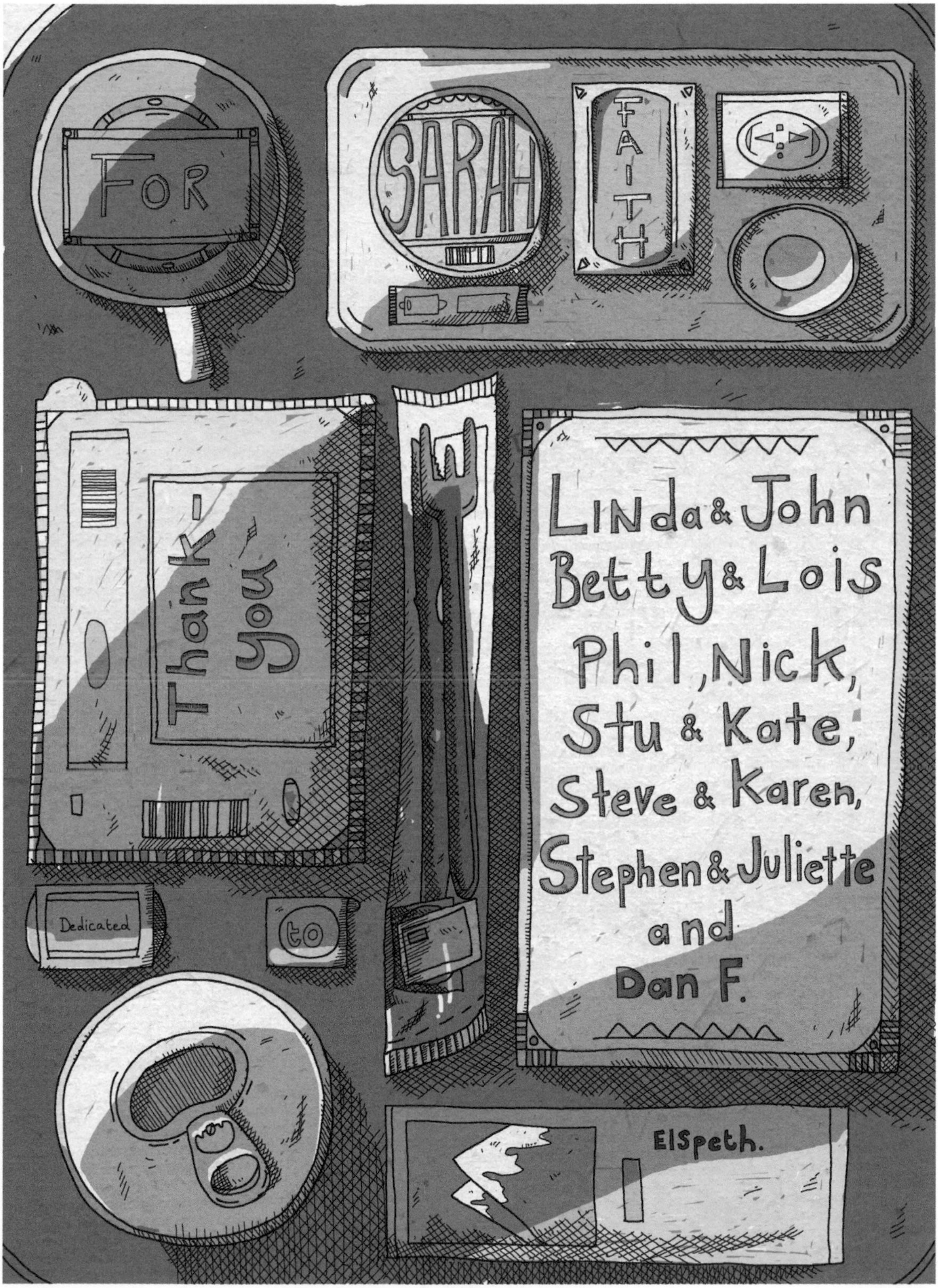
For
SARAH
FAITH
Thank-you
Linda & John
Betty & Lois
Phil, Nick,
Stu & Kate,
Steve & Karen,
Stephen & Juliette
and
Dan F.
Dedicated
to
Elspeth.

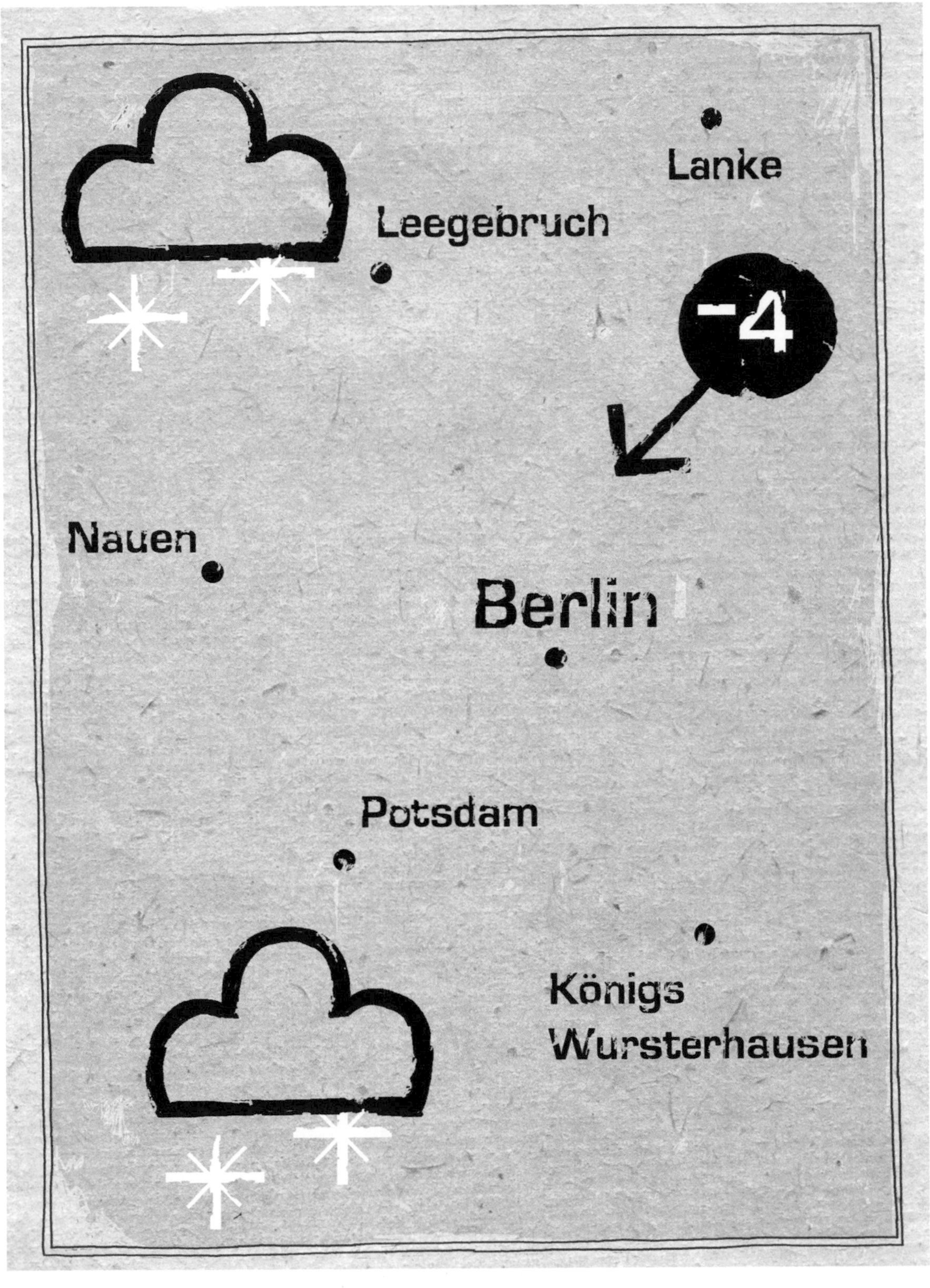
Lanke
Leegebruch
-4
Nauen
Berlin
Potsdam
Königs
Wursterhausen

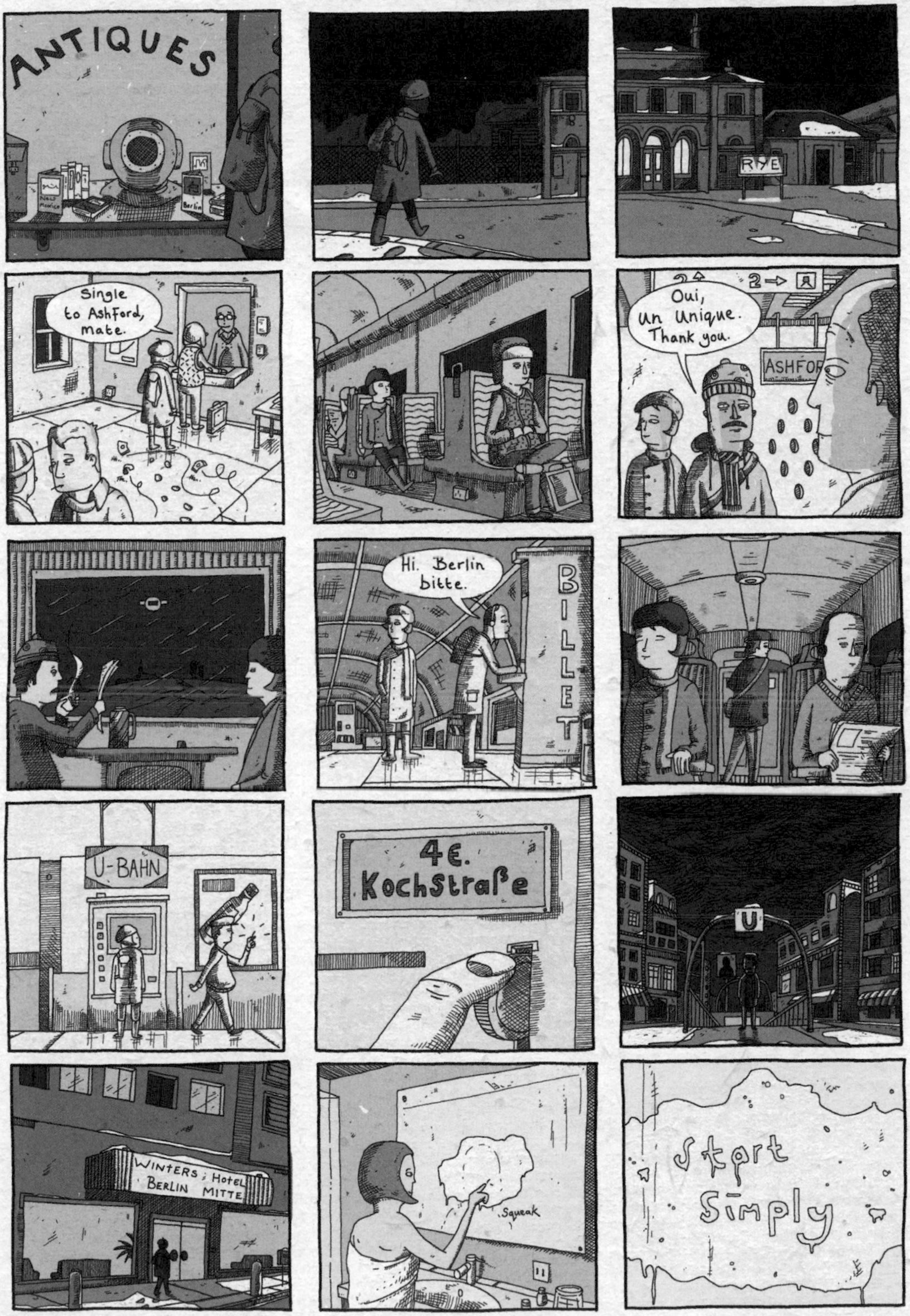
ANTIQUES
Berlin
RYE
Single to AshFord, mate.
Oui, un Unique. Thank you.
ASHFOR
Hi. Berlin bitte.
BILLET
U-BAHN
4€. Kochstraße
U
WINTERS Hotel
BERLIN MITTE
Squeak
Start Simply

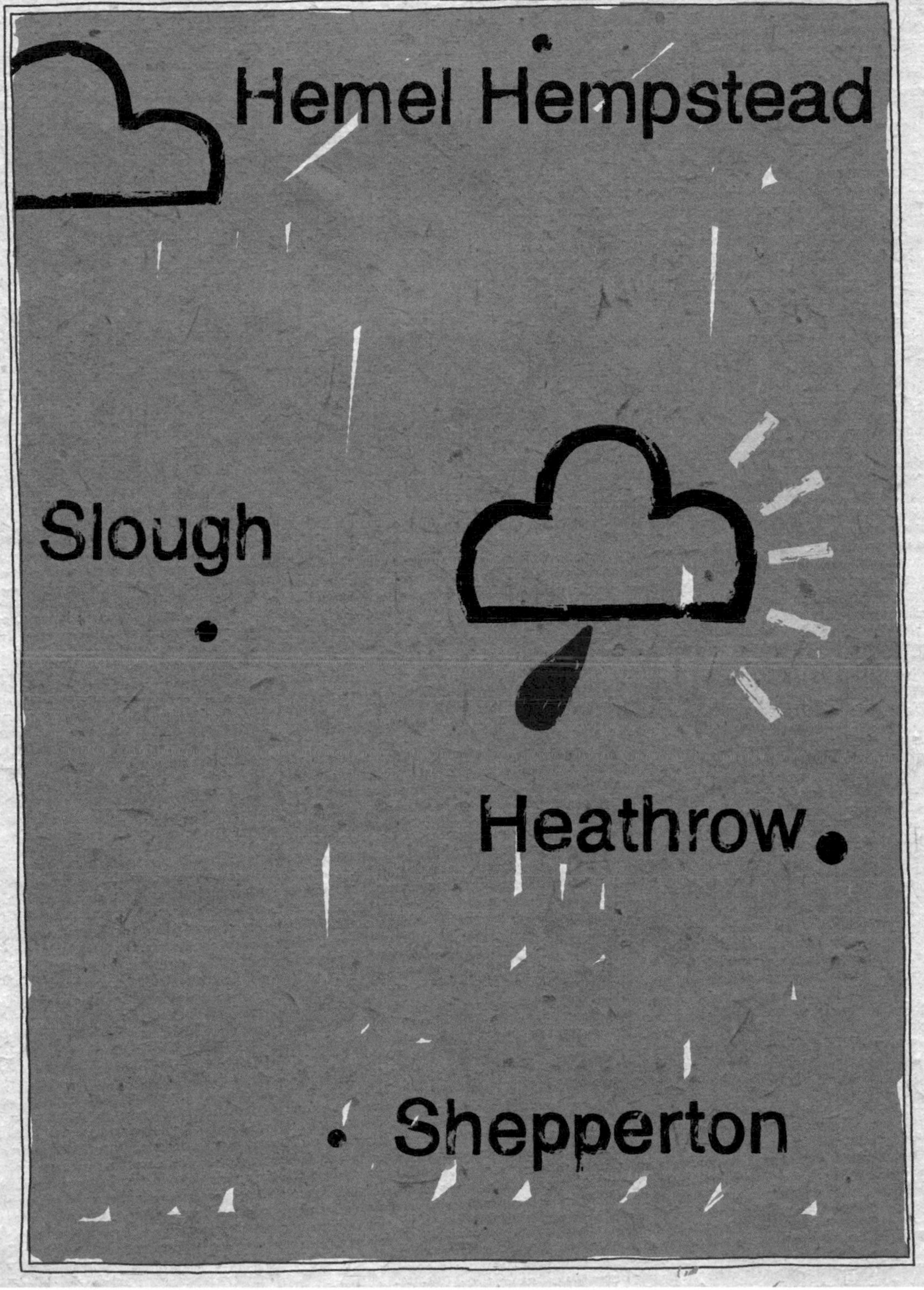
Hemel Hempstead
Slough
Heathrow
Shepperton

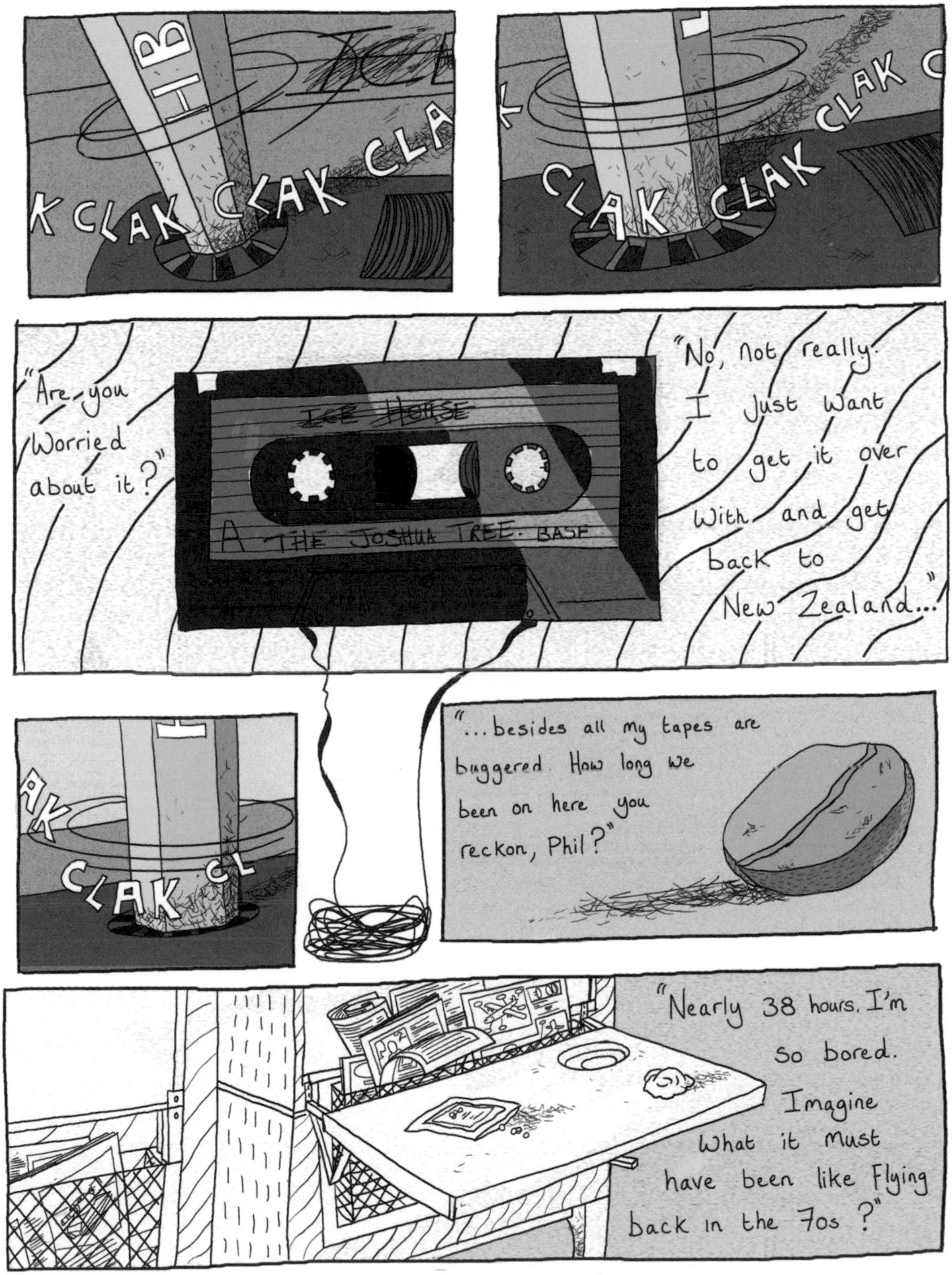
K CLAK CLAK CLA
K
CLAK CLAK CLAK C
"Are you worried about it?"
ICE HOUSE
A THE JOSHUA TREE. BASF
"No, not really. I just want to get it over with and get back to New Zealand..."
AK
CLAK CL
"...besides all my tapes are buggered. How long we been on here you reckon, Phil?"
"Nearly 38 hours. I'm so bored. Imagine what it must have been like flying back in the 70s?"

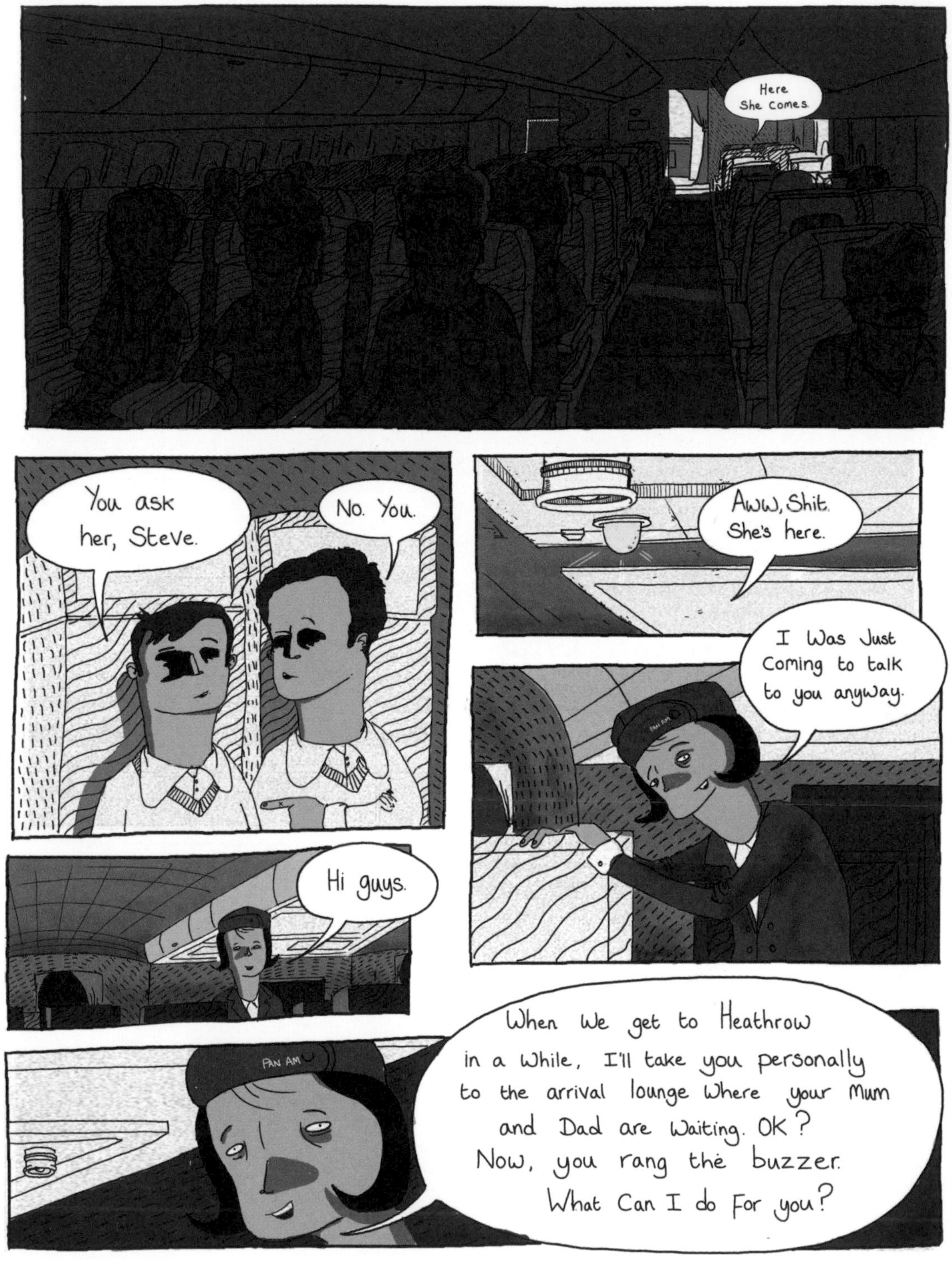
Here She Comes.
You ask her, Steve.
No. You.
Aww, Shit. She's here.
I Was Just Coming to talk to you anyway.
Hi guys.
PAN AM
When We get to Heathrow in a While, I'll take you personally to the arrival lounge Where your Mum and Dad are Waiting. OK? Now, you rang the buzzer. What Can I do For you?

Ahem. Can we get two beers please?
Heineken if you've got it.
click
Sorry boys. I'll see you when we land.
Strewth I'd root her.
Definibely.
Bloody hell Phil!
As your older brother I have to say you're a horny bugger.
D.E.F.I.N.I.T.E.L.Y
So, England doesn't look too different.
Well. From up here anyway.
A dull toothache grey. Like it was being lit by a 40 watt bulb.

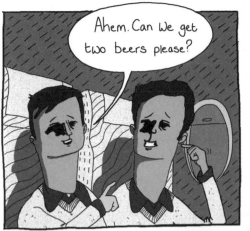

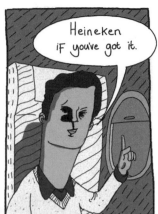

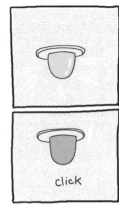

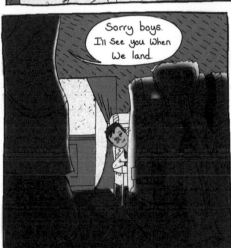

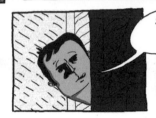

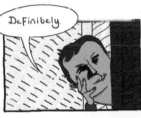

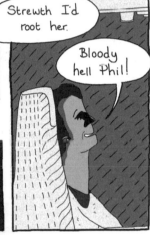

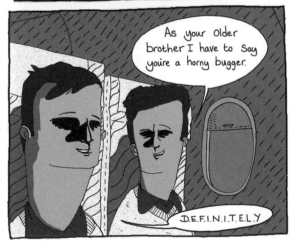

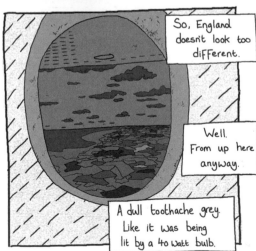

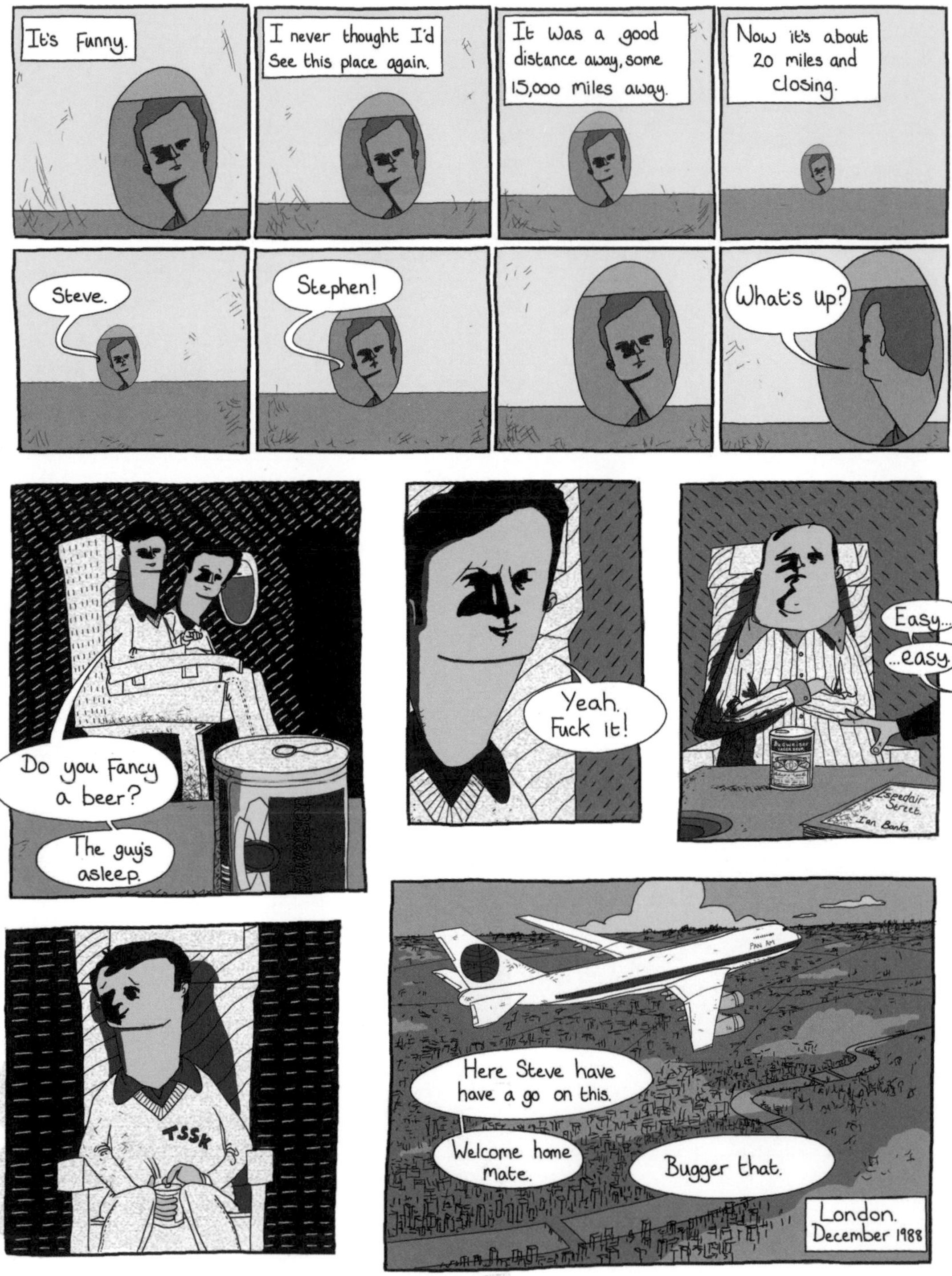
It's Funny.
I never thought I'd See this place again.
It Was a good distance away, some 15,000 miles away.
Now it's about 20 miles and closing.
Steve.
Stephen!
What's up?
Do you Fancy a beer?
The guy's asleep.
Yeah. Fuck it!
Easy...
...easy.
Espedair Street.
Iain Banks
TSSK
PAN AM
Here Steve have have a go on this.
Welcome home mate.
Bugger that.
London. December 1988

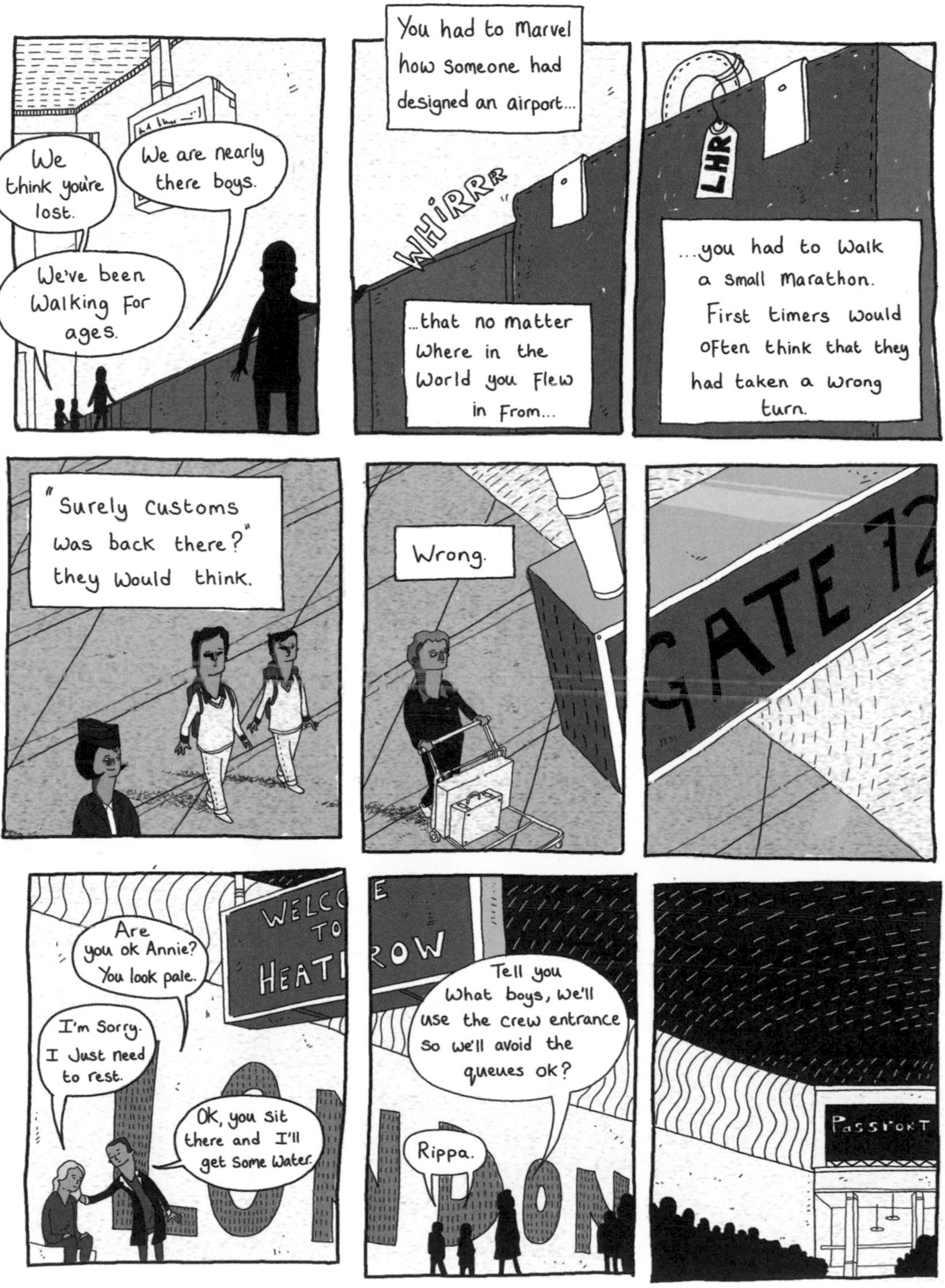
We think you're lost.
We are nearly there boys.
We've been Walking For ages.
You had to Marvel how someone had designed an airport...
WHIRRR
...that no matter Where in the World you Flew in From...
LHR
...you had to Walk a small marathon. First timers would often think that they had taken a Wrong turn.
"Surely customs was back there?" they would think.
Wrong.
GATE 72
WELCO TO HEATHROW
Are you ok Annie? You look pale.
I'm Sorry. I Just need to rest.
Ok, you sit there and I'll get some Water.
LONDON
Tell you What boys, We'll use the crew entrance so we'll avoid the queues ok?
Rippa.
PASSPORT

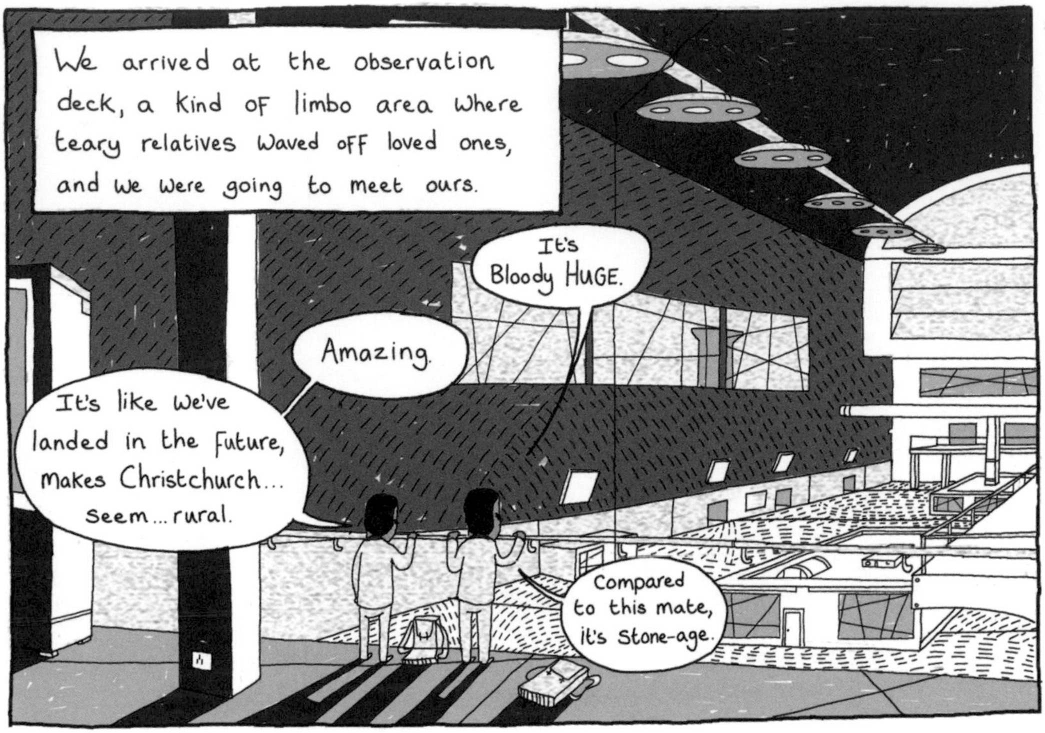
We arrived at the observation deck, a kind of limbo area where teary relatives waved off loved ones, and we were going to meet ours.
It's Bloody HUGE.
Amazing.
It's like we've landed in the future, makes Christchurch... seem... rural.
Compared to this mate, it's Stone-age.

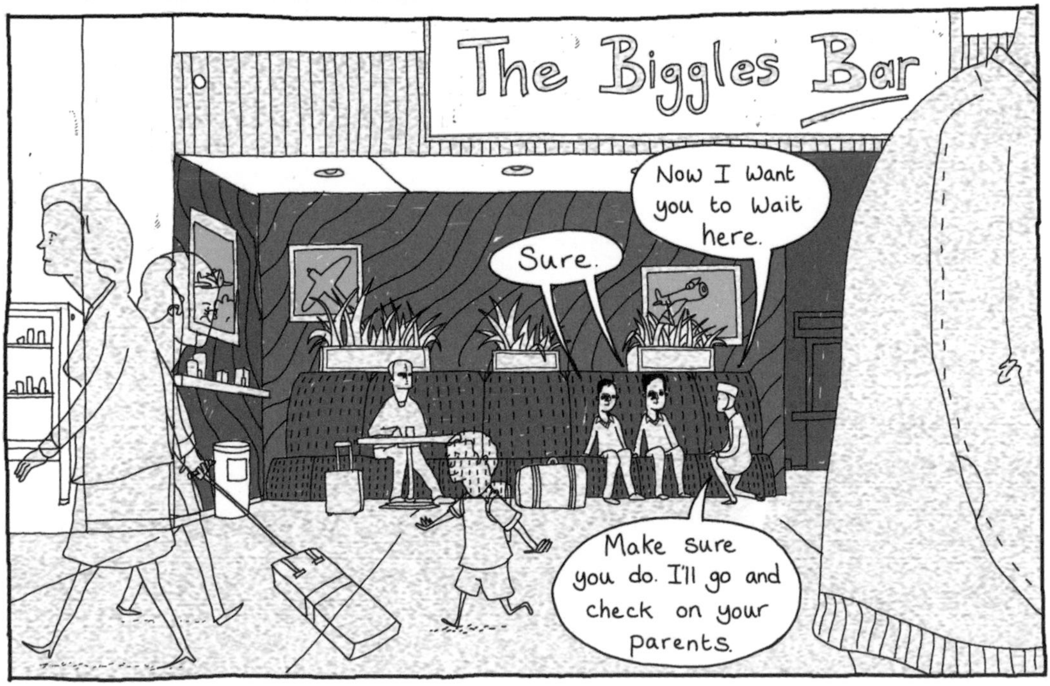
The Biggles Bar
Now I want you to wait here.
Sure.
Make sure you do. I'll go and check on your parents.

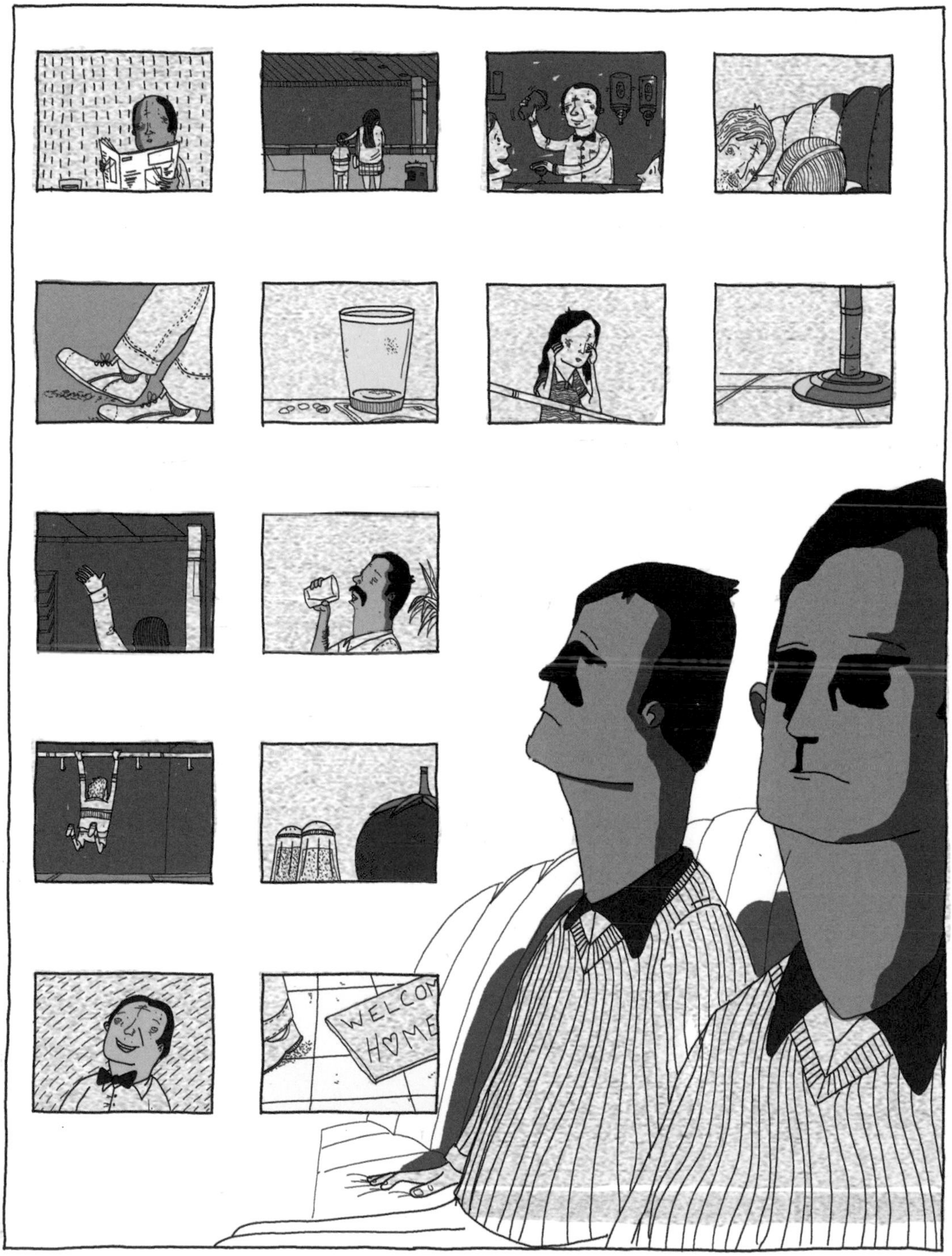
WELCOM
H♥ME

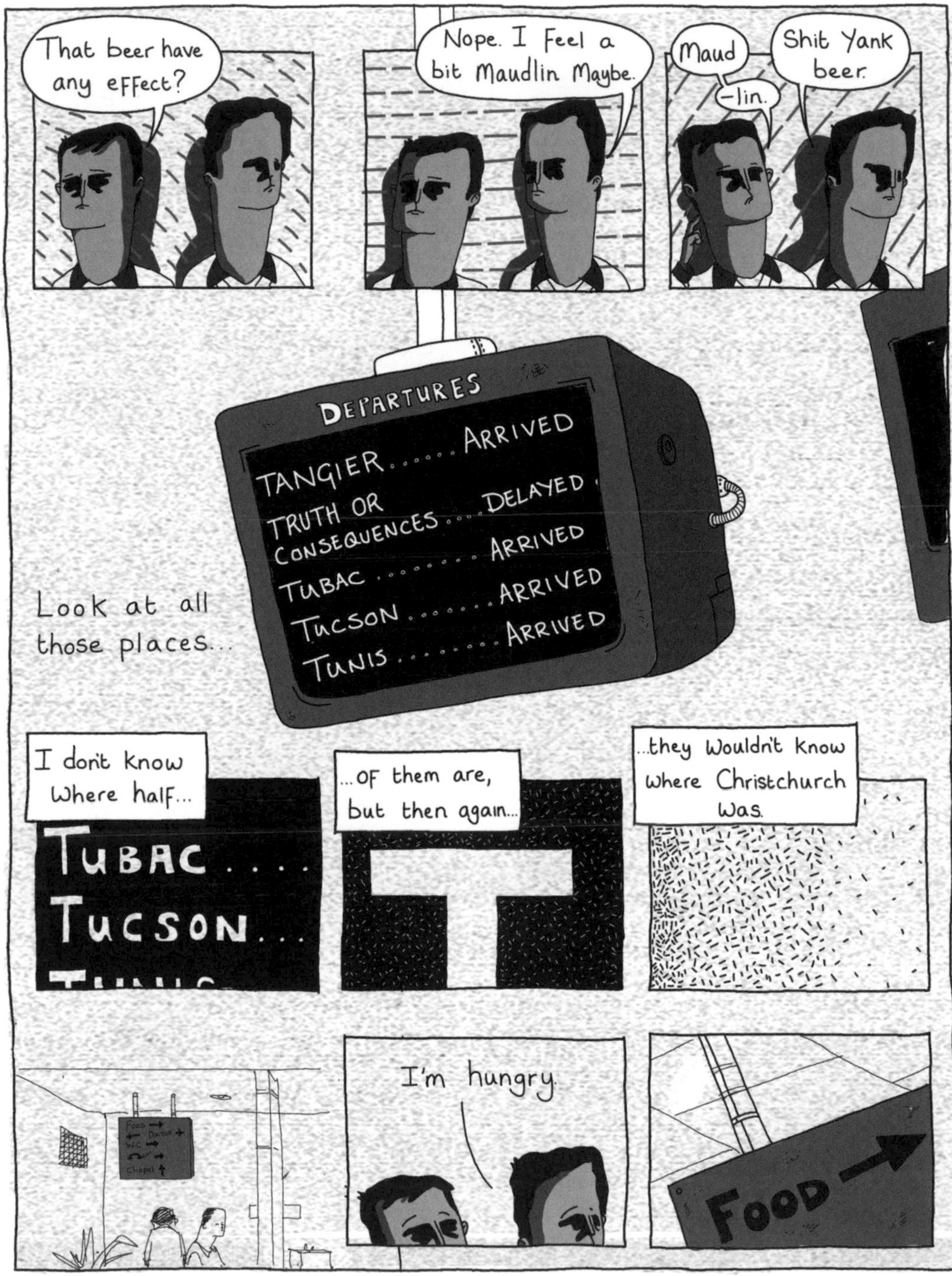

That beer have any effect?
Nope. I feel a bit Maudlin Maybe.
Maud
-lin.
Shit Yank beer.
DEPARTURES
TANGIER .... ARRIVED
TRUTH OR CONSEQUENCES ..... DELAYED
TUBAC .... ARRIVED
TUCSON .... ARRIVED
TUNIS .... ARRIVED
Look at all those places...
I don't know where half...
TUBAC ....
TUCSON ...
...of them are, but then again...
...they wouldn't know where Christchurch was.
I'm hungry.
FOOD

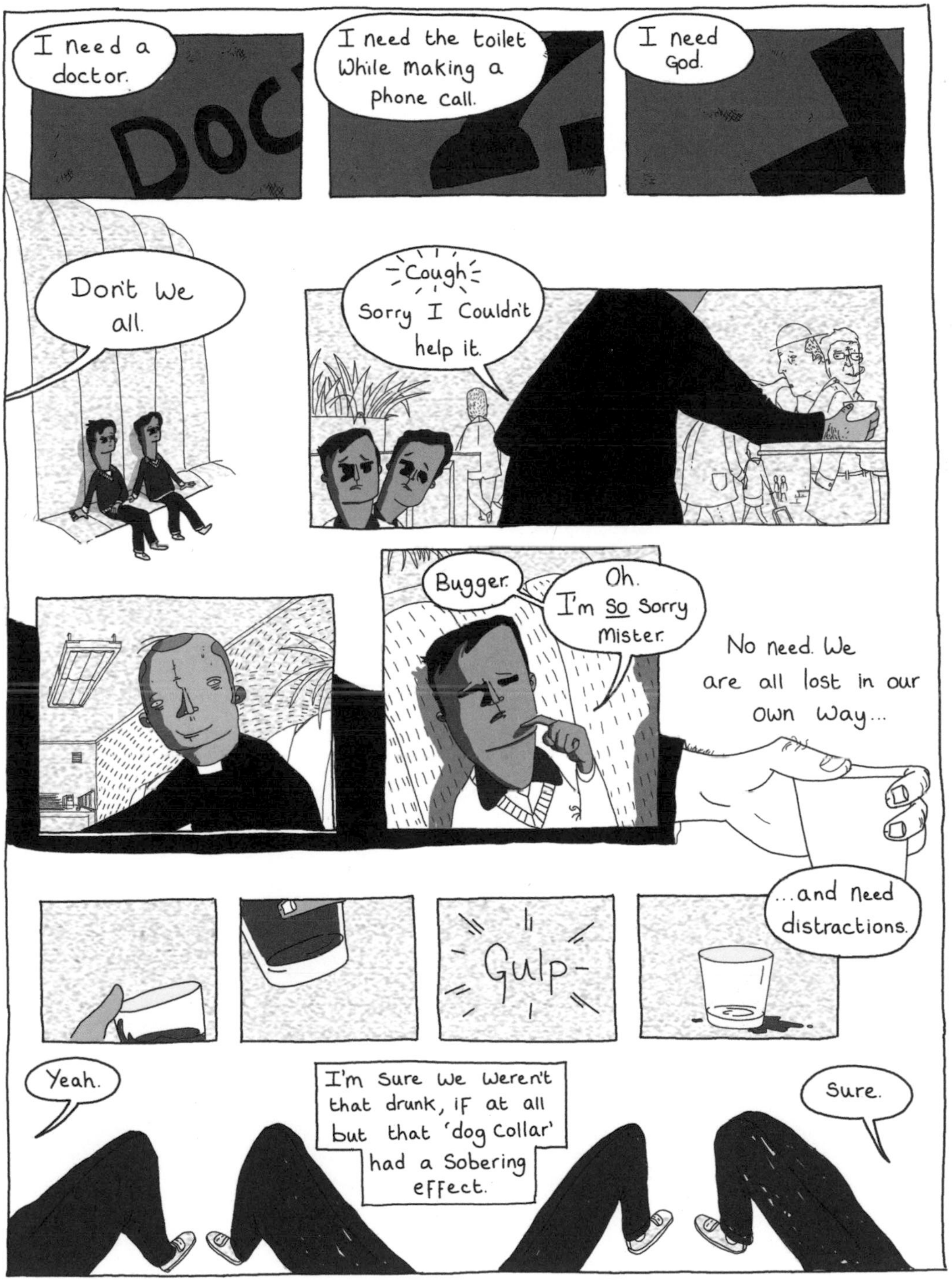
I need a doctor.
DOC
I need the toilet While making a phone call.
I need God.
Don't We all.
Cough
Sorry I Couldn't help it.
Bugger.
Oh. I'm so sorry mister.
No need. We are all lost in our own way...
...and need distractions.
Gulp
Yeah.
I'm sure We Weren't that drunk, if at all but that 'dog Collar' had a Sobering effect.
Sure.

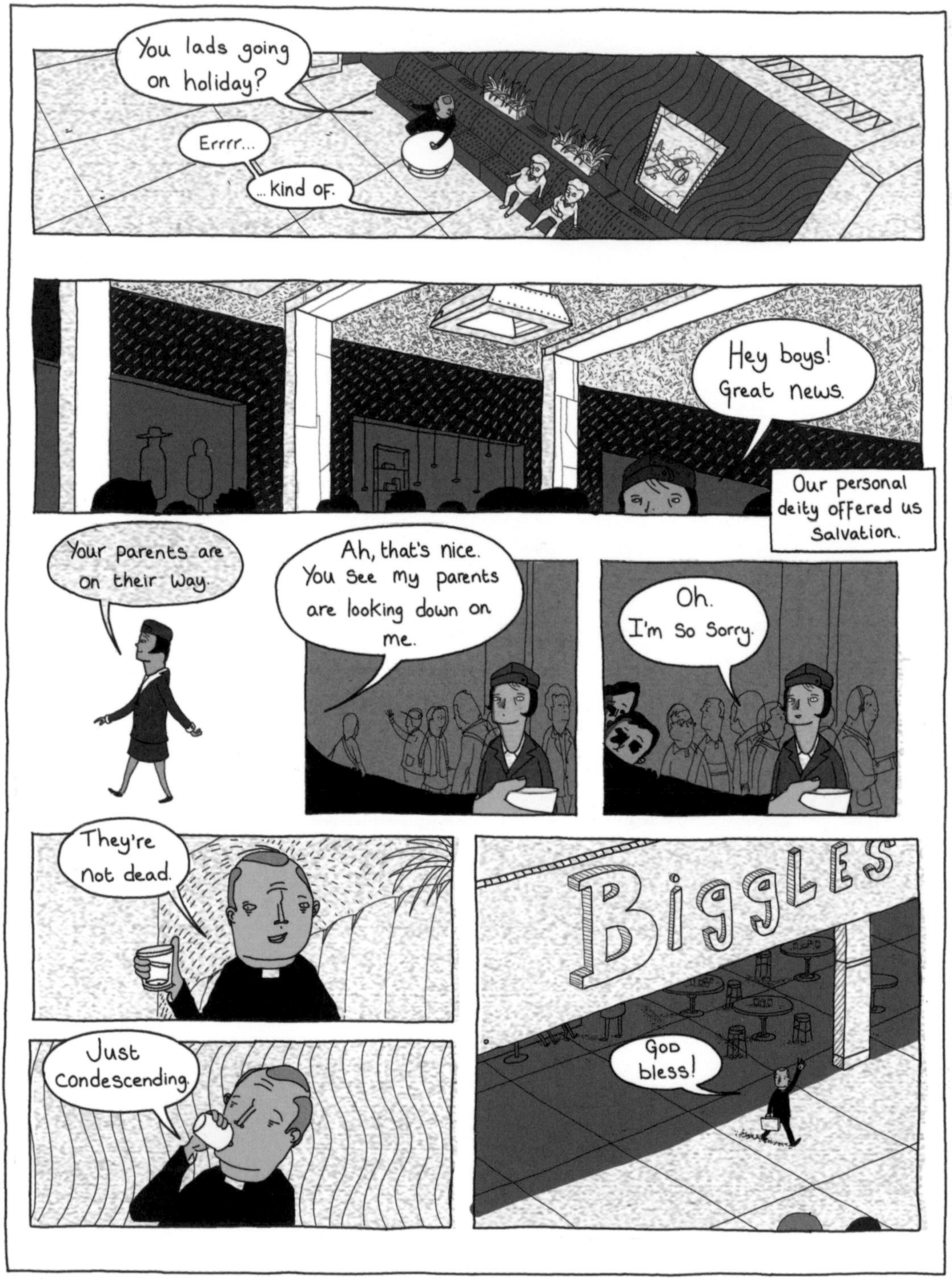
You lads going on holiday?
Errrr...
...kind of.
Hey boys! Great news.
Our personal deity offered us salvation.
Your parents are on their way.
Ah, that's nice. You see my parents are looking down on me.
Oh. I'm so sorry.
They're not dead.
Just condescending.
Biggles
God bless!

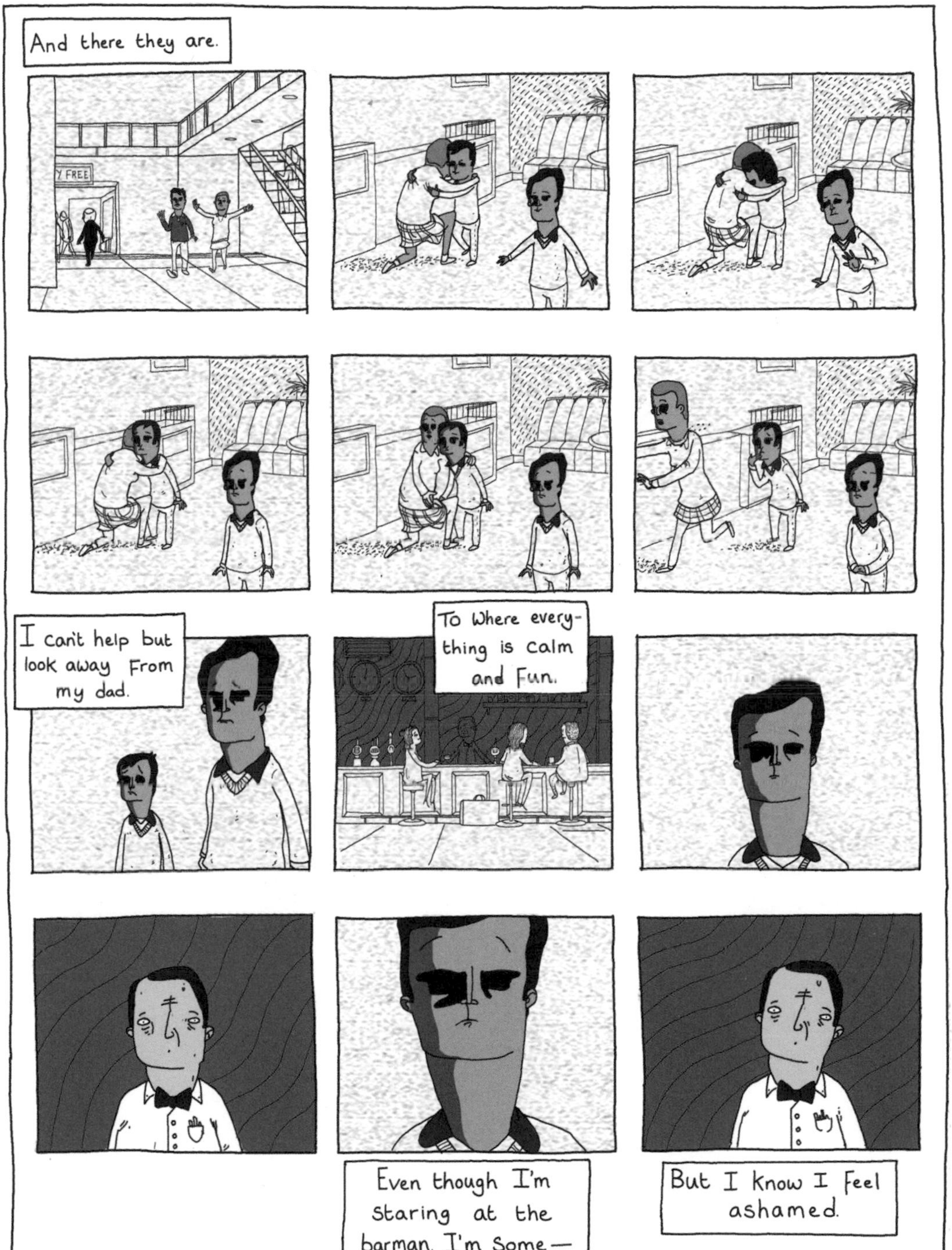
And there they are.
Y FREE
I can't help but look away From my dad.
To Where every-thing is calm and Fun.
Even though I'm staring at the barman. I'm Some—Where else.
But I know I Feel ashamed.

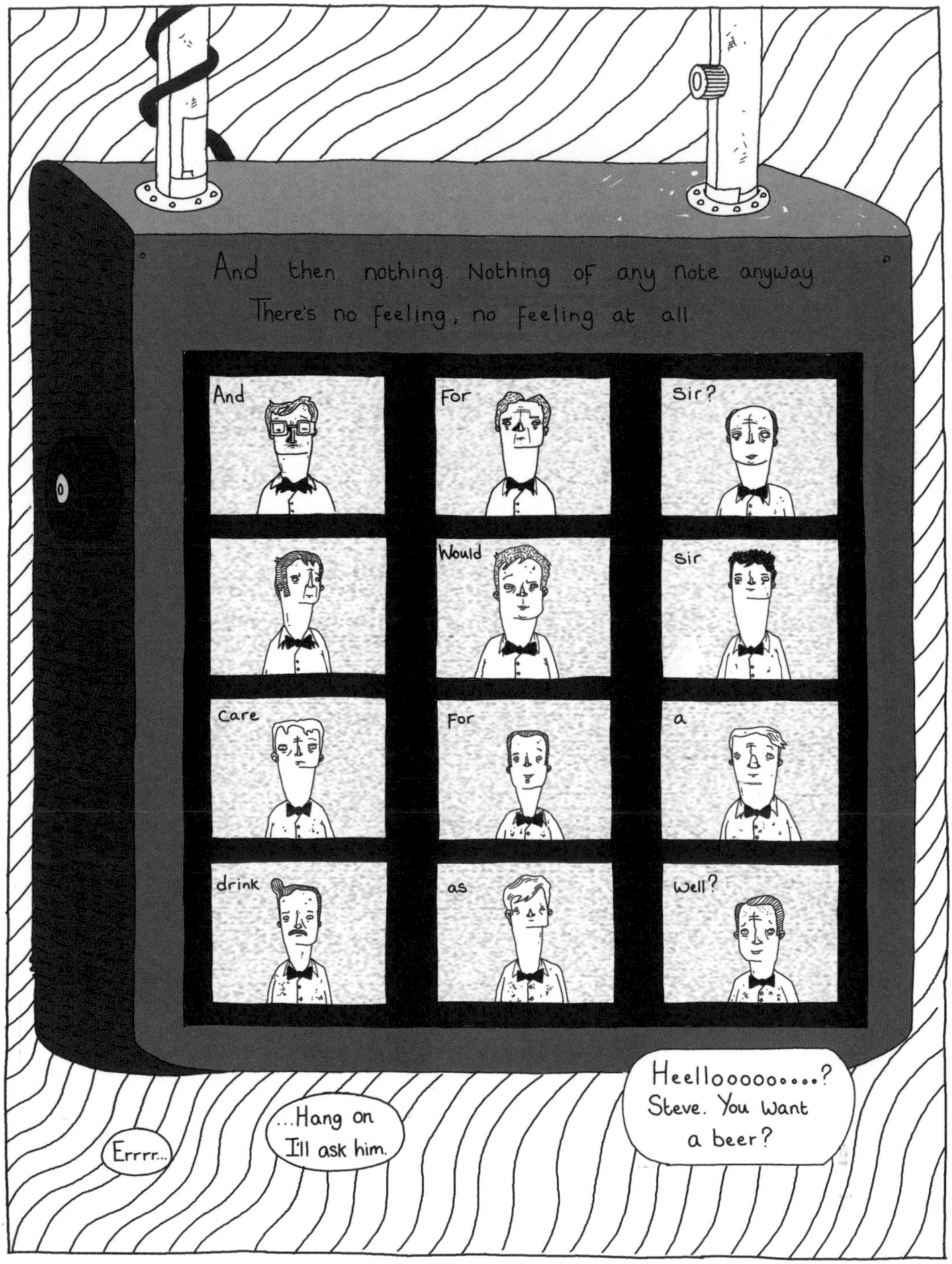

And then nothing. Nothing of any note anyway.
There's no feeling, no feeling at all.
And
For
Sir?
Would
sir
care
for
a
drink
as
well?
Errrr...
...Hang on
I'll ask him.
Heellooooooo...?
Steve. You want
a beer?

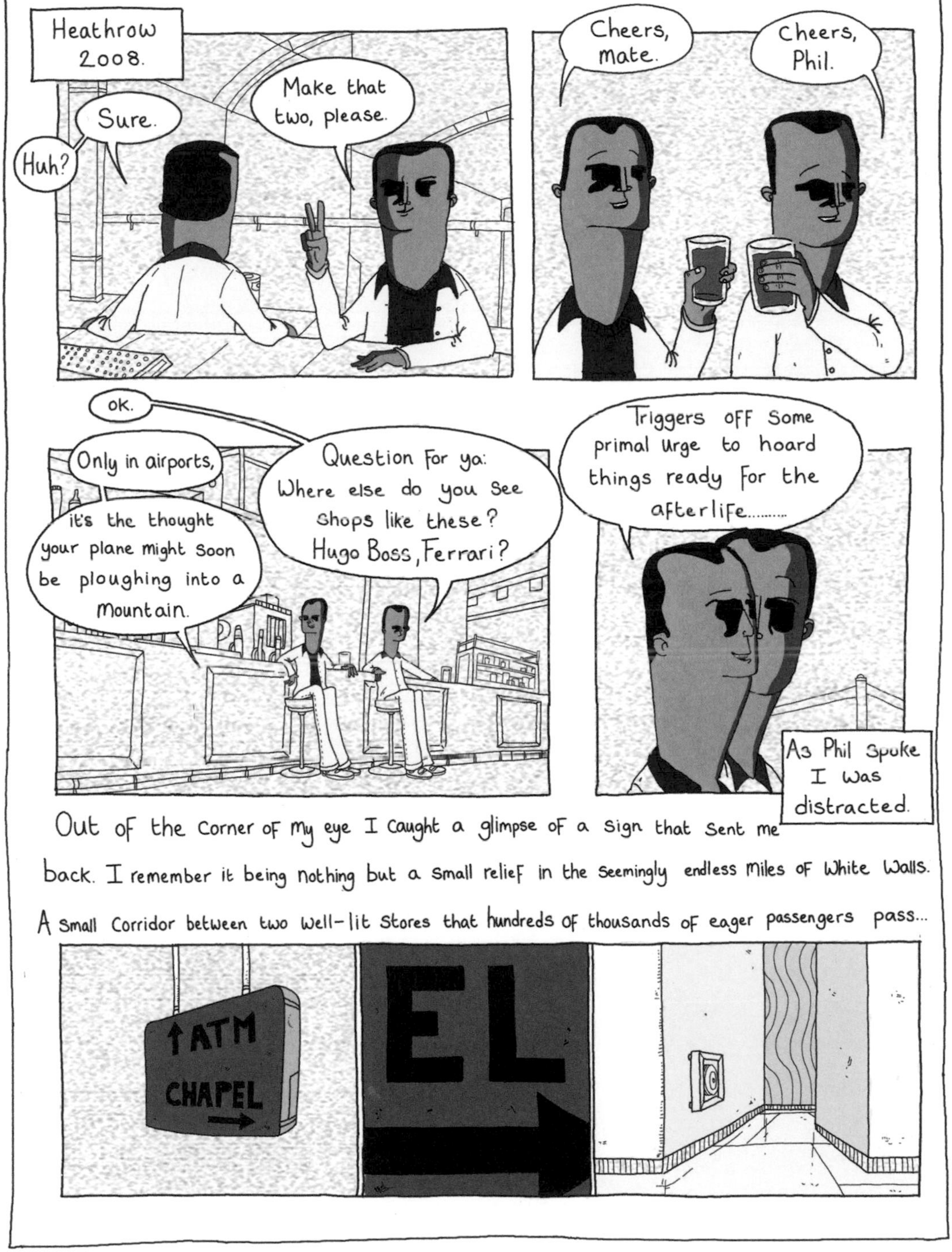
Heathrow 2008.
Make that two, please.
Huh?
Sure.
Cheers, mate.
Cheers, Phil.
Question for ya: Where else do you see shops like these? Hugo Boss, Ferrari?
ok.
Only in airports,
it's the thought your plane might soon be ploughing into a mountain.
Triggers off some primal urge to hoard things ready for the afterlife..........
As Phil spoke I was distracted.
Out of the corner of my eye I caught a glimpse of a sign that sent me back. I remember it being nothing but a small relief in the seemingly endless miles of white walls. A small corridor between two well-lit stores that hundreds of thousands of eager passengers pass...
ATM
CHAPEL
EL

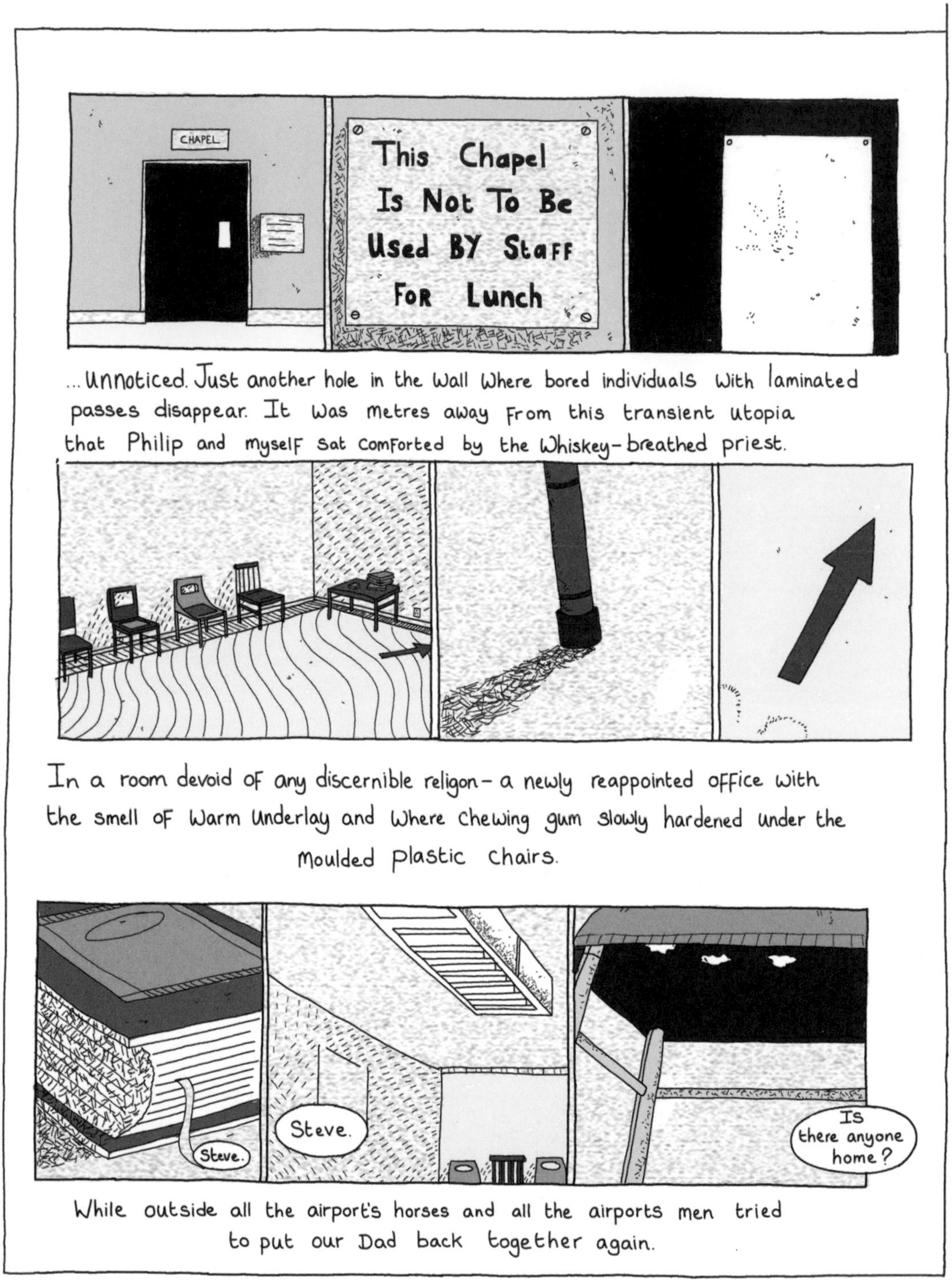
CHAPEL
This Chapel Is Not To Be Used BY Staff For Lunch
...unnoticed. Just another hole in the wall where bored individuals with laminated passes disappear. It was metres away from this transient utopia that Philip and myself sat comforted by the whiskey-breathed priest.
In a room devoid of any discernible religon – a newly reappointed office with the smell of warm underlay and where chewing gum slowly hardened under the moulded plastic chairs.
Steve.
Steve.
Is there anyone home?
While outside all the airport's horses and all the airports men tried to put our Dad back together again.

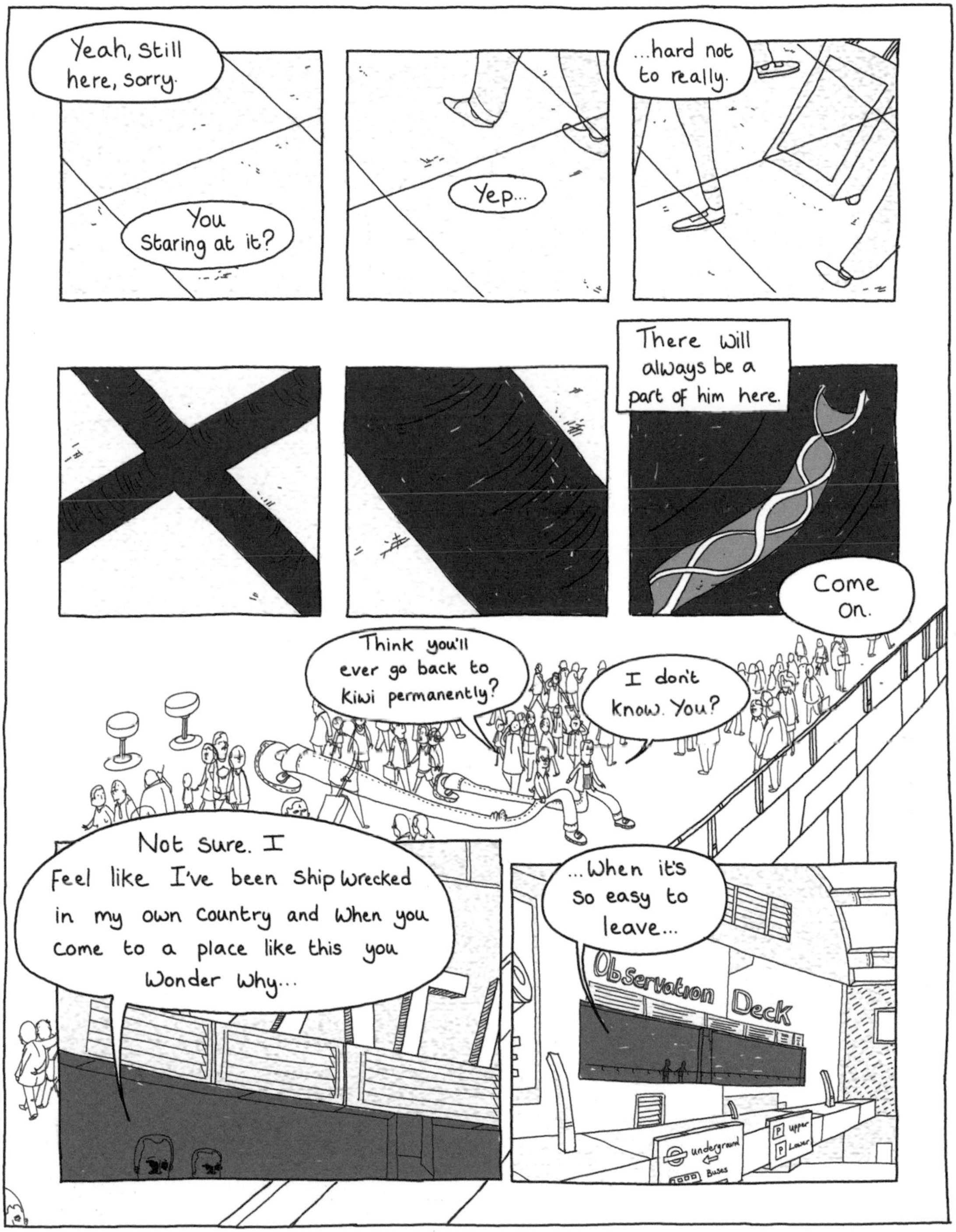
Yeah, still here, sorry.
You staring at it?
Yep...
...hard not to really.
There will always be a part of him here.
Come on.
Think you'll ever go back to Kiwi permanently?
I don't know. You?
Not sure. I feel like I've been shipwrecked in my own country and when you come to a place like this you wonder why...
...When it's so easy to leave...
Observation Deck
underground
Buses
P upper
P Lower

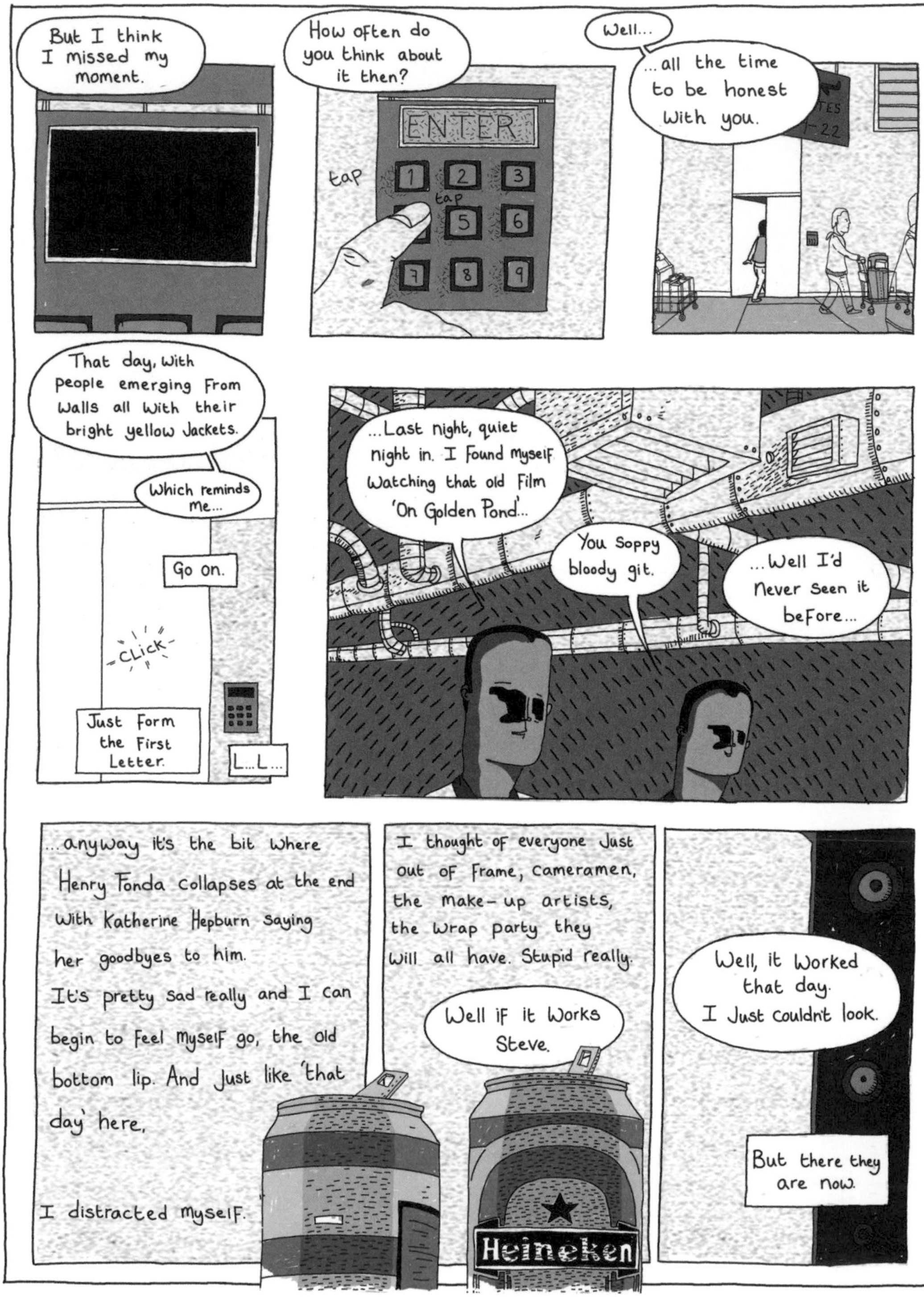
But I think I missed my moment.
How often do you think about it then?
ENTER
tap
1 2 3
tap
5 6
7 8 9
Well...
...all the time to be honest with you.
That day, with people emerging from walls all with their bright yellow jackets.
Which reminds me...
Go on.
CLICK
Just form the first letter.
L...L...
...Last night, quiet night in. I found myself watching that old film 'On Golden Pond'...
You soppy bloody git.
...Well I'd never seen it before...
...anyway it's the bit where Henry Fonda collapses at the end with Katherine Hepburn saying her goodbyes to him. It's pretty sad really and I can begin to feel myself go, the old bottom lip. And just like 'that day' here,
I distracted myself.
I thought of everyone just out of frame, cameramen, the make-up artists, the wrap party they will all have. Stupid really.
Well if it works Steve.
Heineken
Well, it worked that day. I just couldn't look.
But there they are now.

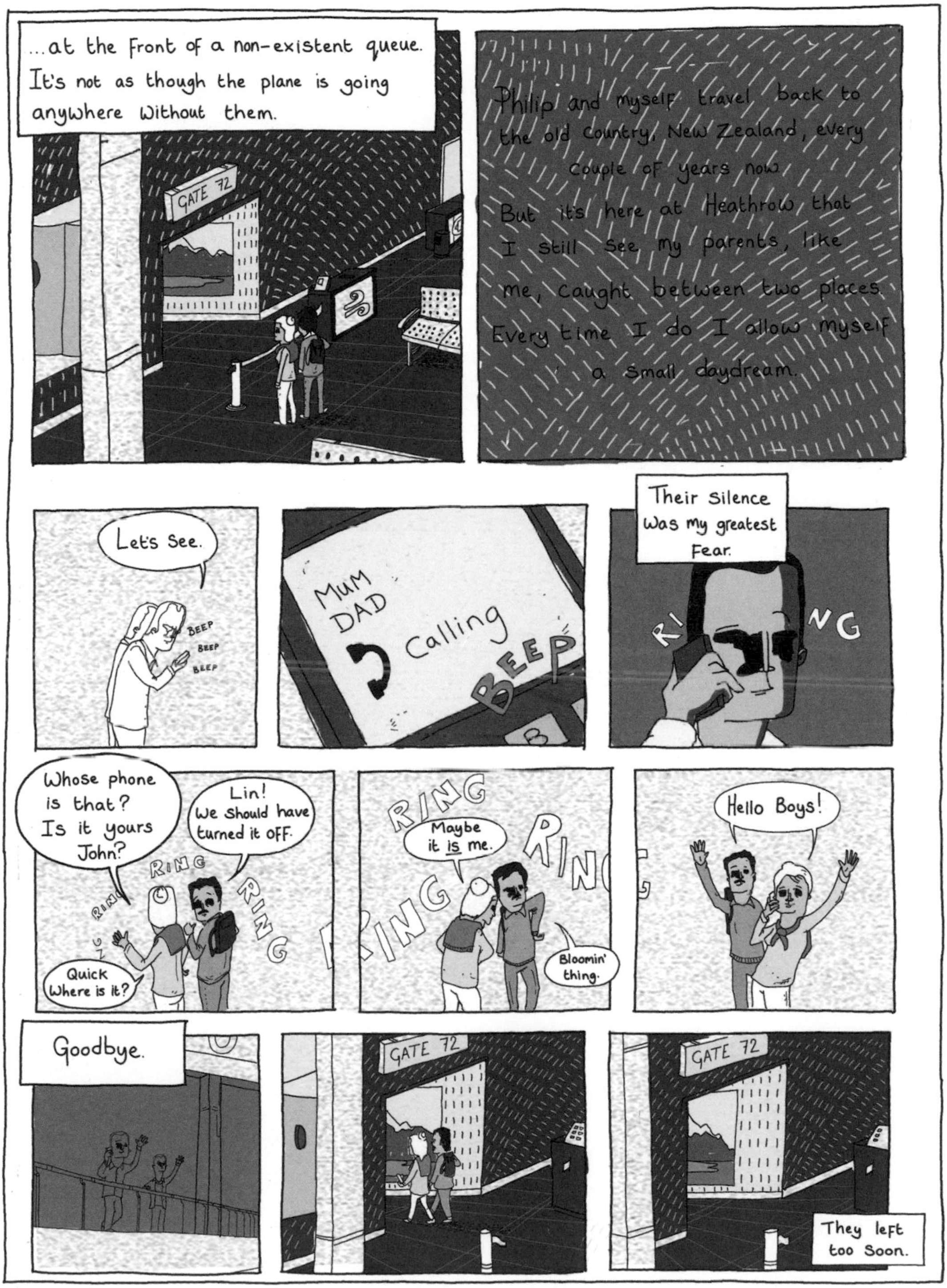

...at the front of a non-existent queue. It's not as though the plane is going anywhere without them.
GATE 72
Philip and myself travel back to the old country, New Zealand, every couple of years now.
But it's here at Heathrow that I still see my parents, like me, caught between two places.
Every time I do I allow myself a small daydream.
Let's see.
BEEP
BEEP
BEEP
MUM DAD
Calling
BEEP
Their silence was my greatest fear.
RING
Whose phone is that? Is it yours John?
Lin! We should have turned it OFF.
RING
RING
RING
Quick Where is it?
RING
Maybe it is me.
RING
RING
Bloomin' thing.
Hello Boys!
Goodbye.
GATE 72
GATE 72
They left too soon.

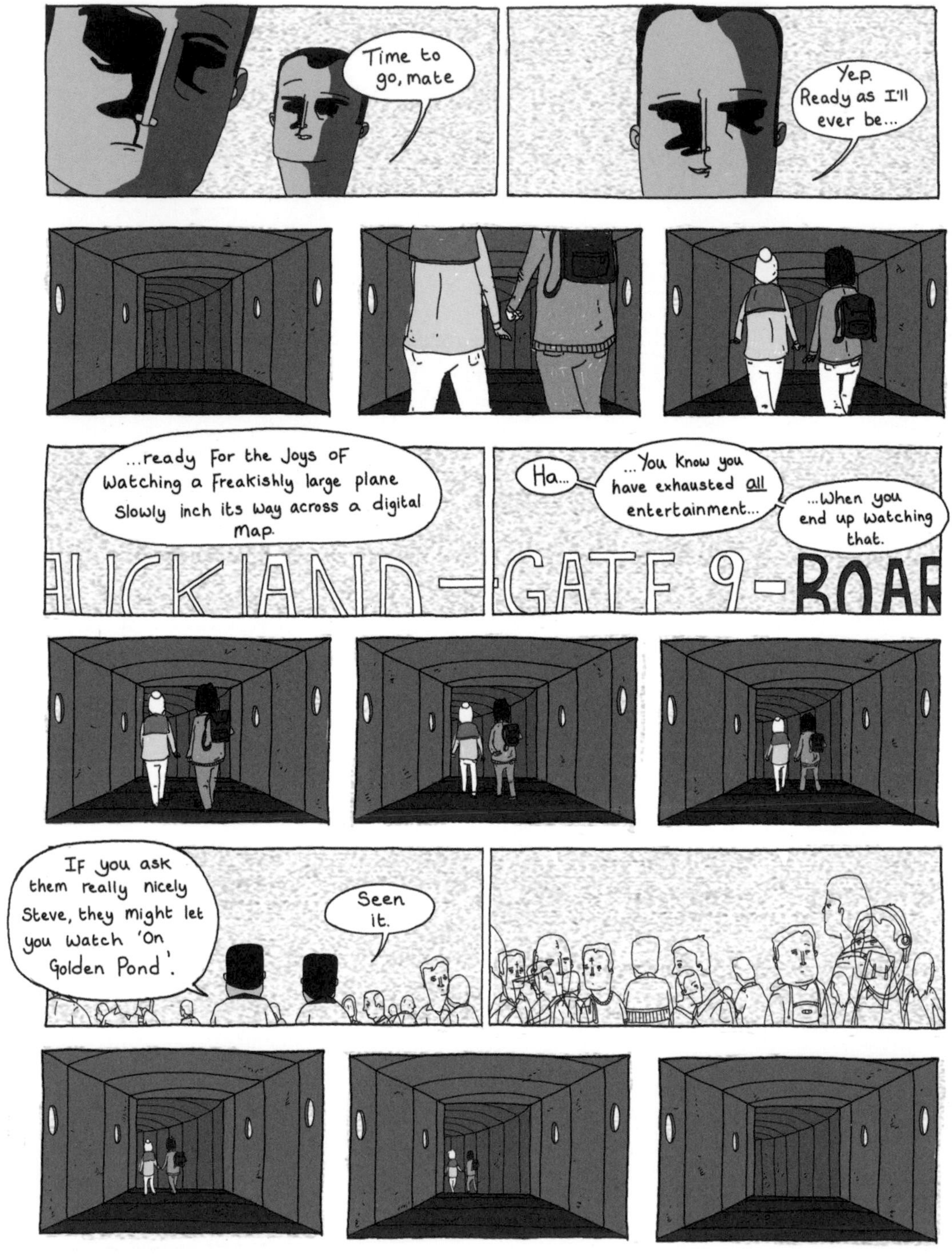
Time to go, mate
Yep. Ready as I'll ever be...
...ready for the Joys of Watching a Freakishly large plane slowly inch its way across a digital map.
Ha...
...You know you have exhausted all entertainment...
...When you end up watching that.
UCKIAND - GATE 9 - BOAR
If you ask them really nicely Steve, they might let you watch 'On Golden Pond'.
Seen it.

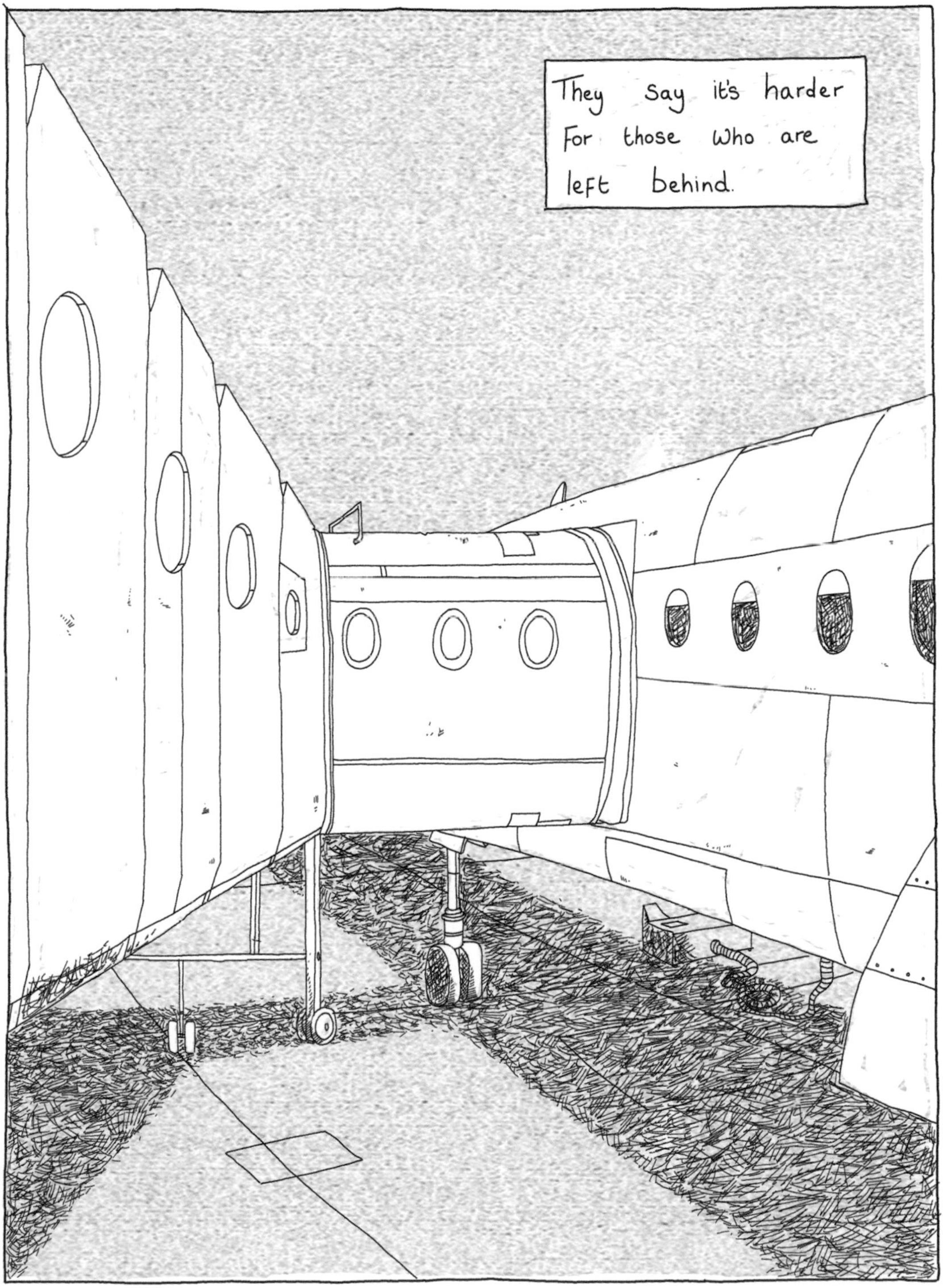
They say it's harder for those who are left behind.

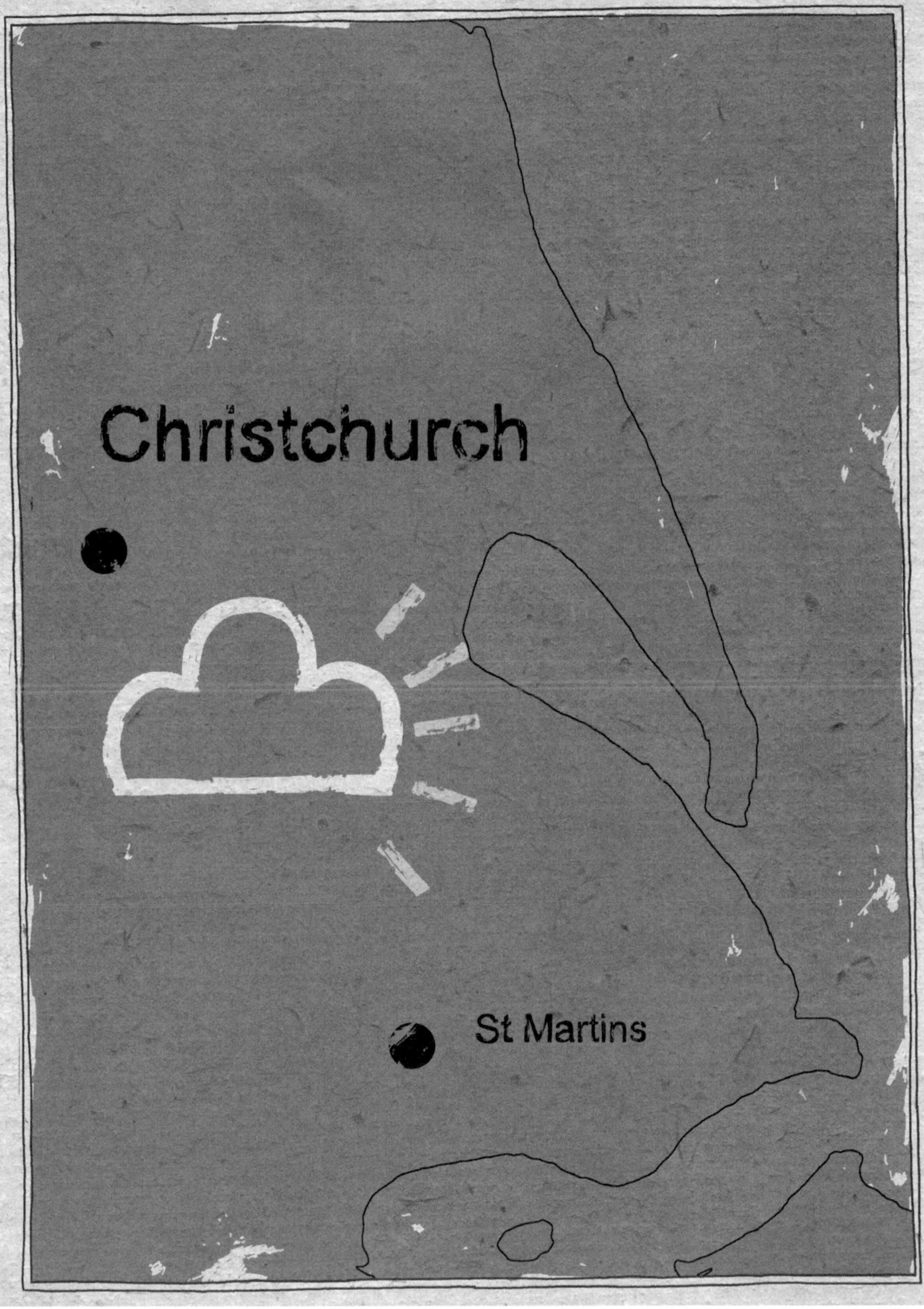
Christchurch
St Martins

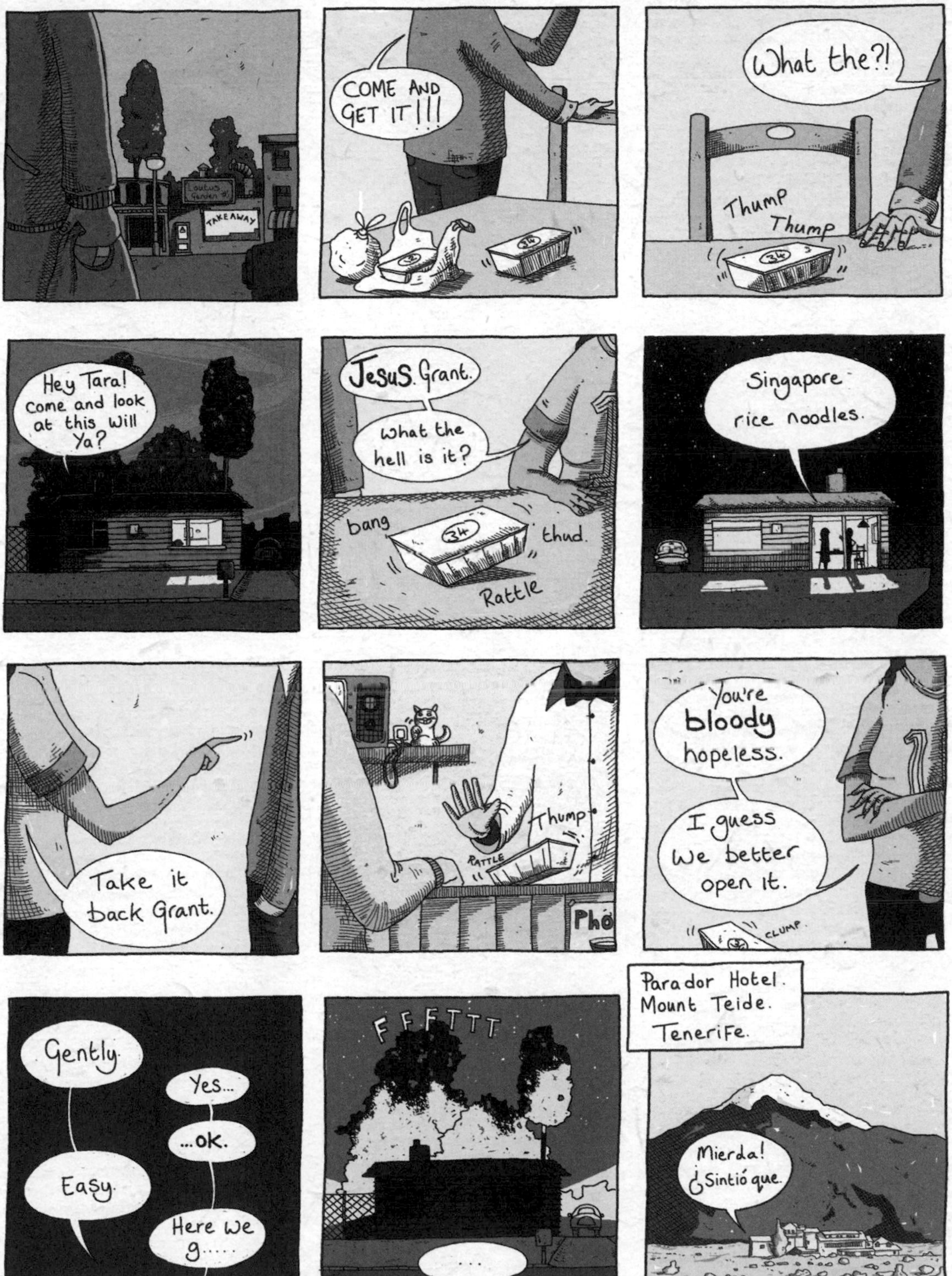

TAKEAWAY
COME AND GET IT!!!
What the?!
Thump Thump
Hey Tara! Come and look at this will Ya?
Jesus. Grant.
what the hell is it?
bang
thud.
Rattle
Singapore rice noodles.
Take it back Grant.
Thump
RATTLE
Phô
You're bloody hopeless.
I guess we better open it.
CLUMP.
Gently.
Easy.
Yes...
...ok.
Here we g.....
FFFTTT
...
Parador Hotel. Mount Teide. Tenerife.
Mierda! ¿Sintió que.

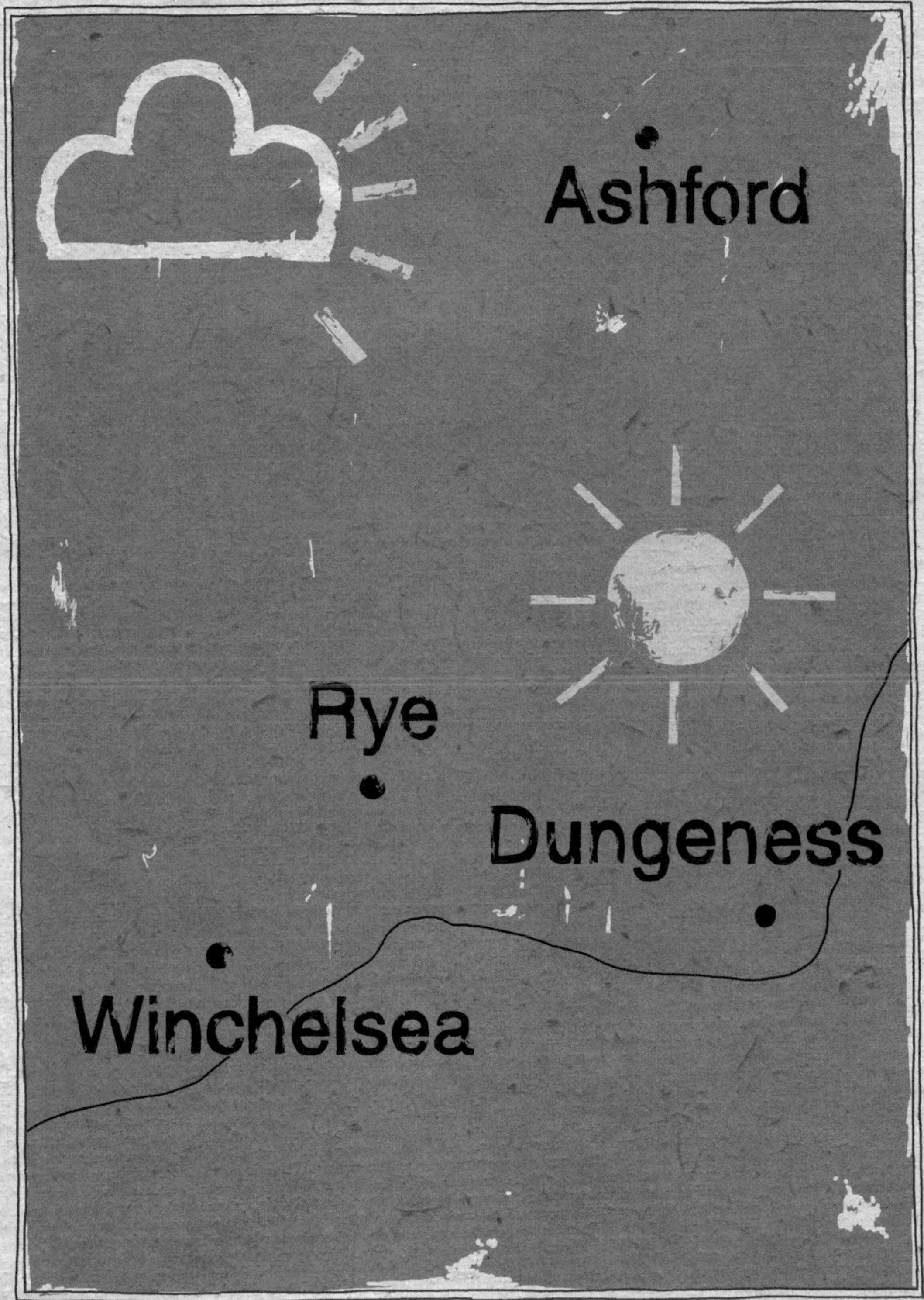
Ashford
Rye
Dungeness
Winchelsea

JUNE 1983
MY DARLING,
I MISS YOU SO MUCH
ALREADY. THESE THINGS
I HAVE SEEN ON MY
JOURNEY.

The Start of a Street Funnel.

A Strung-up C-90.

Broken Computer.

Man stealing mail.

Couple arguing over a broken-down car.

Dumped Fridge in a lay-by with a bird nesting in it.

London disappearing in the rear-view mirror of a hitched ride.

Spinning tea cups at a 'Singles Night Fun Fair.'

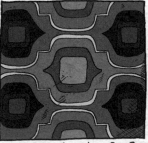

Wallpaper in the B+B.

Passing Satellite

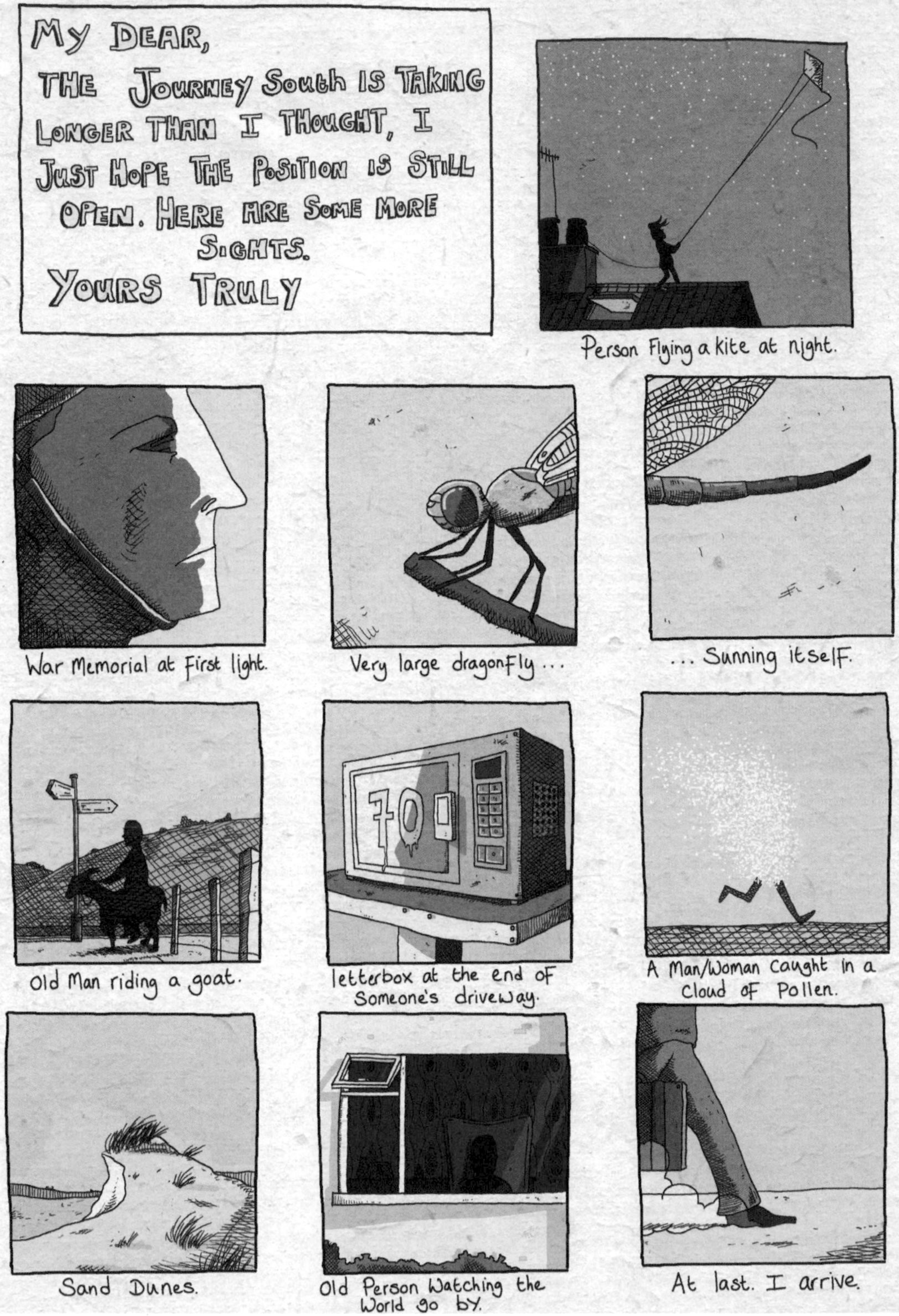
MY DEAR,
THE JOURNEY SOUTH IS TAKING LONGER THAN I THOUGHT, I JUST HOPE THE POSITION IS STILL OPEN. HERE ARE SOME MORE SIGHTS.
YOURS TRULY
Person Flying a kite at night.
War Memorial at First light.
Very large dragonFly ...
... Sunning itselF.
Old Man riding a goat.
letterbox at the end of Someone's driveway.
70
A Man/Woman caught in a Cloud of Pollen.
Sand Dunes.
Old Person Watching the World go by.
At last. I arrive.

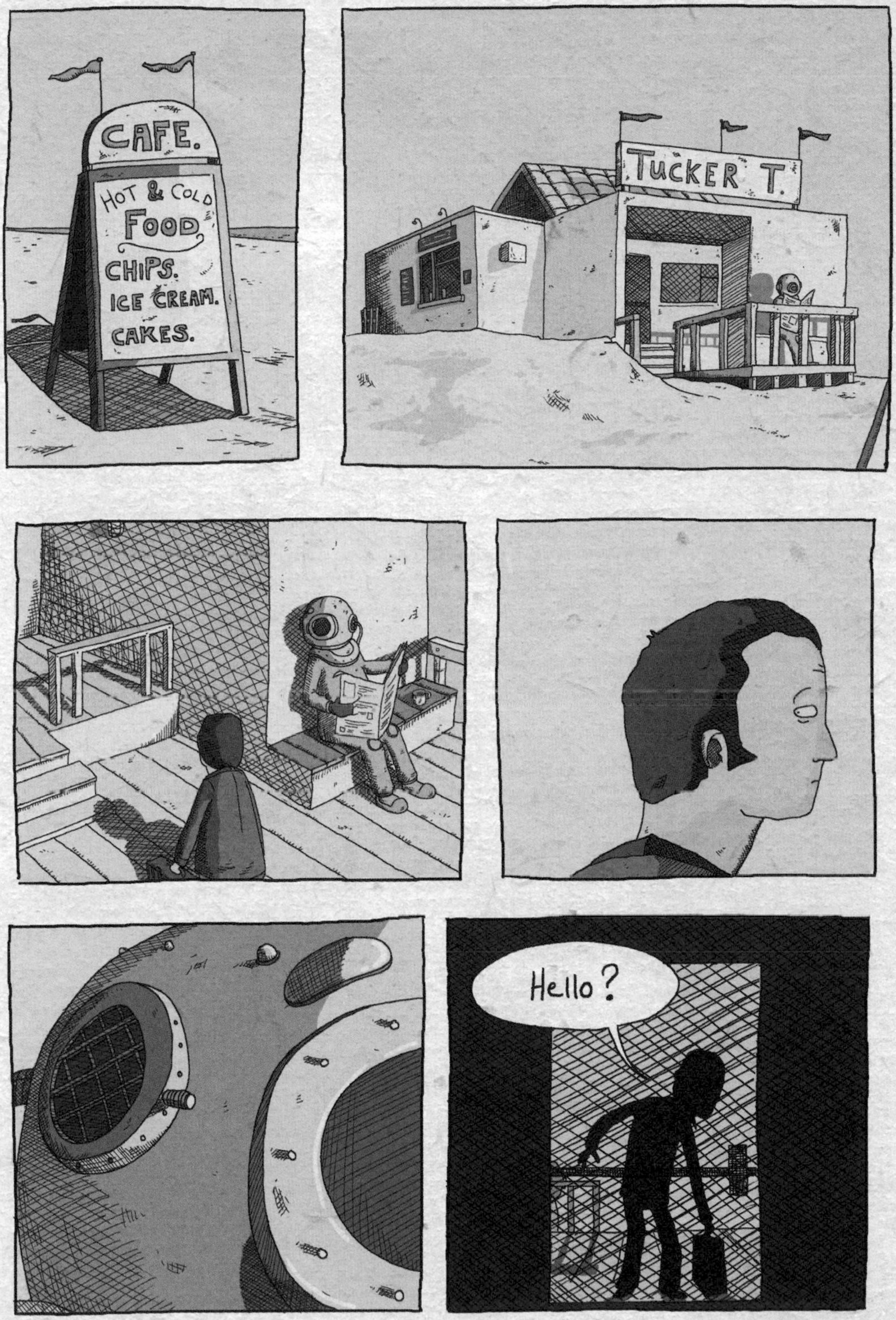
CAFE.
HOT & COLD
FOOD
CHIPS.
ICE CREAM.
CAKES.
TUCKER T.
Hello?

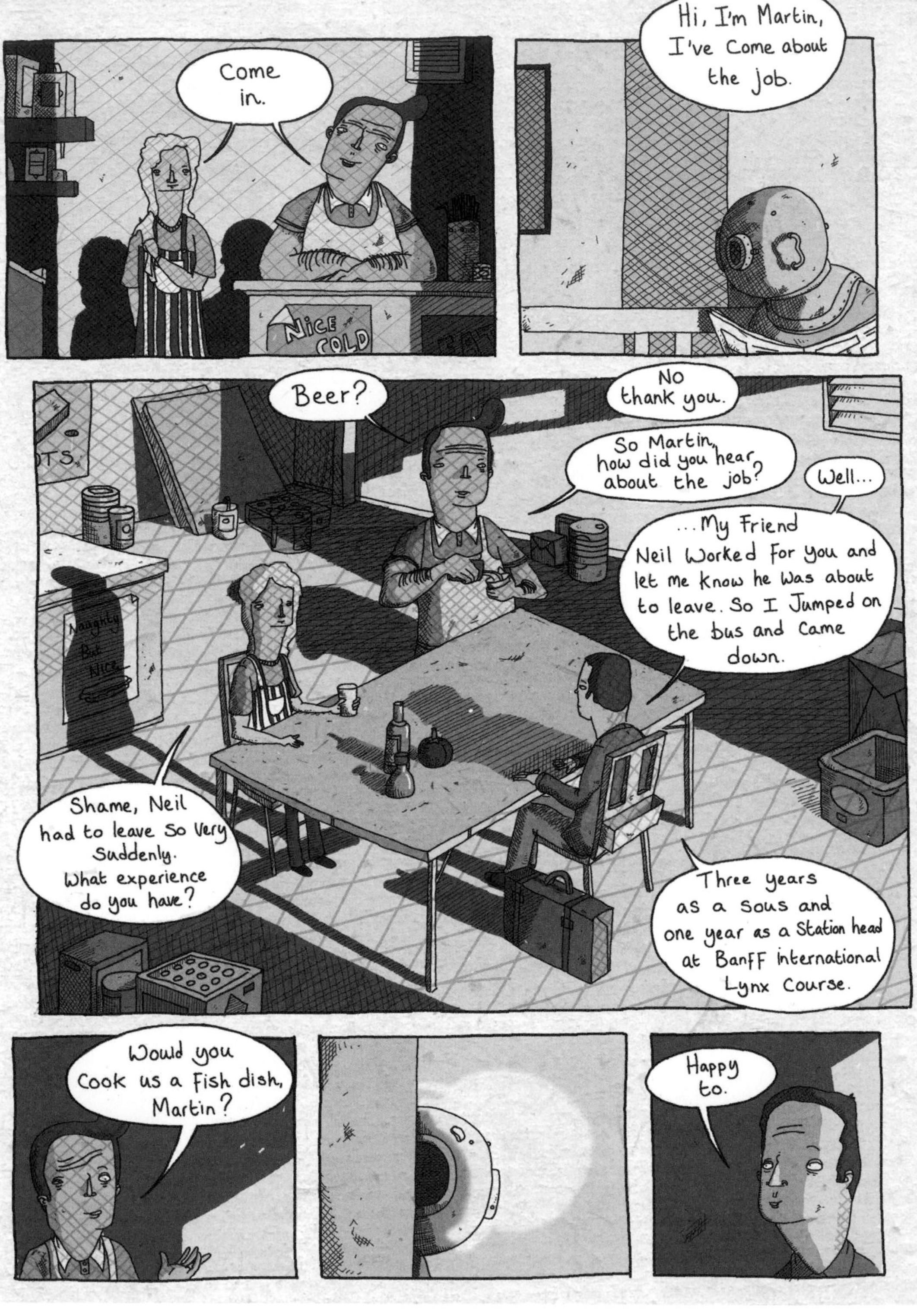

Come in.
NICE COLD
Hi, I'm Martin, I've Come about the job.
Beer?
No thank you.
So Martin, how did you hear about the job?
Well...
...My Friend Neil Worked For you and let me know he Was about to leave. So I Jumped on the bus and Came down.
Naughty But Nice
Shame, Neil had to leave So Very Suddenly. What experience do you have?
Three years as a Sous and one year as a Station head at BanFF International Lynx Course.
Would you Cook us a Fish dish, Martin?
Happy to.

3 Rye Bay Scallops.
1 Granny Smith Apple.
1 Good Quality black pudding.
½ a litre of Chicken Stock.
200 MIS of local Cider.
50 grams of butter.

1. Peel the apple.

Core, then slice into 1cm thick Slices.

2.

Reduce Cider in a pan until it looks like a Syrup. Add stock and reduce Further. Whisk in a little butter at a time.

3.

Strain through Sieve.

4.

Pan Fry Apple Slices in a little butter.

5. Fry black pudding

6.

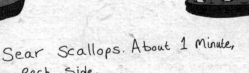

Sear Scallops. About 1 Minute, each Side.

7.

Place :-
Black Pudding on the base
Followed by the Apple Slice
then the Scallop and
Finish With the Syrup over the top.

That's it get it all in.

Come on.

Martin, that was delicious. Here at Tucker T's we do however cook slightly more... basic dishes...

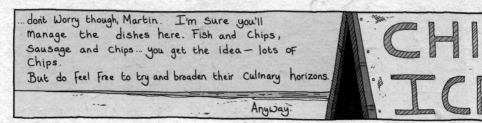

...don't worry though, Martin. I'm sure you'll manage the dishes here. Fish and Chips, Sausage and chips... you get the idea — lots of chips.
But do feel free to try and broaden their culinary horizons.

Anyway.

CHI
ICH

Let me show you around...

...right...

This will be your digs. It's simple but I think you'll find it comfortable. Best views in the county.......

...This is...... the sun deck, most of the customers sit here...

Your main service hatch, you can use the other one around the corner. But best stay with this........

Bring this in every night.

TUCKER T

...and the mail box.

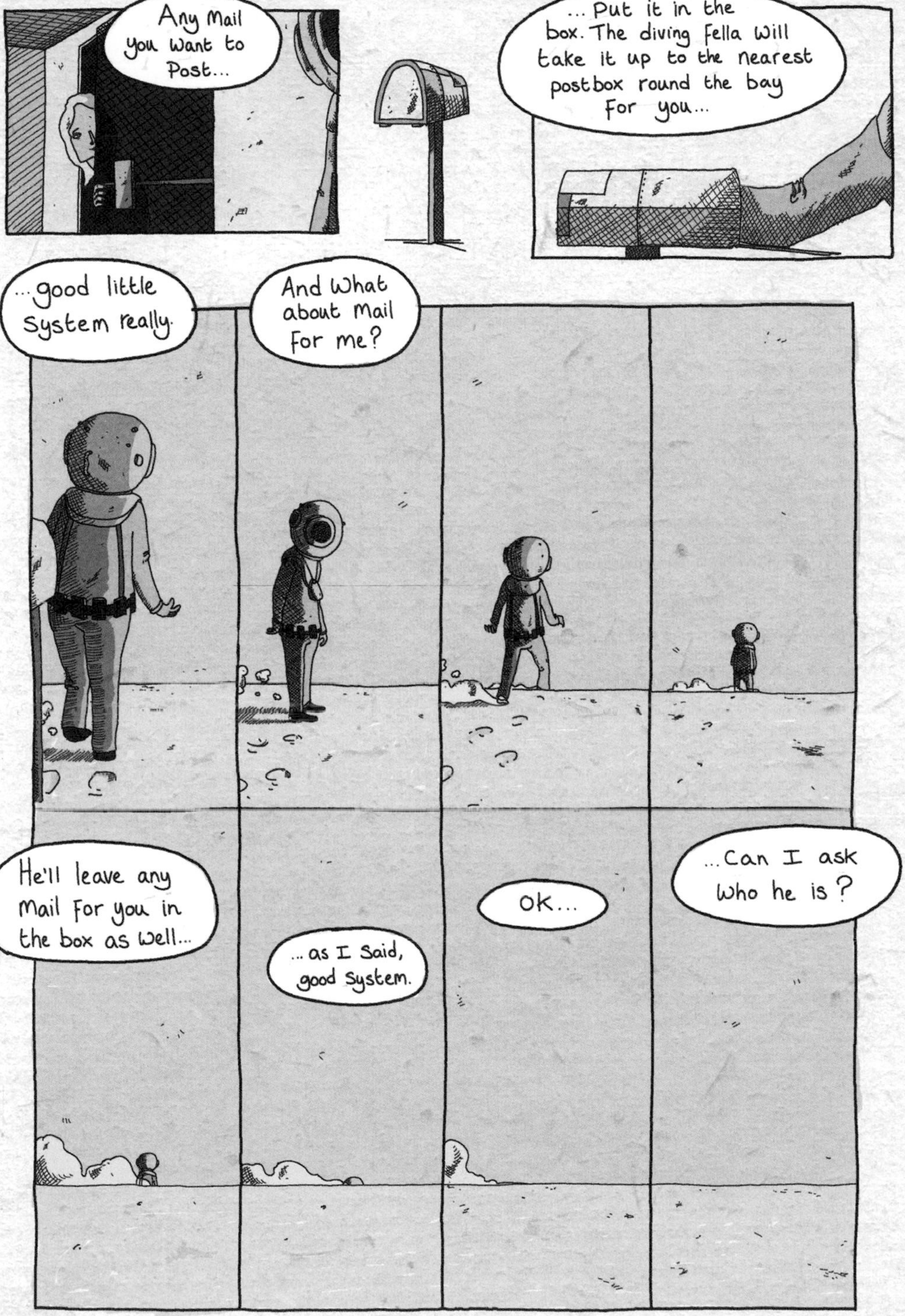
Any Mail you Want to Post...
... Put it in the box. The diving fella Will take it up to the nearest postbox round the bay for you...
...good little system really.
And What about Mail for me?
He'll leave any Mail for you in the box as well...
... as I said, good system.
OK...
...Can I ask Who he is?

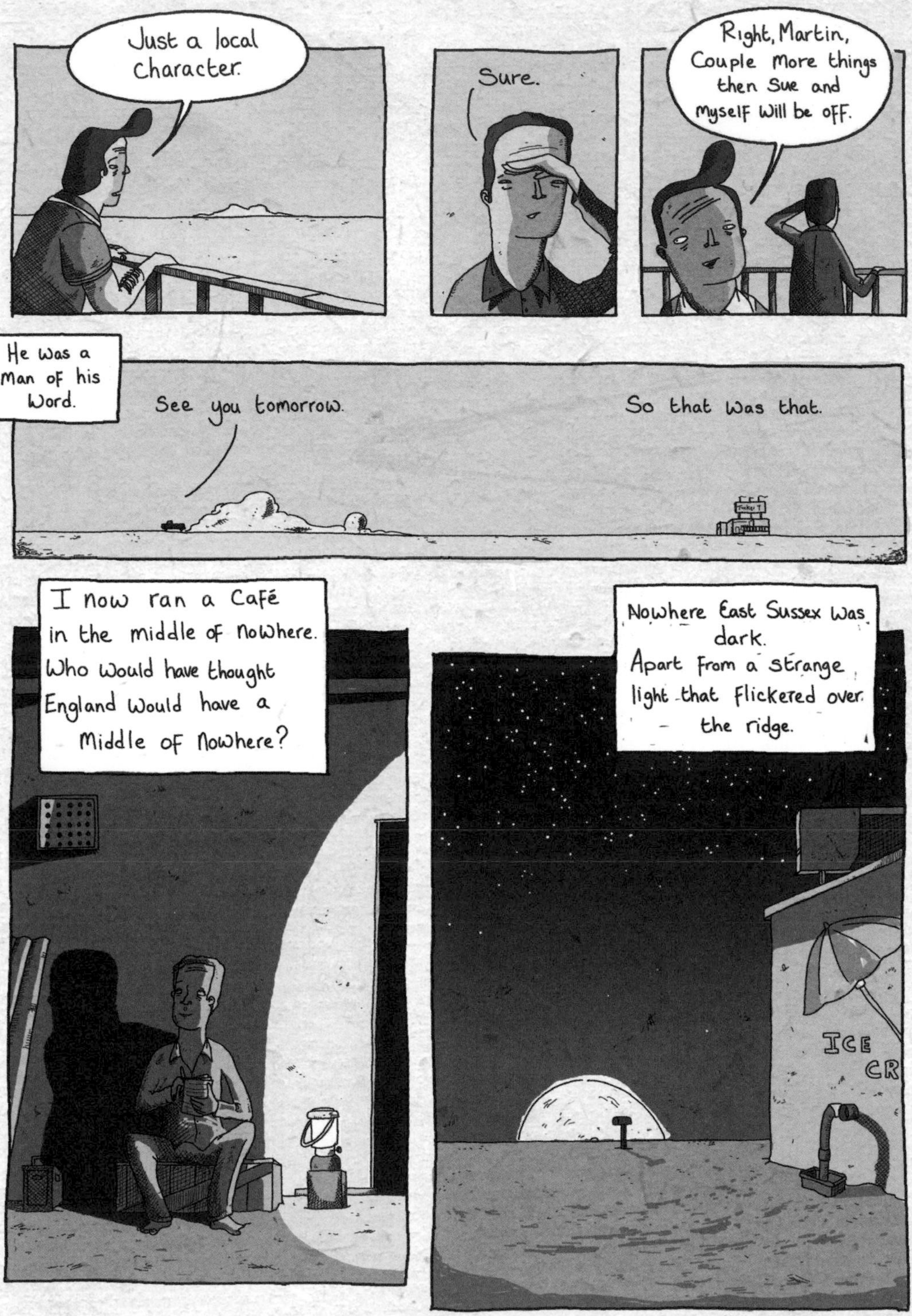

Just a local character.
Sure.
Right, Martin, Couple more things then Sue and myself will be off.
He was a man of his word.
See you tomorrow.
So that was that.
I now ran a Café in the middle of nowhere. Who would have thought England would have a Middle of Nowhere?
Nowhere East Sussex was dark. Apart from a strange light that flickered over the ridge.
ICE
CR

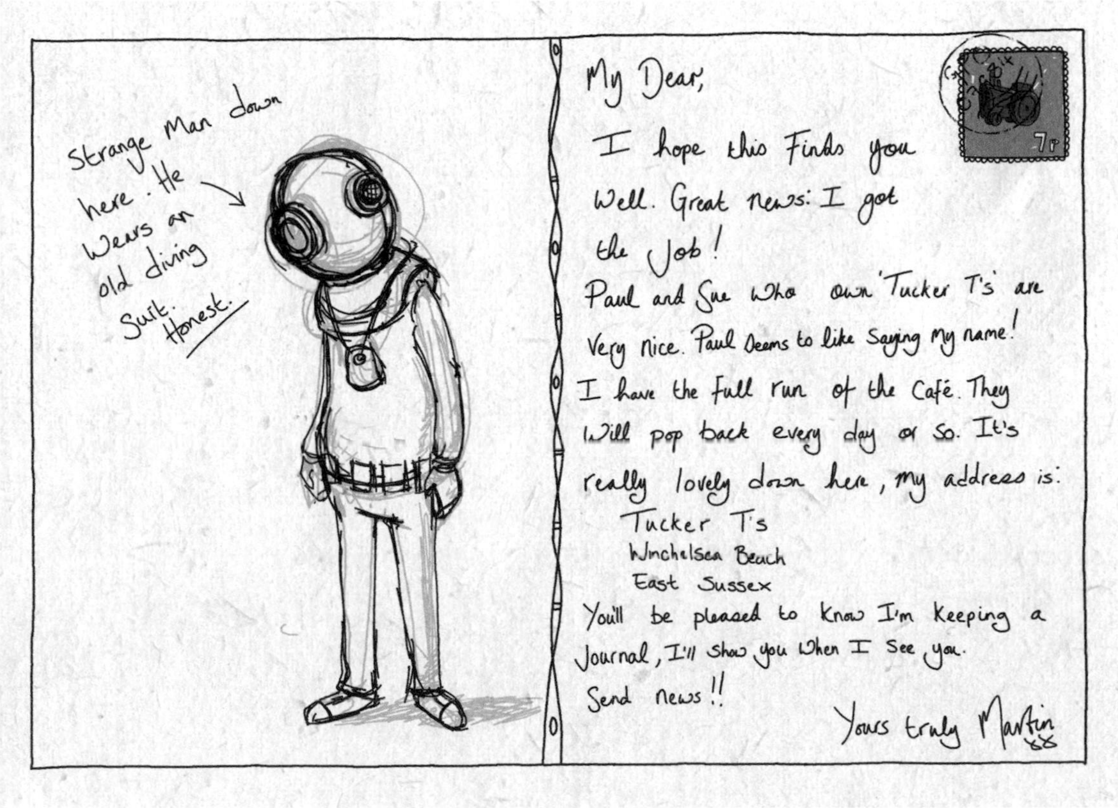
Strange Man down here. He Wears an old diving Suit. Honest.
7p
My Dear,
I hope this Finds you Well. Great news: I got the Job!
Paul and Sue who own 'Tucker T's' are Very nice. Paul seems to like Saying my name!
I have the full run of the Café. They Will pop back every day or so. It's really lovely down here, my address is:
Tucker T's
Winchelsea Beach
East Sussex
You'll be pleased to know I'm Keeping a Journal, I'll show you When I See you.
Send news!!
Yours truly Martin xx

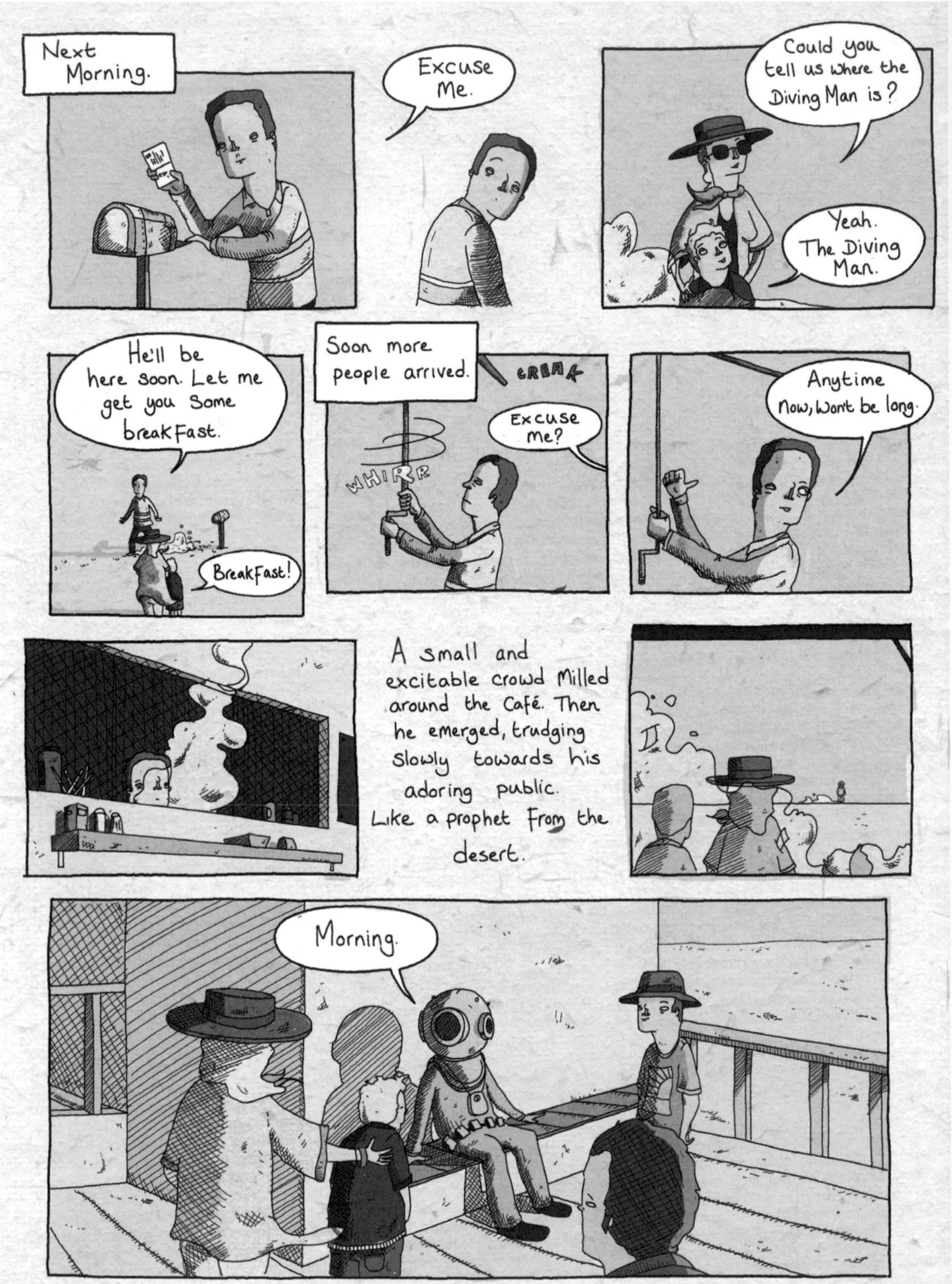

Next Morning.
Excuse Me.
Could you tell us where the Diving Man is?
Yeah. The Diving Man.
He'll be here soon. Let me get you some breakfast.
Breakfast!
Soon more people arrived.
CREAK
WHIRR
Excuse me?
Anytime now, Won't be long.
A small and excitable crowd milled around the Café. Then he emerged, trudging slowly towards his adoring public. Like a prophet from the desert.
Morning.

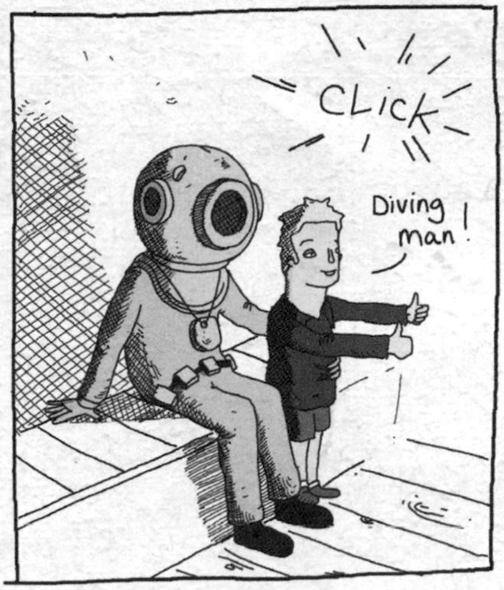
CLICK
Diving man!

For the whole day he sat and had his photo taken, one after another with the excitable hordes.

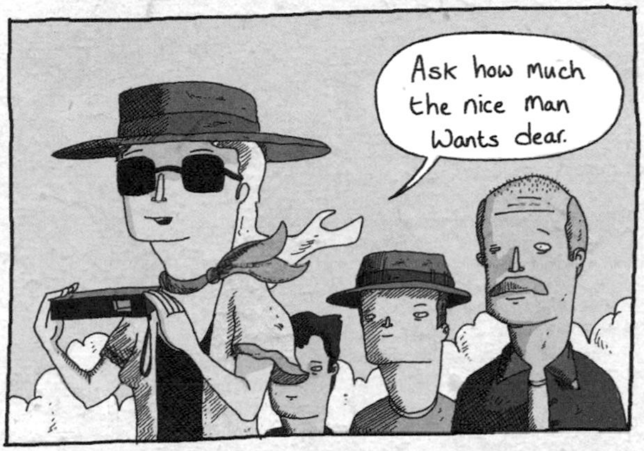
Ask how much the nice man Wants dear.

With every suggestion of money he patiently raised his hand and shook his head.

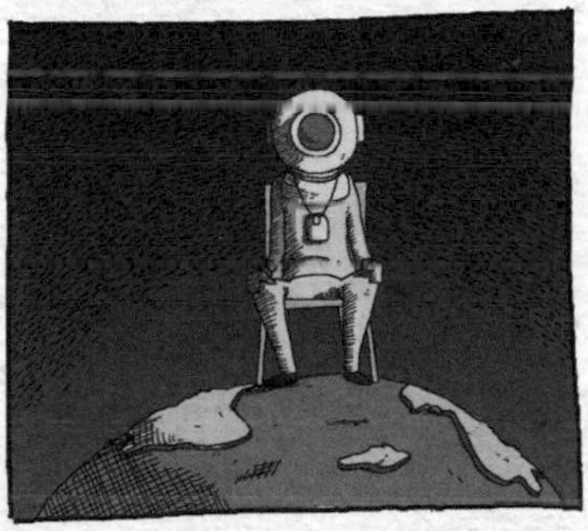

He would only ask for two things from the gathered tourists. He would ask them if they had any finished-with paperbacks with them or which country they planned to holiday in next. Then he would simply ask they send him a postcard.

I'm not sure how many people honoured their promise but he accepted their promises with good grace. I did see him a few times accept a beer.

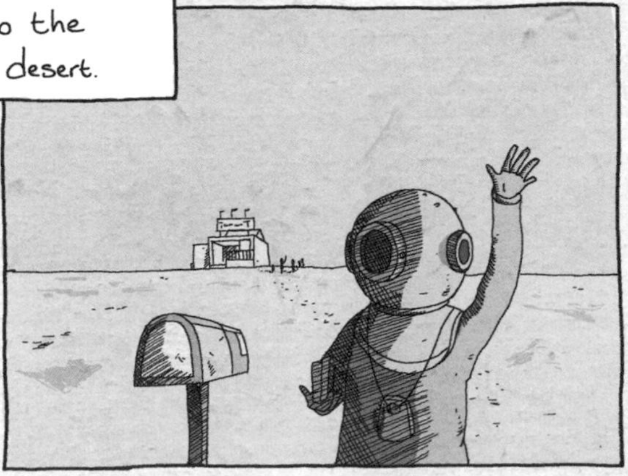
And then back into the desert.

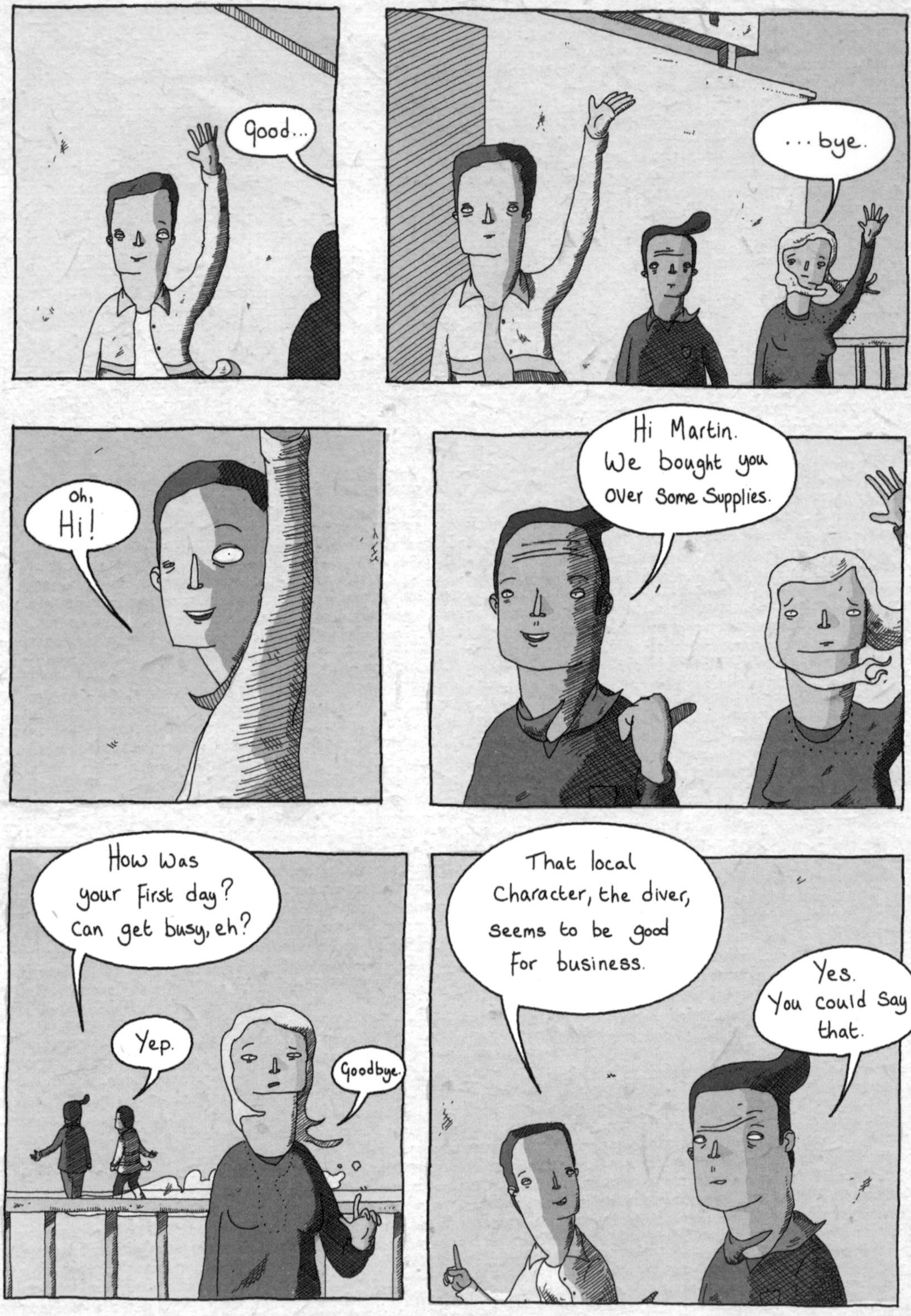
good...
...bye.
Oh, Hi!
Hi Martin. We bought you over some supplies.
How was your first day? Can get busy, eh?
Yep.
Goodbye.
That local character, the diver, seems to be good for business.
Yes. You could say that.

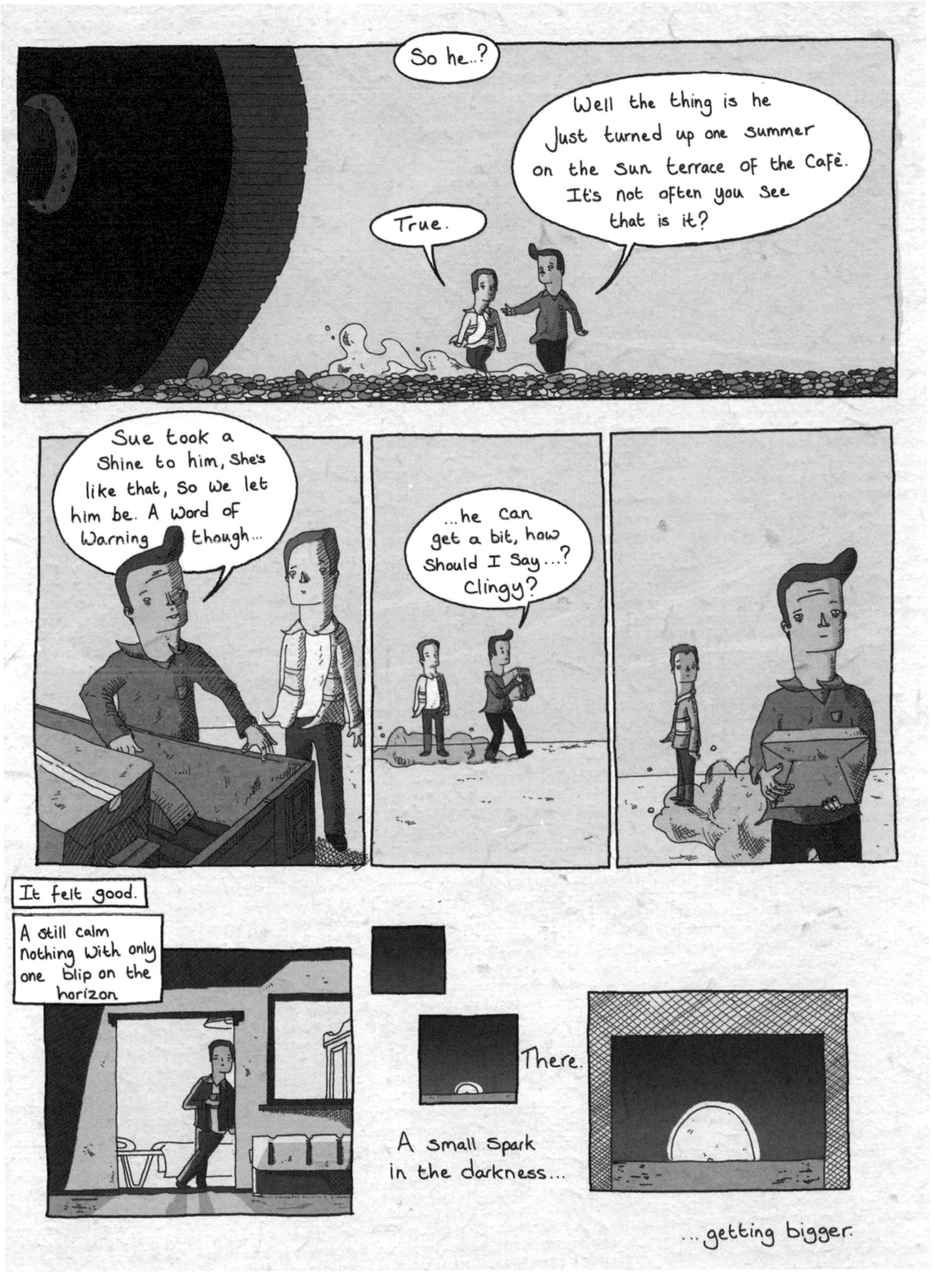

So he..?
Well the thing is he Just turned up one summer on the sun terrace of the Cafè. It's not often you see that is it?
True.
Sue took a shine to him, she's like that, so we let him be. A word of warning though...
...he can get a bit, how should I say...? Clingy?
It felt good.
A still calm nothing with only one blip on the horizon
There.
A small spark in the darkness...
...getting bigger.

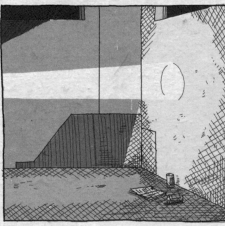

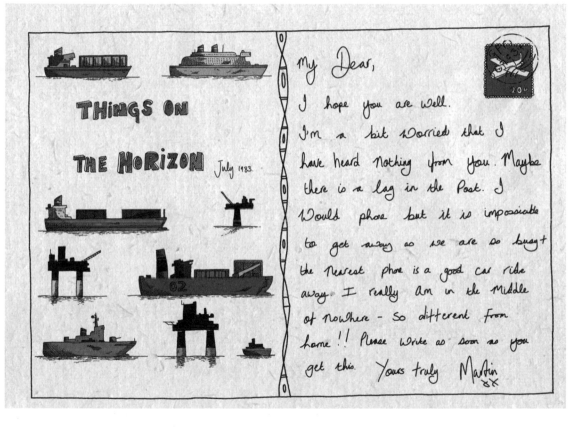

THINGS ON
THE HORIZON

July 1983.

My Dear,

I hope you are Well.
I'm a bit Worried that I
have heard Nothing from you. Maybe
there is a lag in the Post. I
Would phone but it is impossible
to get away as we are so busy +
the nearest phone is a good car ride
away. I really am in the Middle
of Nowhere - so different from
home!! Please Write as soon as you
get this. Yours truly Martin
xx

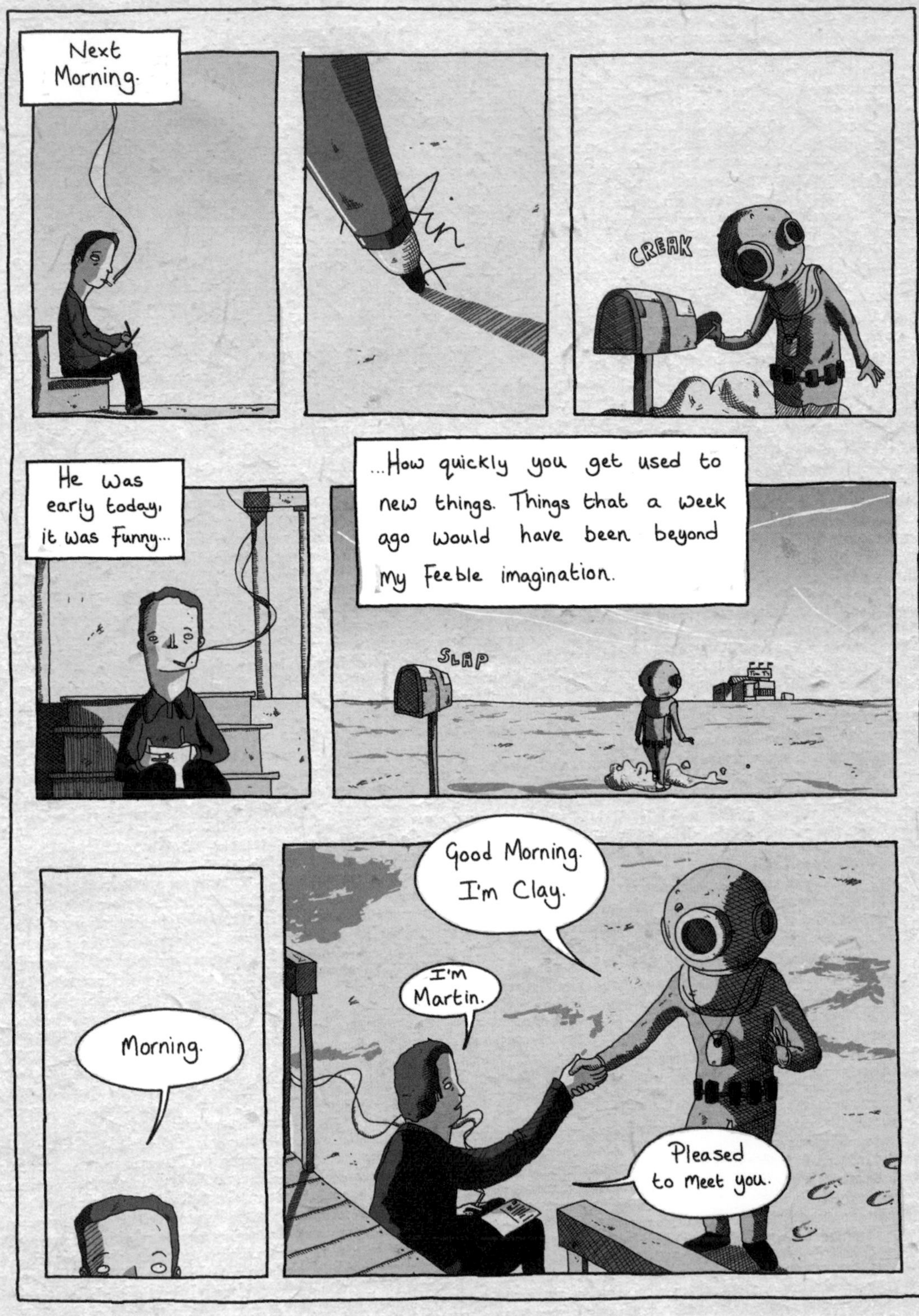
Next Morning.
CREAK
He was early today, it was Funny...
...How quickly you get used to new things. Things that a week ago would have been beyond my Feeble imagination.
SLAP
Morning.
Good Morning. I'm Clay.
I'm Martin.
Pleased to meet you.

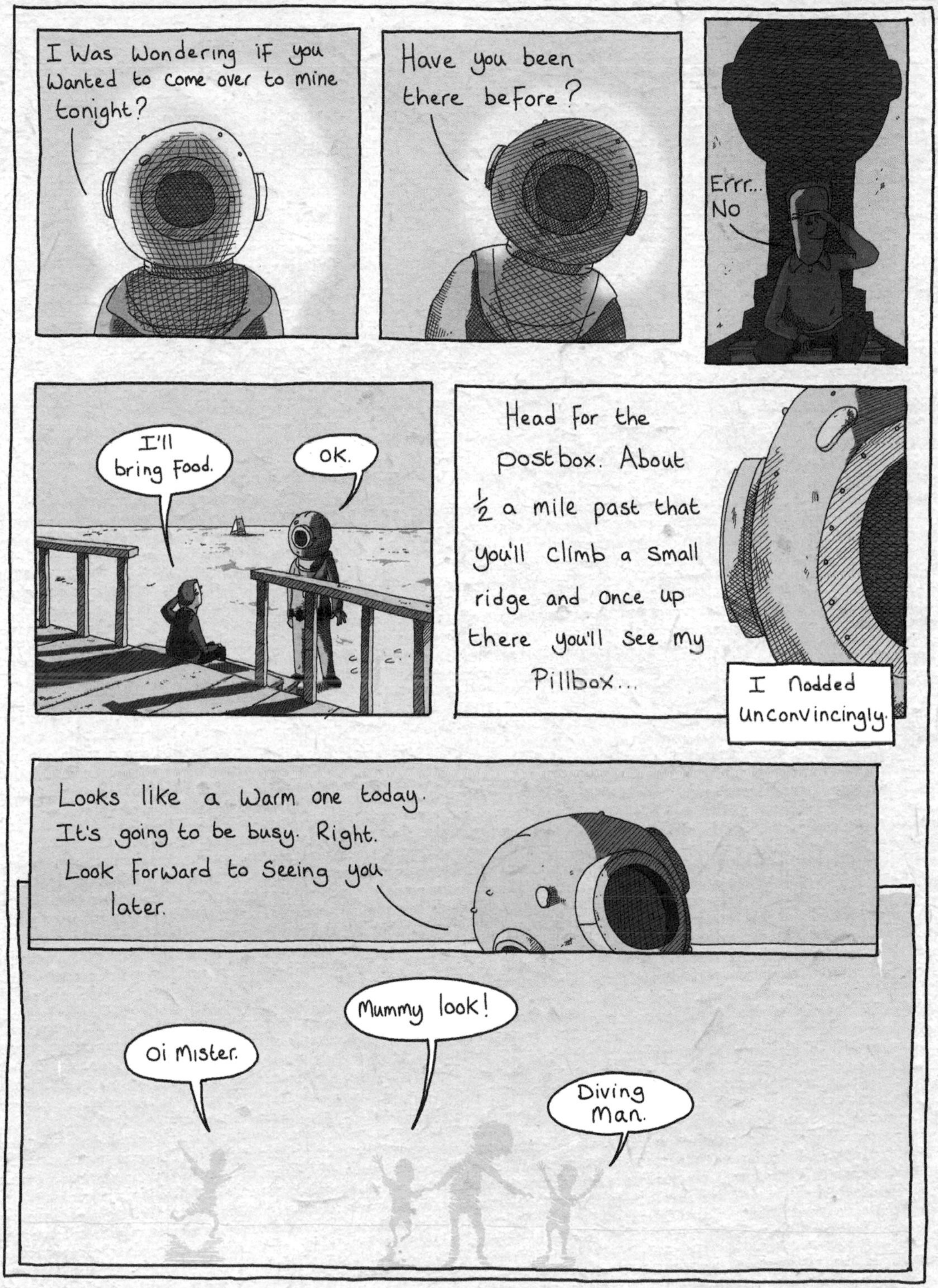
I Was Wondering if you Wanted to come over to mine tonight?
Have you been there before?
Errr... No
I'll bring Food.
OK.
Head for the postbox. About ½ a mile past that you'll climb a small ridge and once up there you'll see my Pillbox...
I Nodded Unconvincingly.
Looks like a Warm one today. It's going to be busy. Right. Look Forward to Seeing you later.
Oi Mister.
Mummy look!
Diving Man.

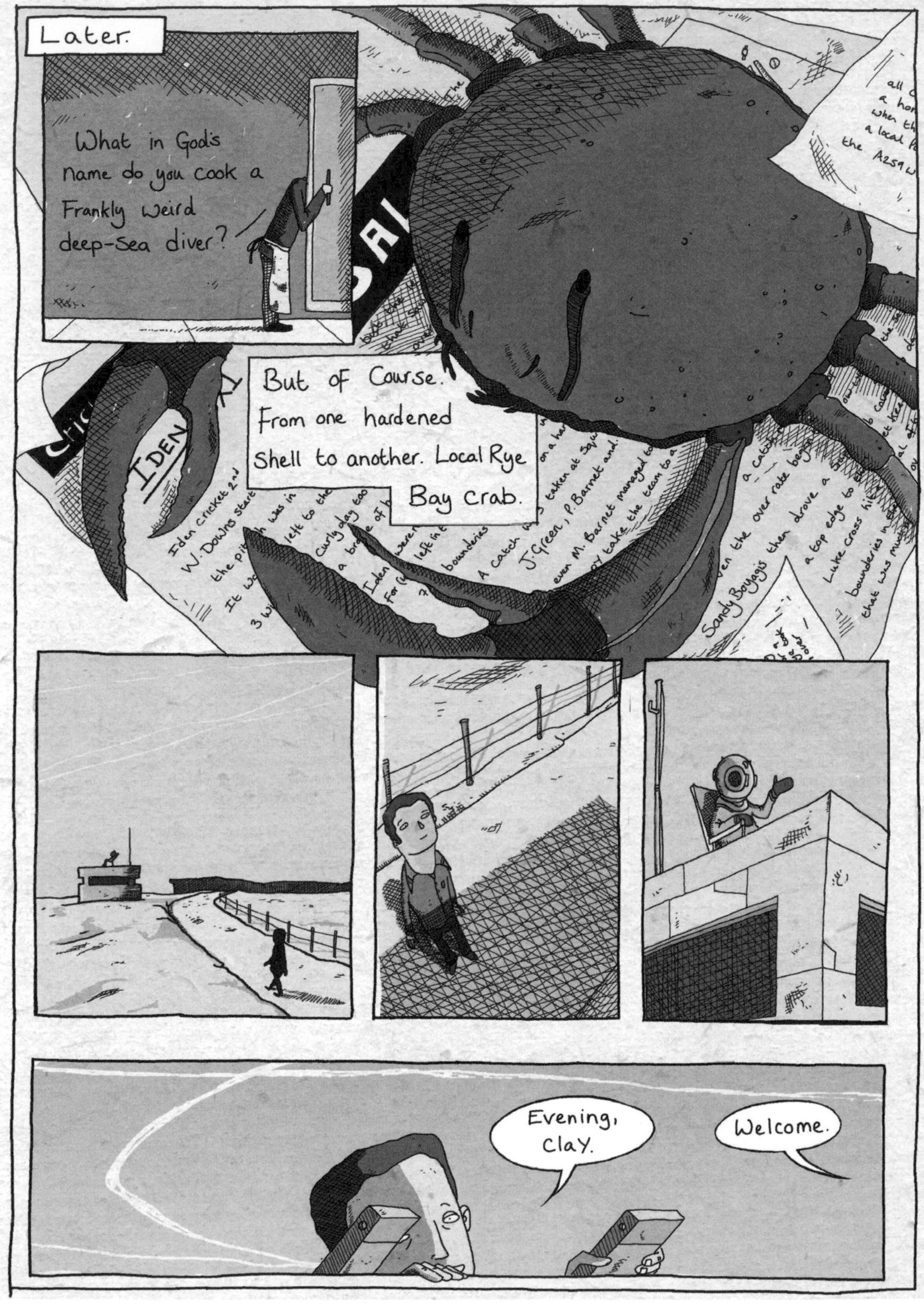
Later.
What in God's name do you cook a Frankly weird deep-sea diver?
But of Course. From one hardened Shell to another. Local Rye Bay crab.
Evening, Clay.
Welcome.

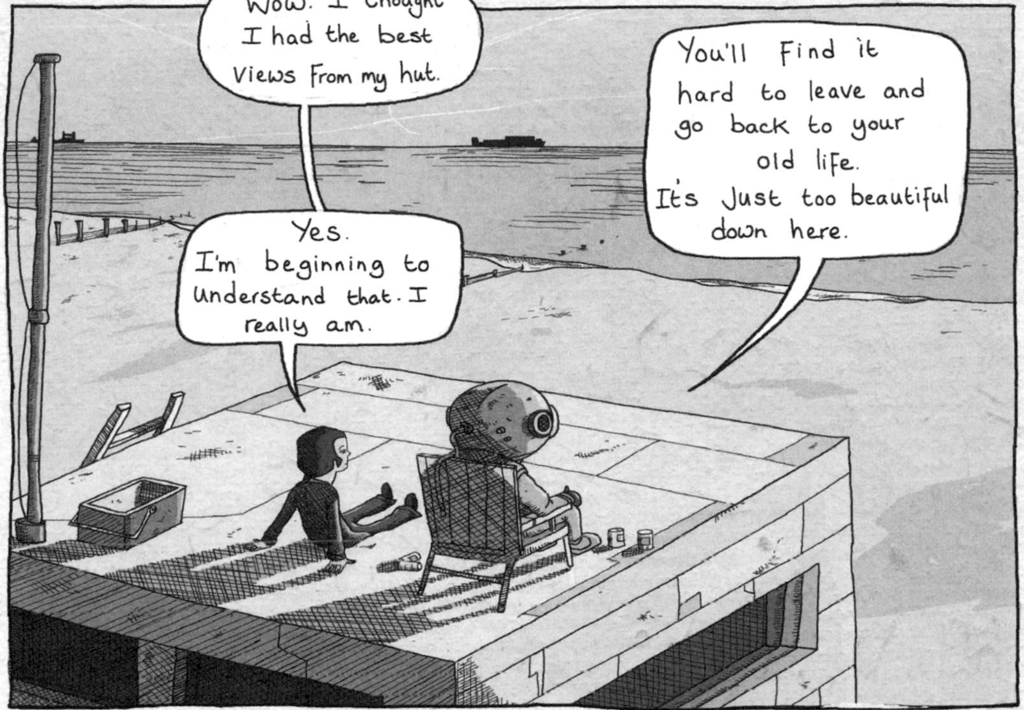
Wow. I thought I had the best views from my hut.
You'll find it hard to leave and go back to your old life. It's just too beautiful down here.
Yes. I'm beginning to understand that. I really am.

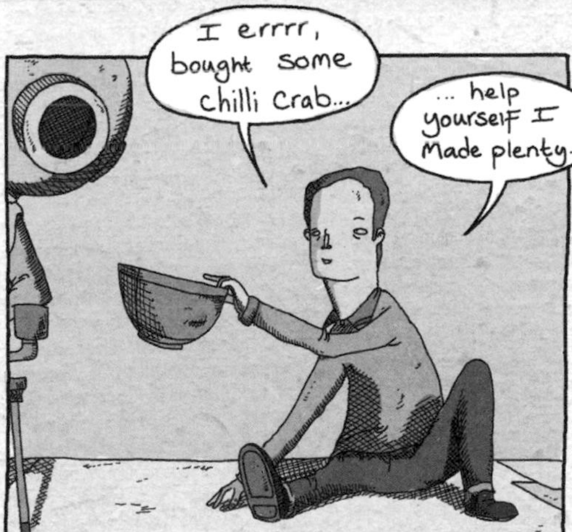
I errrr, bought some chilli crab...
... help yourself I made plenty.

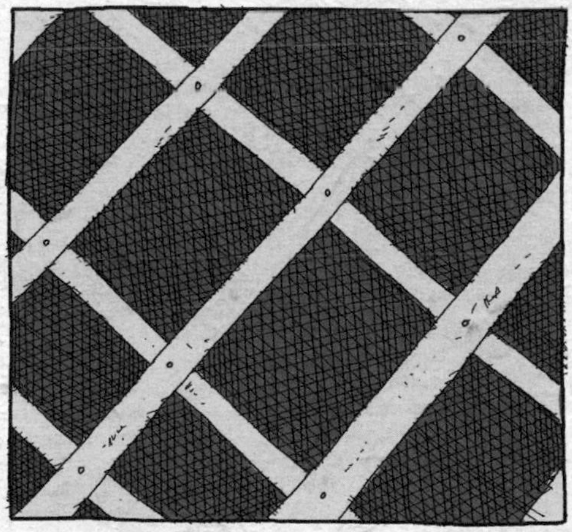

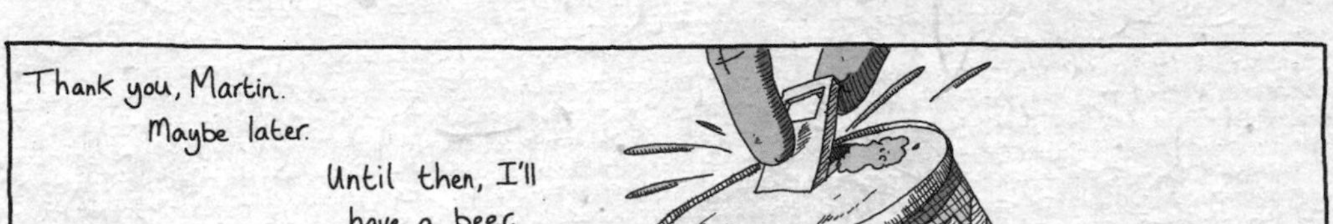
Thank you, Martin.
Maybe later.
Until then, I'll have a beer.

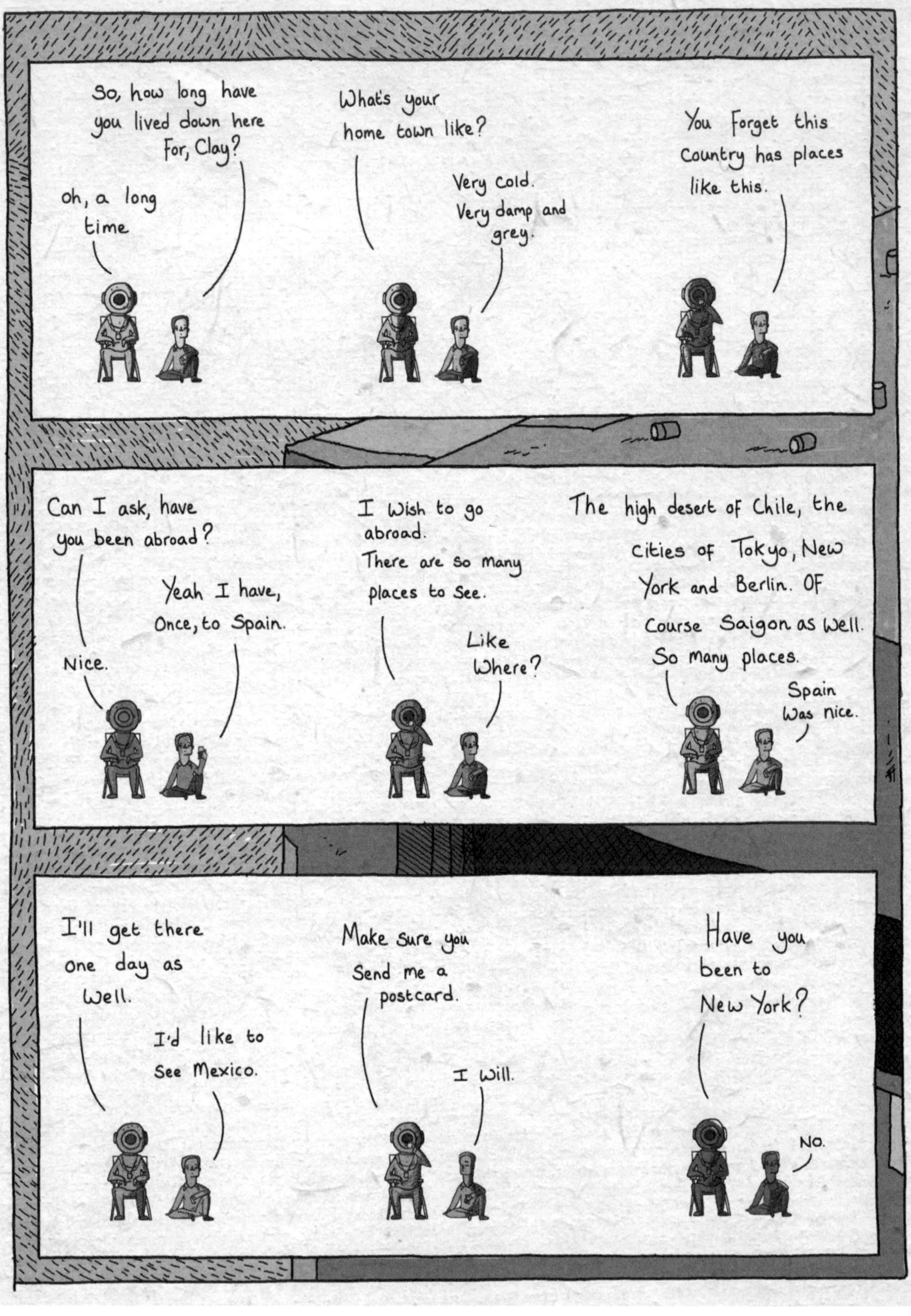
So, how long have you lived down here For, Clay?
Oh, a long time
What's your home town like?
Very cold. Very damp and grey.
You Forget this Country has places like this.
Can I ask, have you been abroad?
Yeah I have, Once, to Spain.
Nice.
I Wish to go abroad. There are so many places to see.
Like Where?
The high desert of Chile, the cities of Tokyo, New York and Berlin. OF Course Saigon as Well. So many places.
Spain Was nice.
I'll get there one day as Well.
I'd like to See Mexico.
Make sure you Send me a postcard.
I Will.
Have you been to New York?
No.

We talked, drank plenty of beers and watched the boats twinkle and slide along the horizon.

Then his head lolled to one side. He went silent.

Slowly...

... Very slowly.

Nothing.

Just the touch of a damp heavy weave fabric.

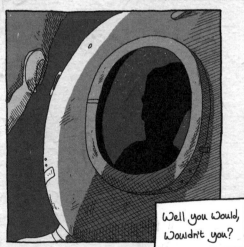

Well you would, wouldn't you?

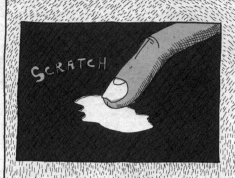

SCRATCH

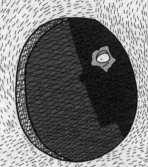

It was like looking at a seabed being pummelled by a huge wave. An invisible tsunami churning the contents where a head should be.

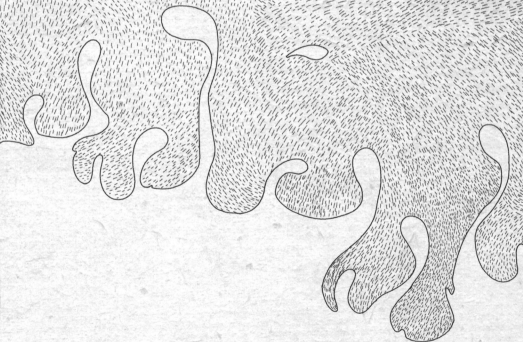

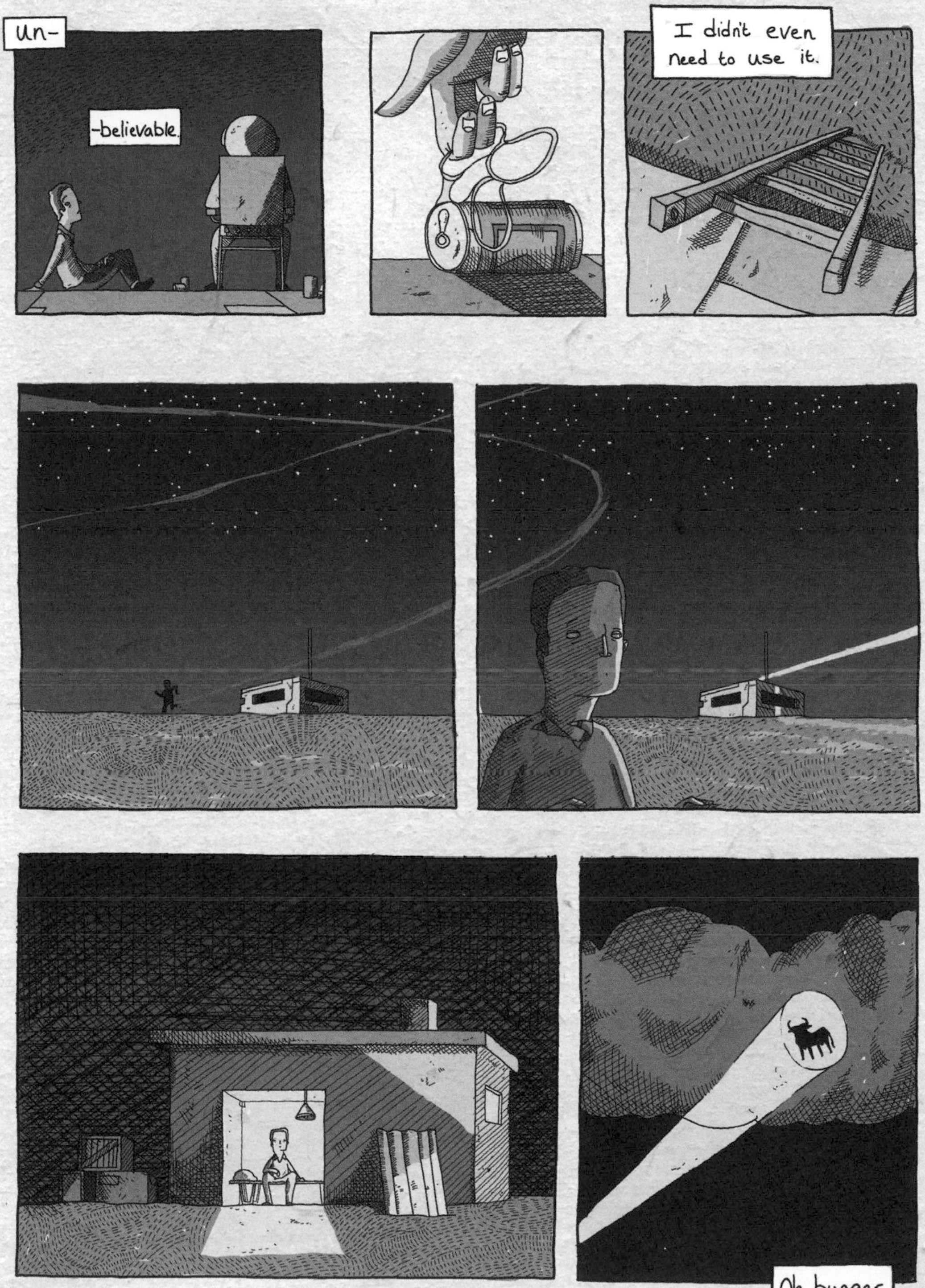
Un-
-believable.
I didn't even need to use it.
Oh, bugger.

Strange things just along the Coast in Denge. Got there at night it took _so_ long to hike to them!

My Dear,

Why have you not Written?

Is it Something I have done? Have I done something Wrong?

I miss you so much. Perhaps the cards have got lost in the post. I check the postbox every Morning, and Clay (the diving man) takes mine for me. As I said in a previous postcard I am so busy in the Cafe, it is impossible to get away to a phone box. Every day — and I mean _every_ day has been so Warm and beautiful.

In that sense I can't complain!

I've become friends with the diving man, he is a bit odd, but it's nice to have a friend down here.

~~He does this thing with~~ ← ignore that!

I hope this gets through and I get to see your handwriting soon. Yours truly Martin

25p

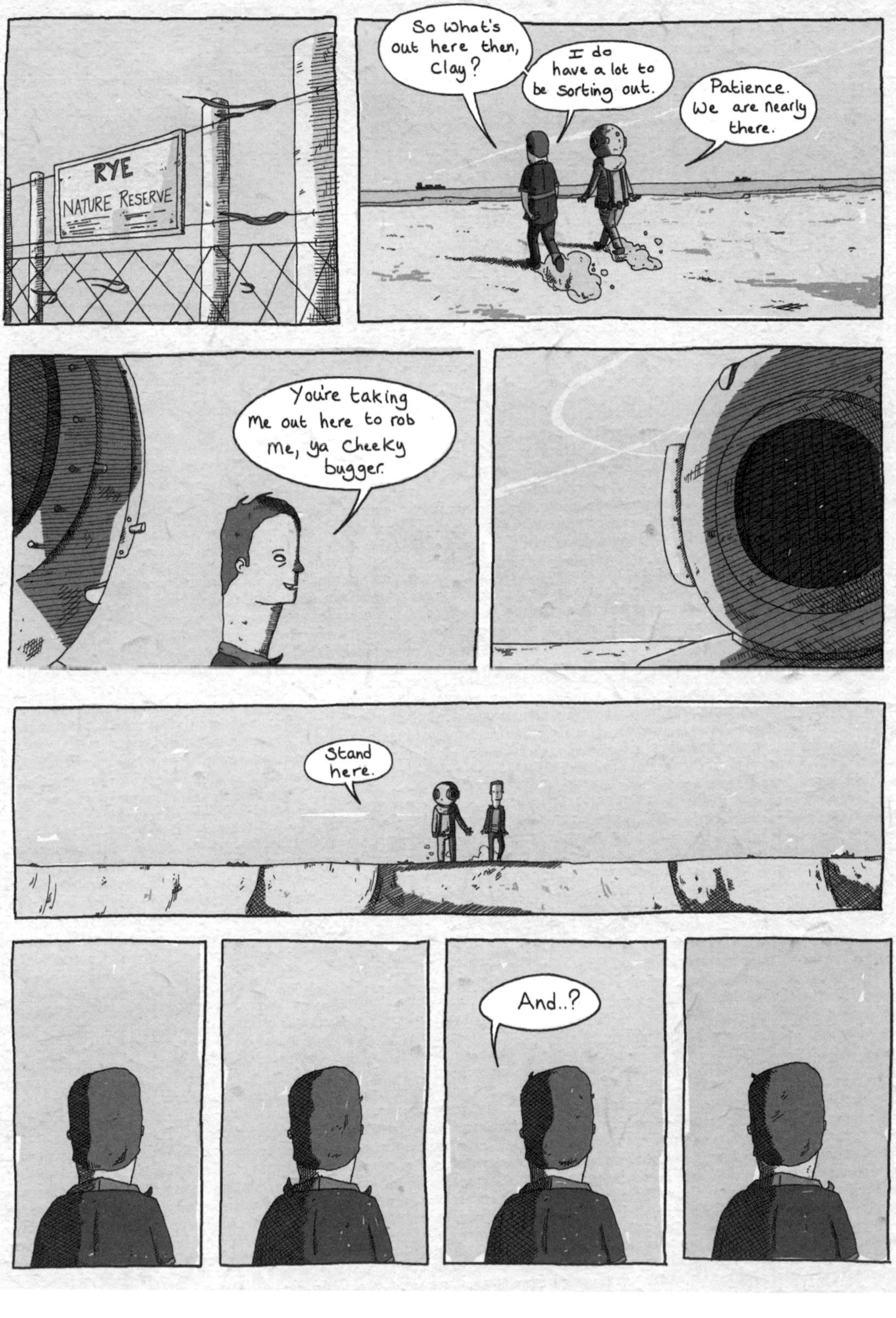
RYE
NATURE RESERVE
So what's out here then, Clay?
I do have a lot to be sorting out.
Patience. We are nearly there.
You're taking me out here to rob me, ya cheeky bugger.
Stand here.
And..?

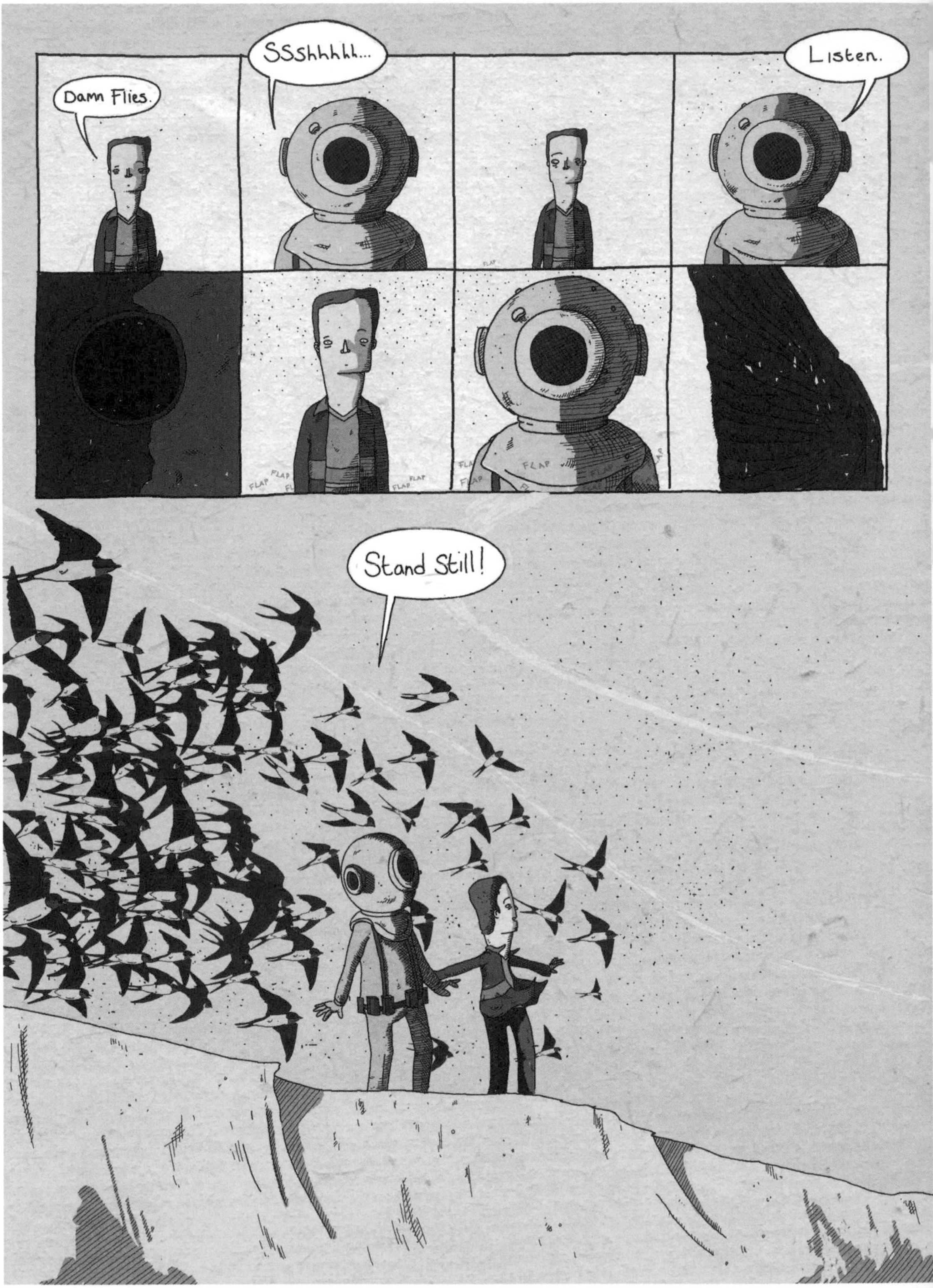
Damn Flies.
SSshhhhh...
Listen.
FLAP
FLAP FLAP
FLAP FLAP
FLAP
FLAP
Stand Still!

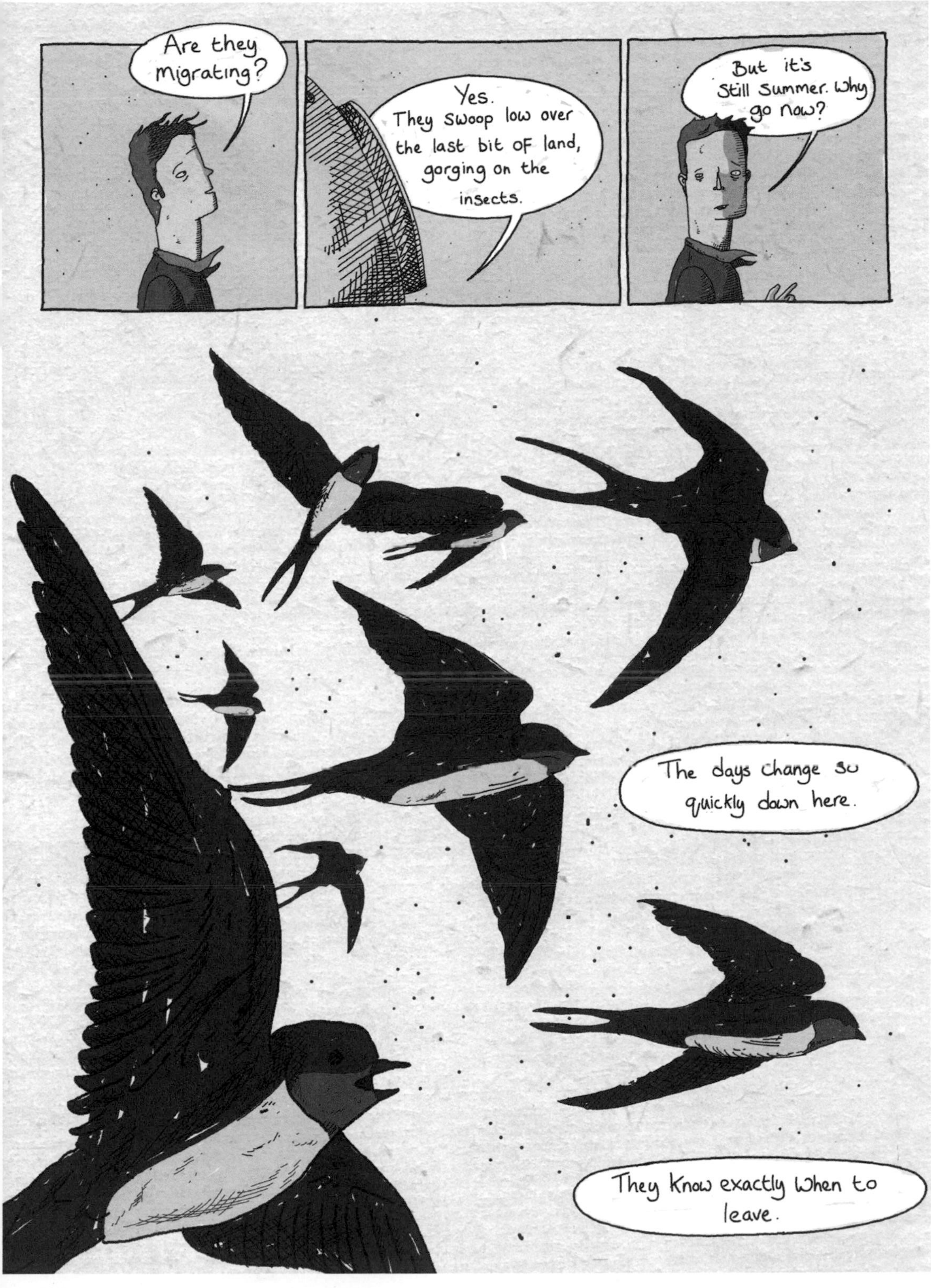
Are they migrating?
Yes. They swoop low over the last bit of land, gorging on the insects.
But it's still summer. Why go now?
The days change so quickly down here.
They know exactly when to leave.

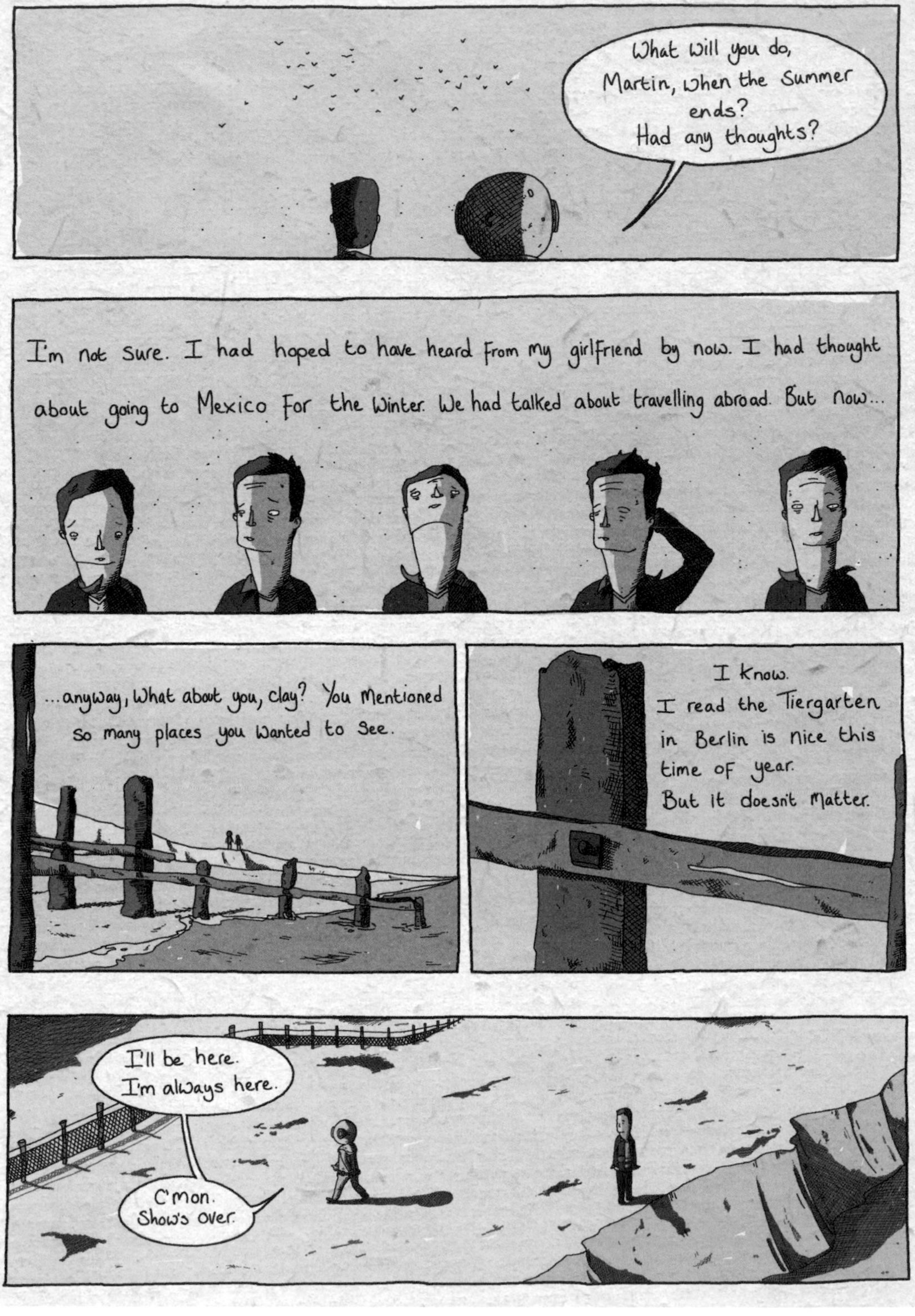
What will you do, Martin, when the Summer ends? Had any thoughts?
I'm not sure. I had hoped to have heard from my girlfriend by now. I had thought about going to Mexico for the winter. We had talked about travelling abroad. But now...
...anyway, what about you, clay? You mentioned so many places you wanted to see.
I know. I read the Tiergarten in Berlin is nice this time of year. But it doesn't matter.
I'll be here. I'm always here.
C'mon. Show's over.

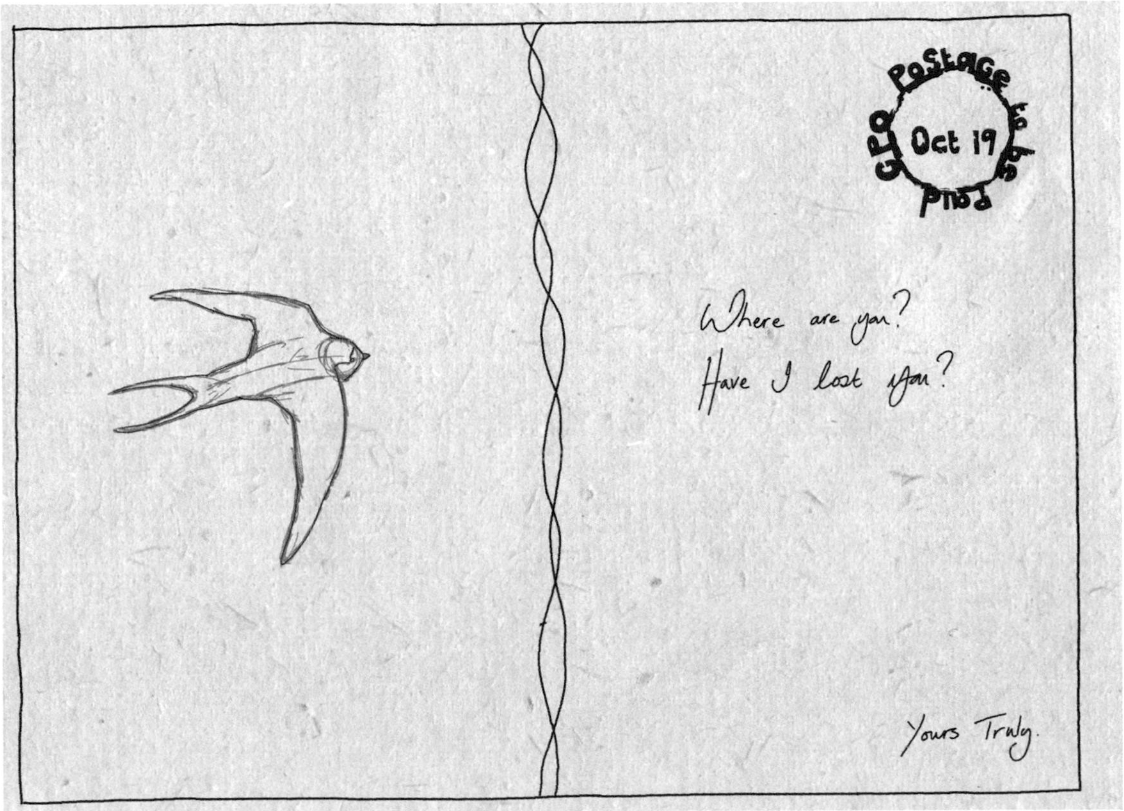
GPO Postage to be Paid
Oct 19
Where are you?
Have I lost you?
Yours Truly.

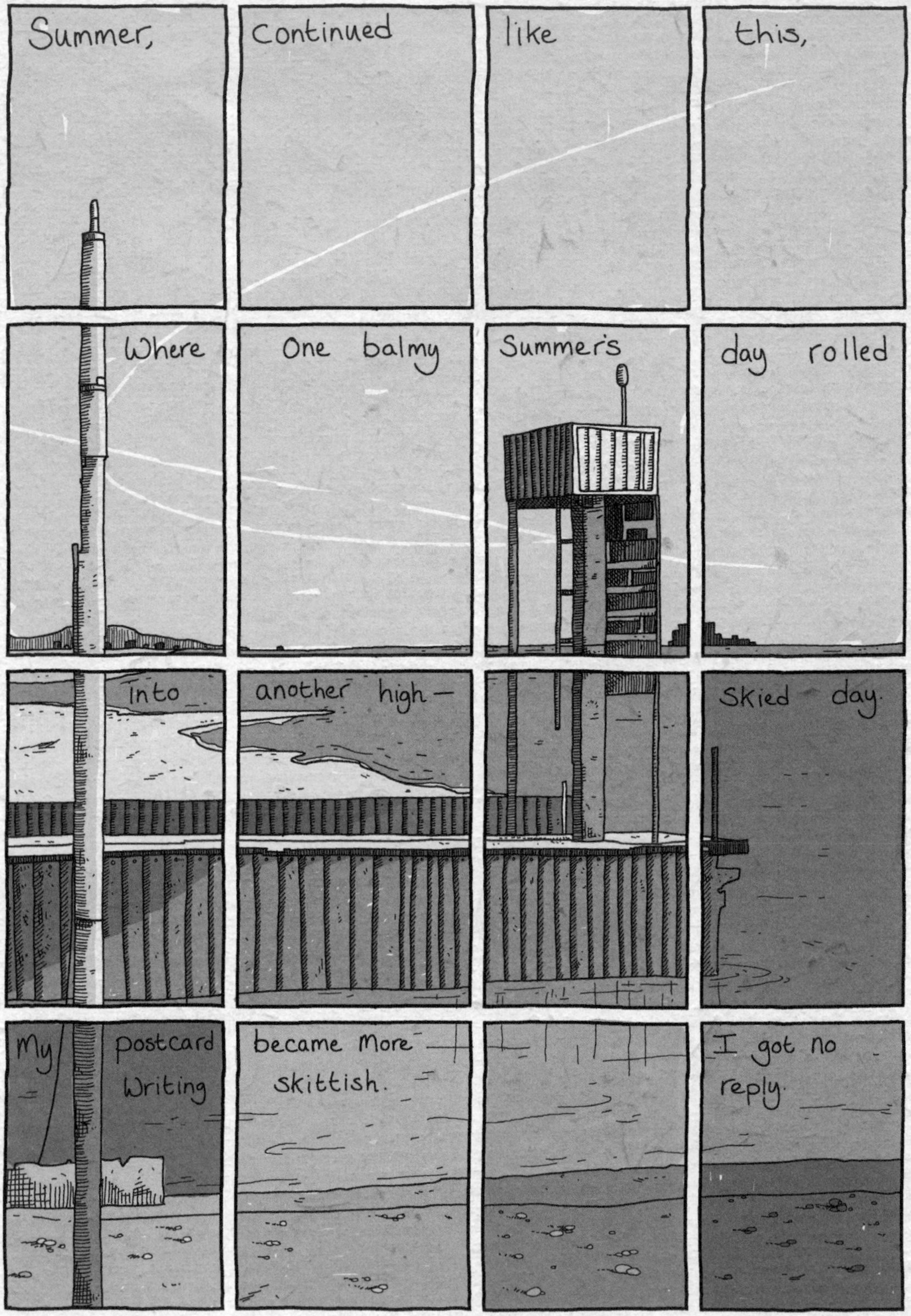
Summer,
continued
like
this,
Where
One balmy
Summer's
day rolled
into
another high-
Skied day.
My
postcard Writing
became more skittish.
I got no reply.

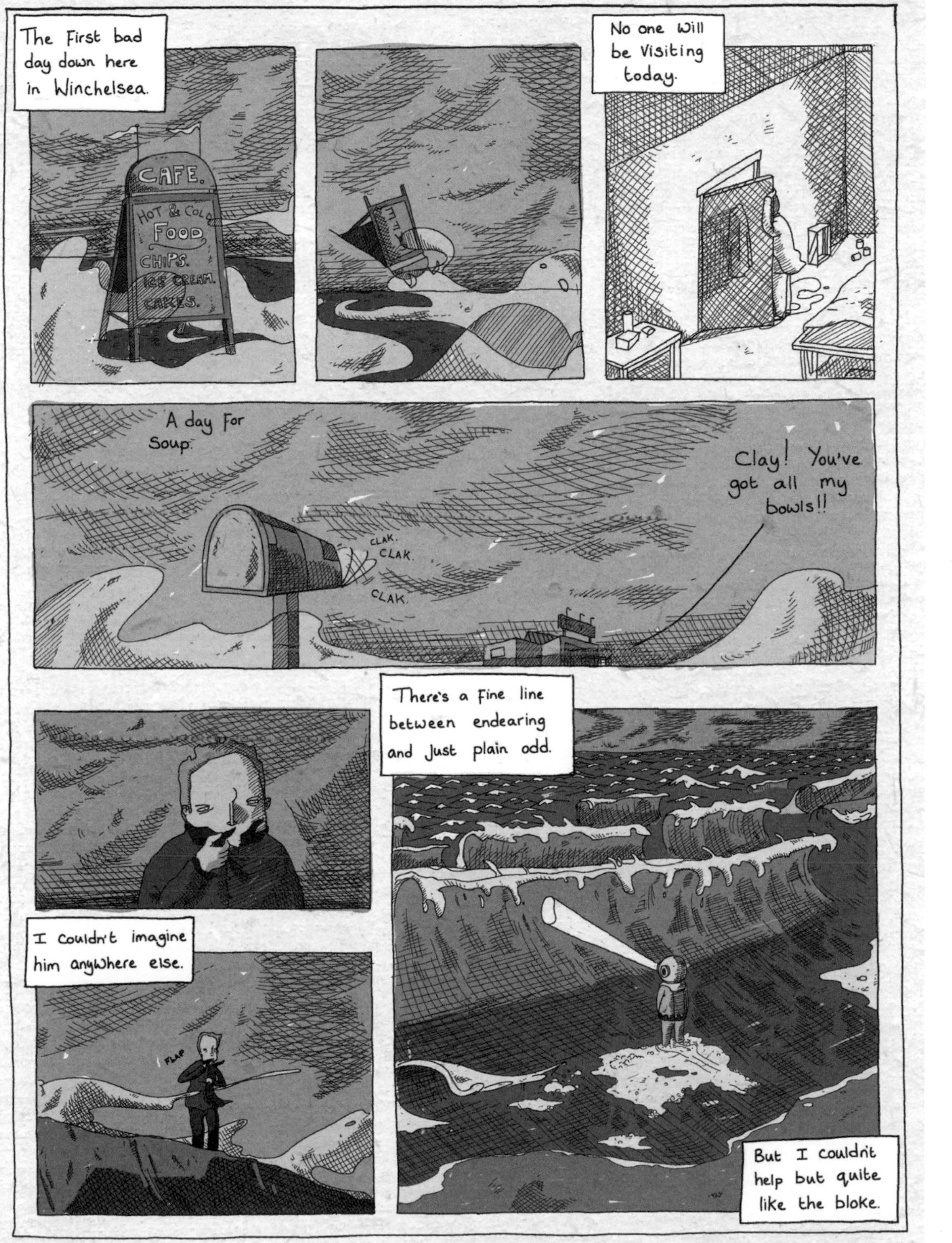

The First bad day down here in Winchelsea.
CAFE.
HOT & COLD
FOOD
CHIPS.
ICE CREAM.
CAKES.
No one will be Visiting today.
A day For Soup.
CLAK.
CLAK.
CLAK.
Clay! You've got all my bowls!!
There's a Fine line between endearing and Just plain odd.
I couldn't imagine him anywhere else.
FLAP
But I couldn't help but quite like the bloke.

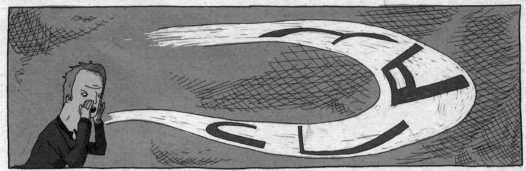

He wasn't going to hear a thing.

Instead of merely taking a peek inside his head, I was now tip-toeing into it.

All the gifted books and promised postcards.

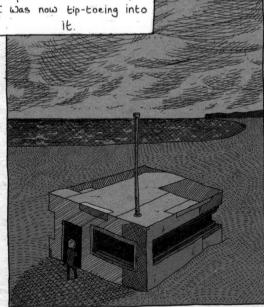

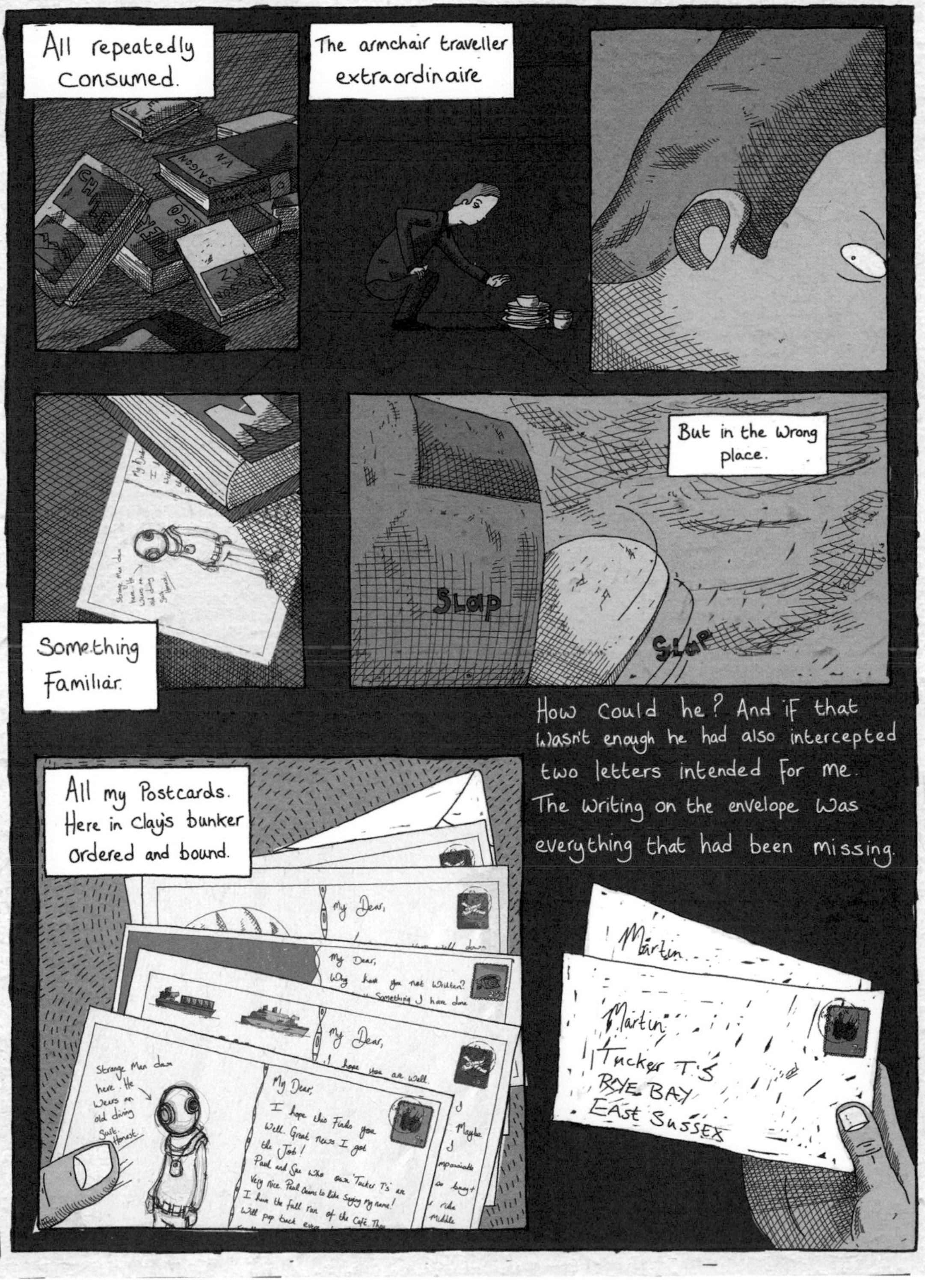

All repeatedly consumed.
The armchair traveller extraordinaire
Something Familiar.
But in the Wrong place.
SLAP
SLAP
How could he? And if that wasn't enough he had also intercepted two letters intended for me. The writing on the envelope was everything that had been missing.
All my Postcards. Here in Clay's bunker ordered and bound.
My Dear,
My Dear,
Why have you not Written?
Something I have done
My Dear,
I hope you are well.
Strange Man down here. He Wears an old diving Suit. Honest.
My Dear,
I hope this Finds you Well. Great news I got the Job!
Paul and Sue who own 'Tucker T's' are Very nice. Paul seems to like Saying my name!
I have the full run of the Café. They Will pop back
Martin
Martin
Tucker T's
RYE BAY
East Sussex

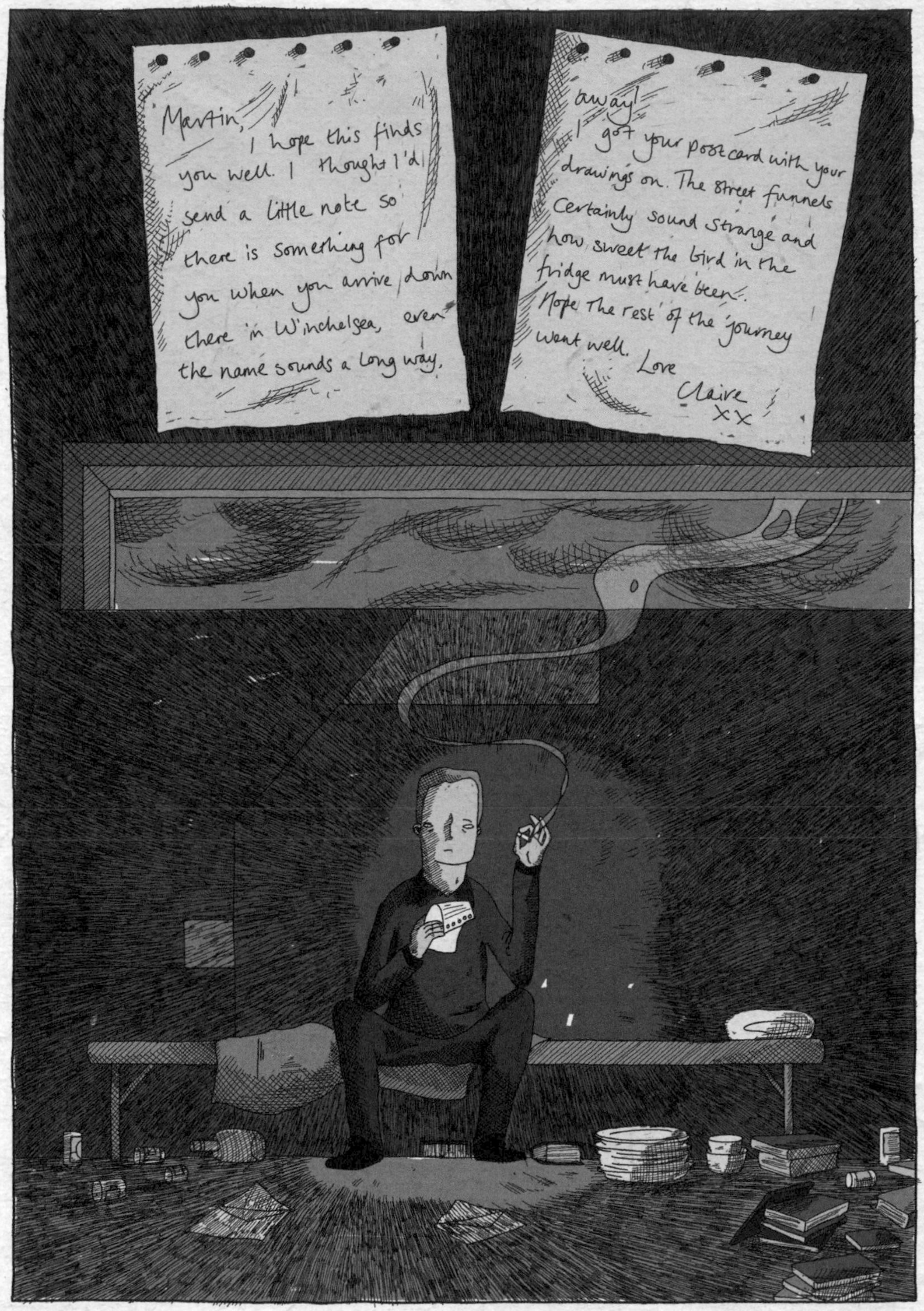

Martin,
I hope this finds you well. I thought I'd send a little note so there is something for you when you arrive down there in Winchelsea, even the name sounds a long way
away!
I got your postcard with your drawings on. The street funnels certainly sound strange and how sweet the bird in the fridge must have been.
Hope the rest of the journey went well.
Love
Claire
xx

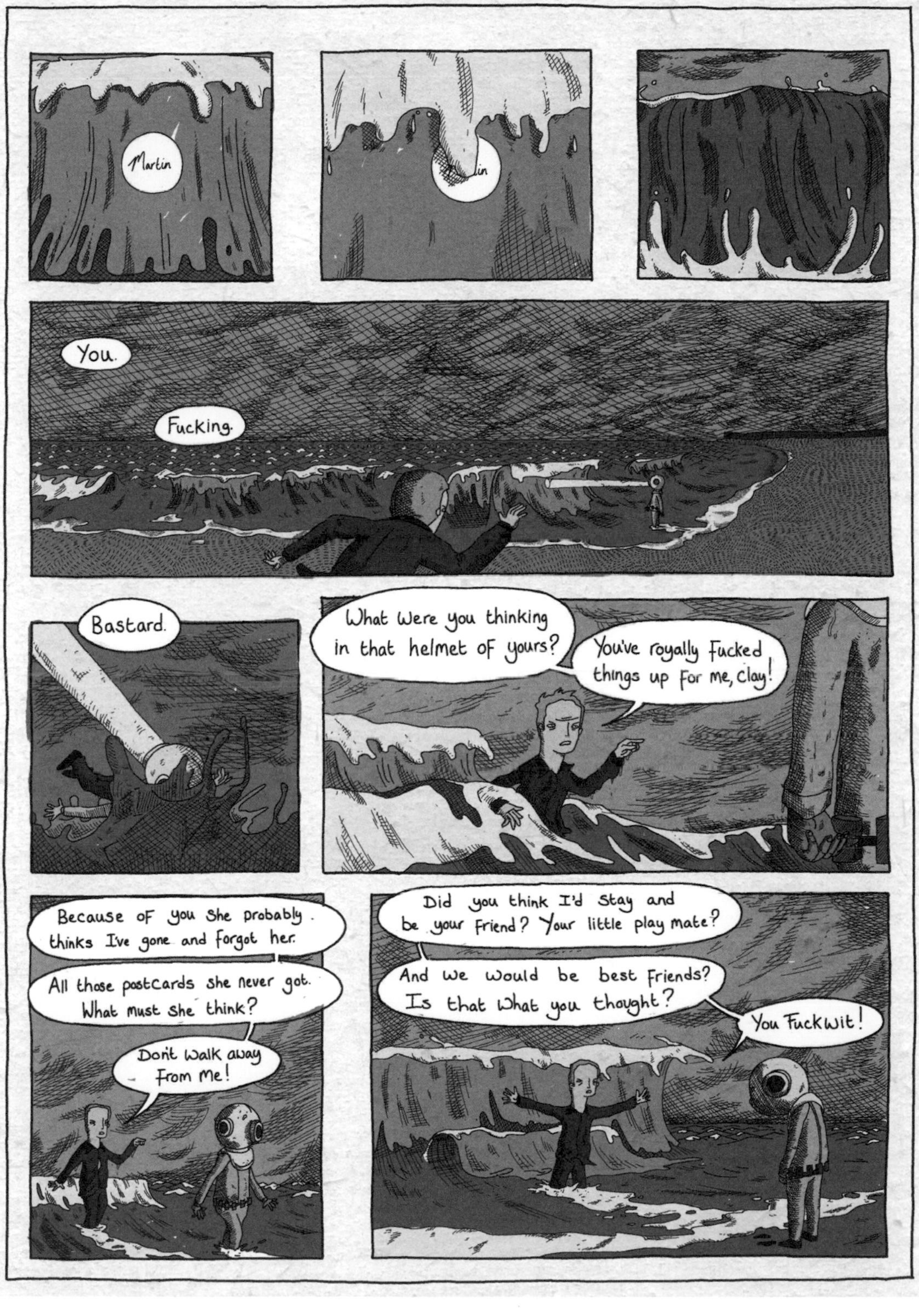

Martin
in
You.
Fucking.
Bastard.
What were you thinking in that helmet of yours?
You've royally fucked things up for me, clay!
Because of you she probably thinks I've gone and forgot her.
All those postcards she never got. What must she think?
Don't walk away from me!
Did you think I'd stay and be your friend? Your little play mate?
And we would be best friends? Is that what you thought?
You fuckwit!

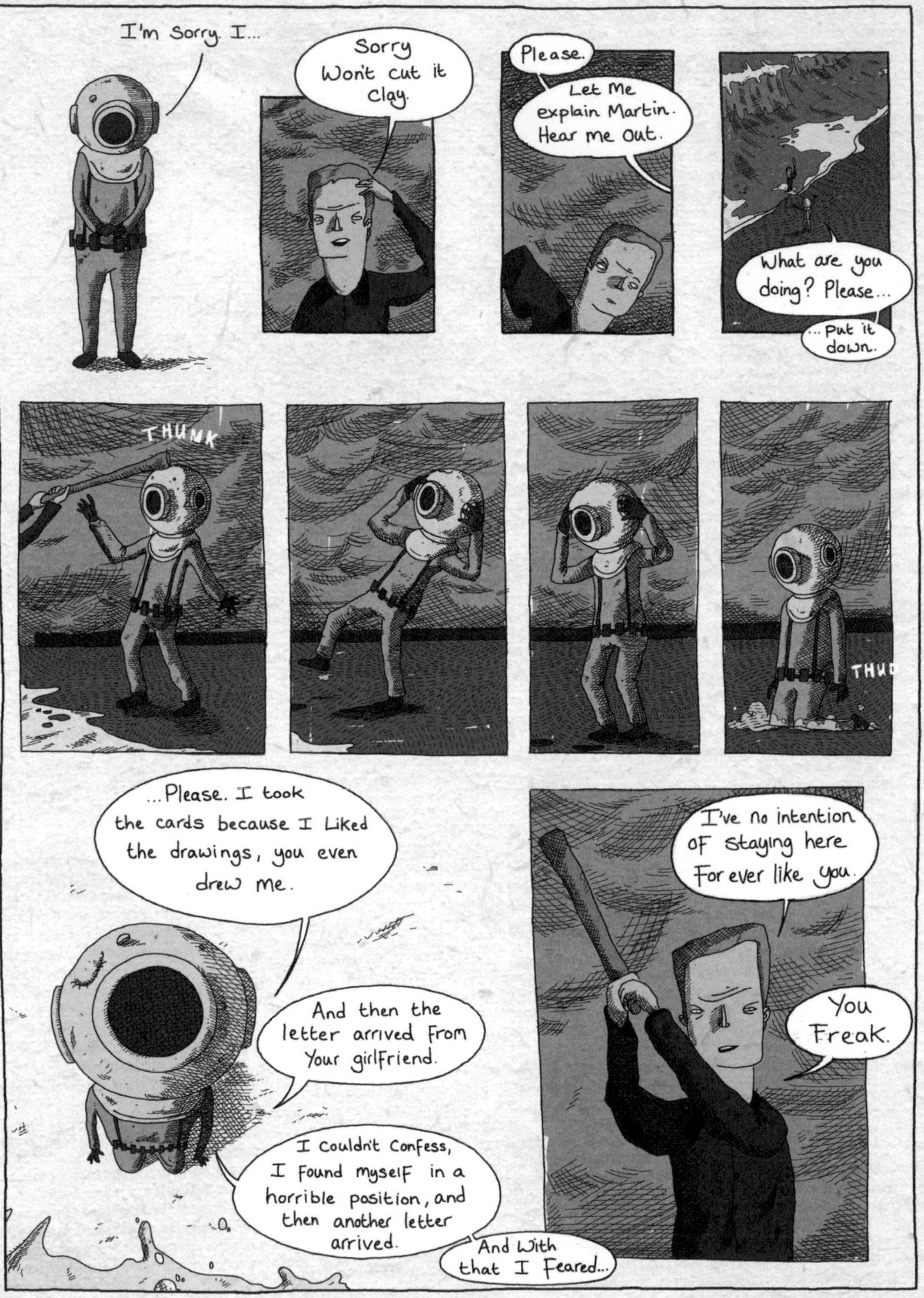
I'm Sorry. I...
Sorry Won't cut it Clay.
Please.
Let Me explain Martin. Hear me out.
What are you doing? Please...
...Put it down.
THUNK
THUD
...Please. I took the cards because I Liked the drawings, you even drew me.
And then the letter arrived From Your girlFriend.
I couldn't Confess, I Found myself in a horrible position, and then another letter arrived.
And With that I Feared...
I've no intention oF staying here For ever like you.
You Freak.

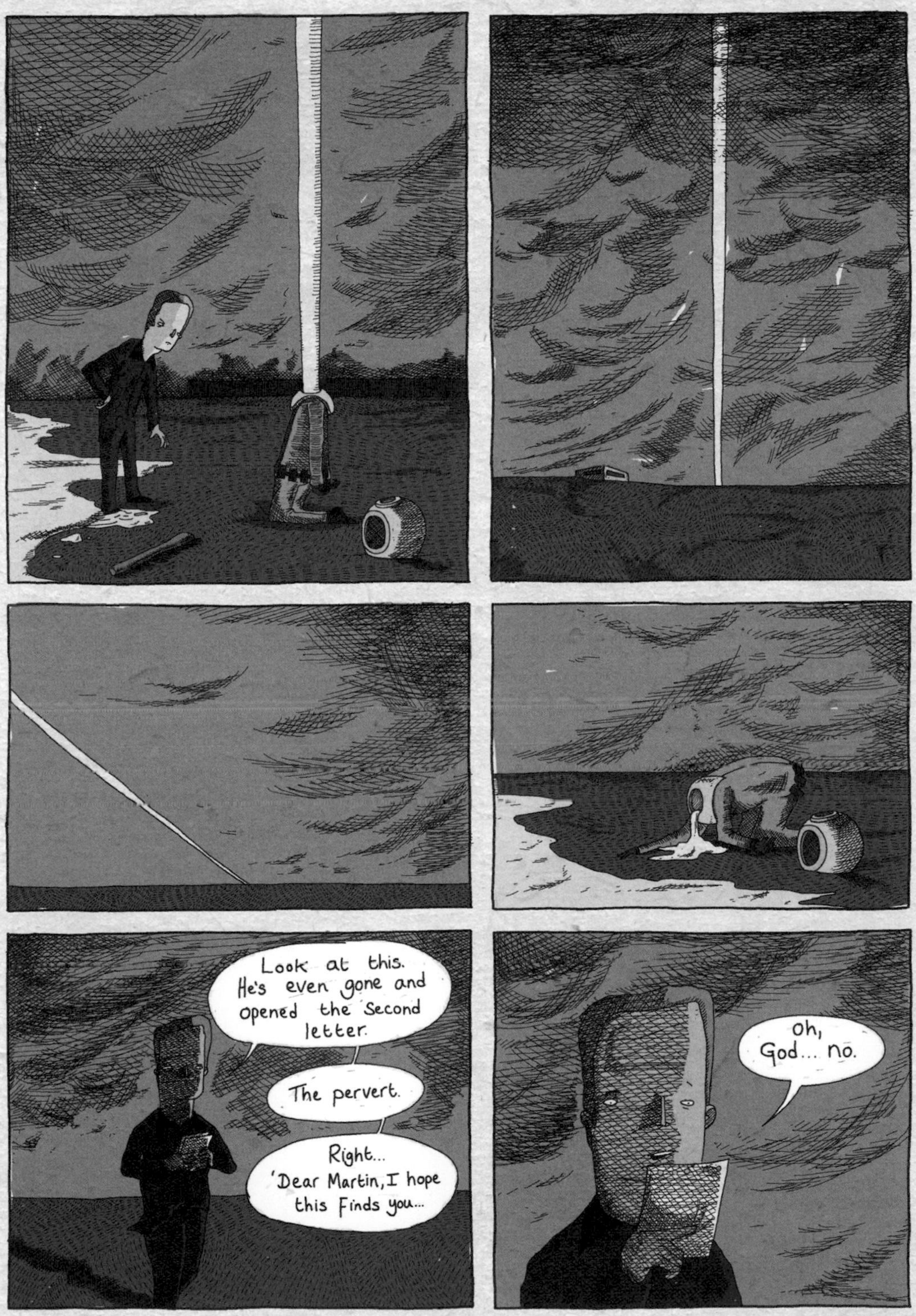
Look at this.
He's even gone and opened the Second letter.
The pervert.
Right...
'Dear Martin, I hope this Finds you...
Oh,
God.... no.

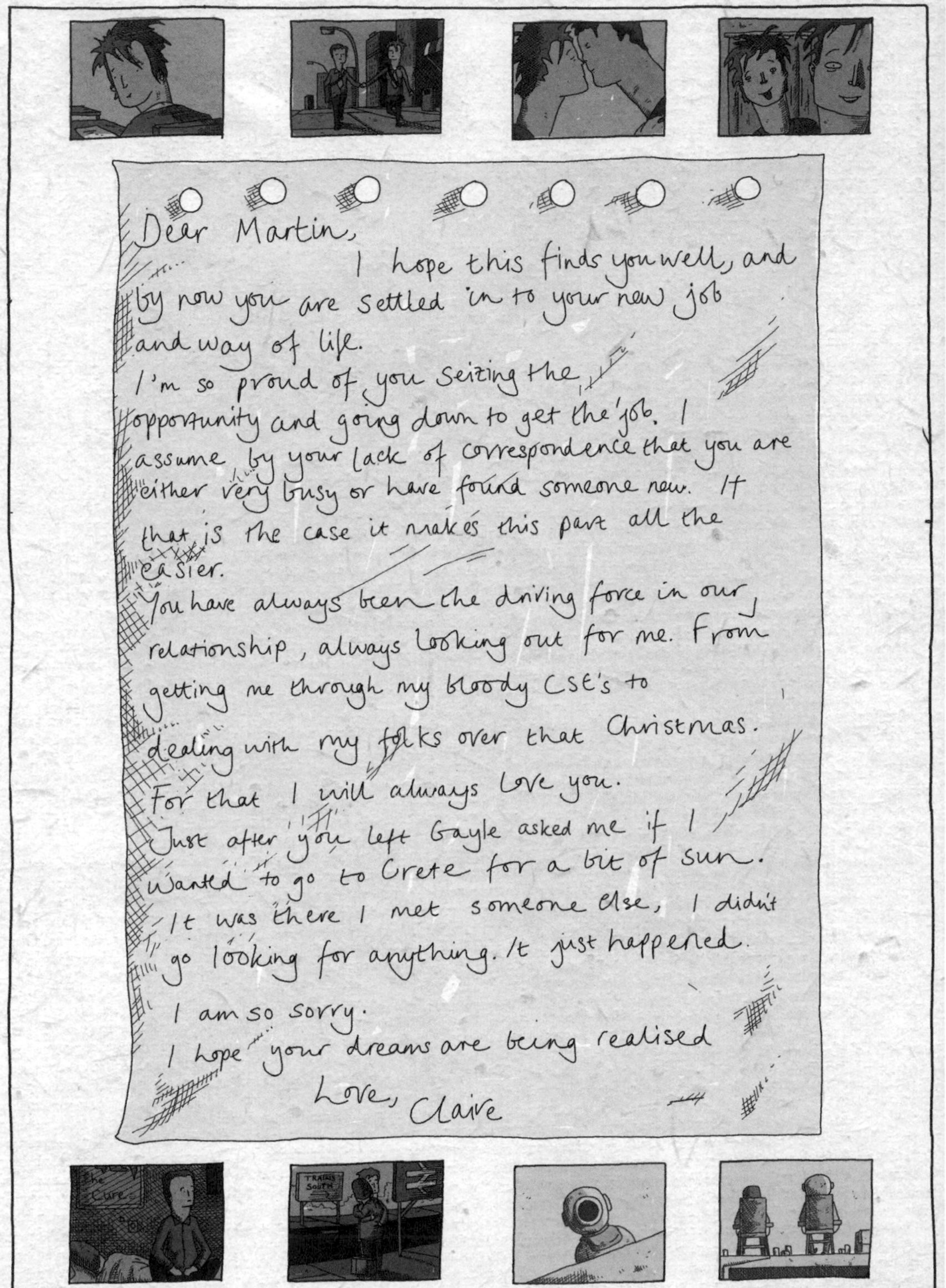
The Cure
TRAINS SOUTH

Dear Martin,

I hope this finds you well, and by now you are settled in to your new job and way of life.

I'm so proud of you seizing the opportunity and going down to get the job. I assume by your lack of correspondence that you are either very busy or have found someone new. If that is the case it makes this part all the easier.

You have always been the driving force in our relationship, always looking out for me. From getting me through my bloody CSE's to dealing with my folks over that Christmas. For that I will always love you.

Just after you left Gayle asked me if I wanted to go to Crete for a bit of sun. It was there I met someone else, I didn't go looking for anything. It just happened.

I am so sorry.

I hope your dreams are being realised

Love, Claire

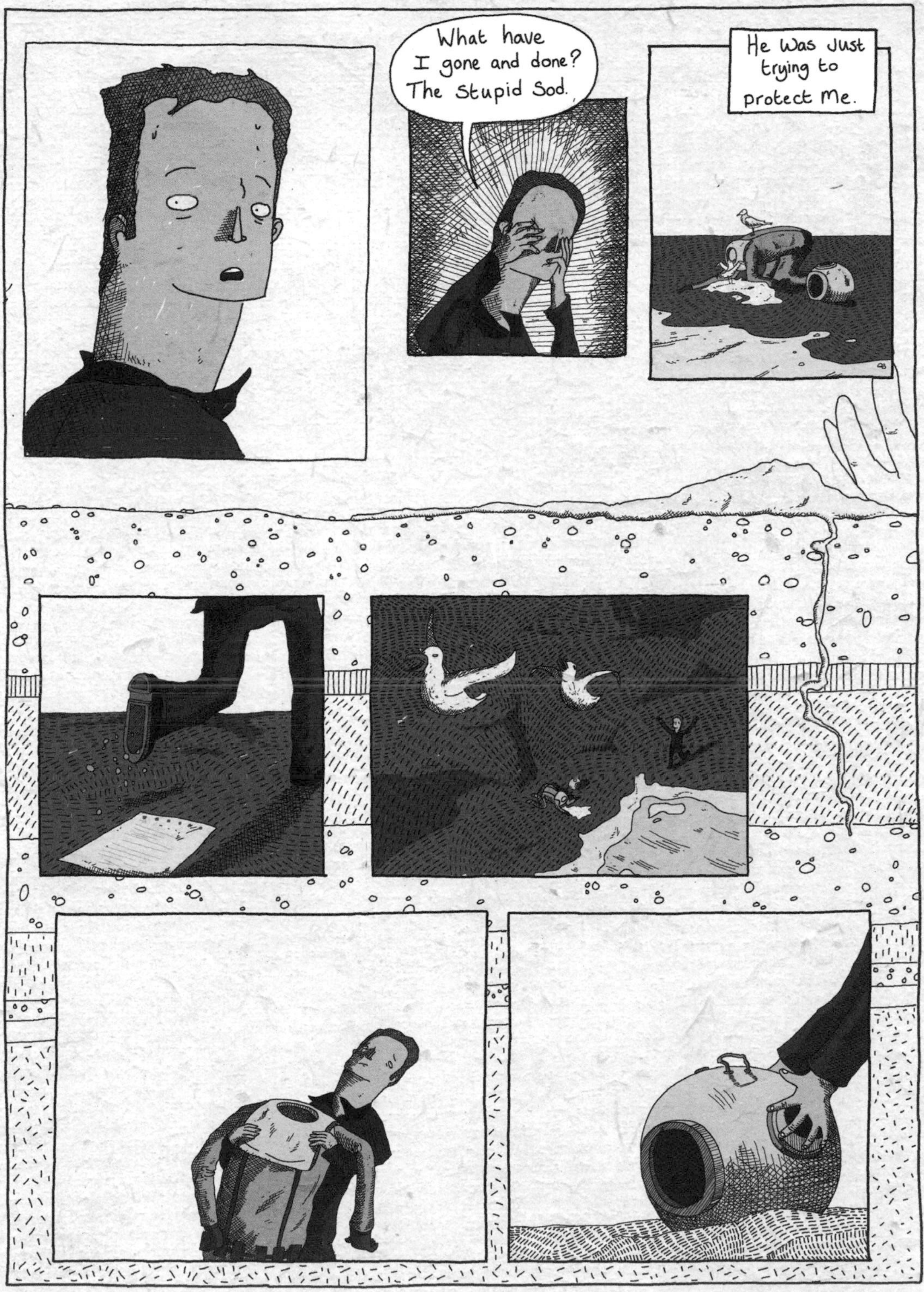
What have I gone and done? The stupid sod.
He was just trying to protect me.

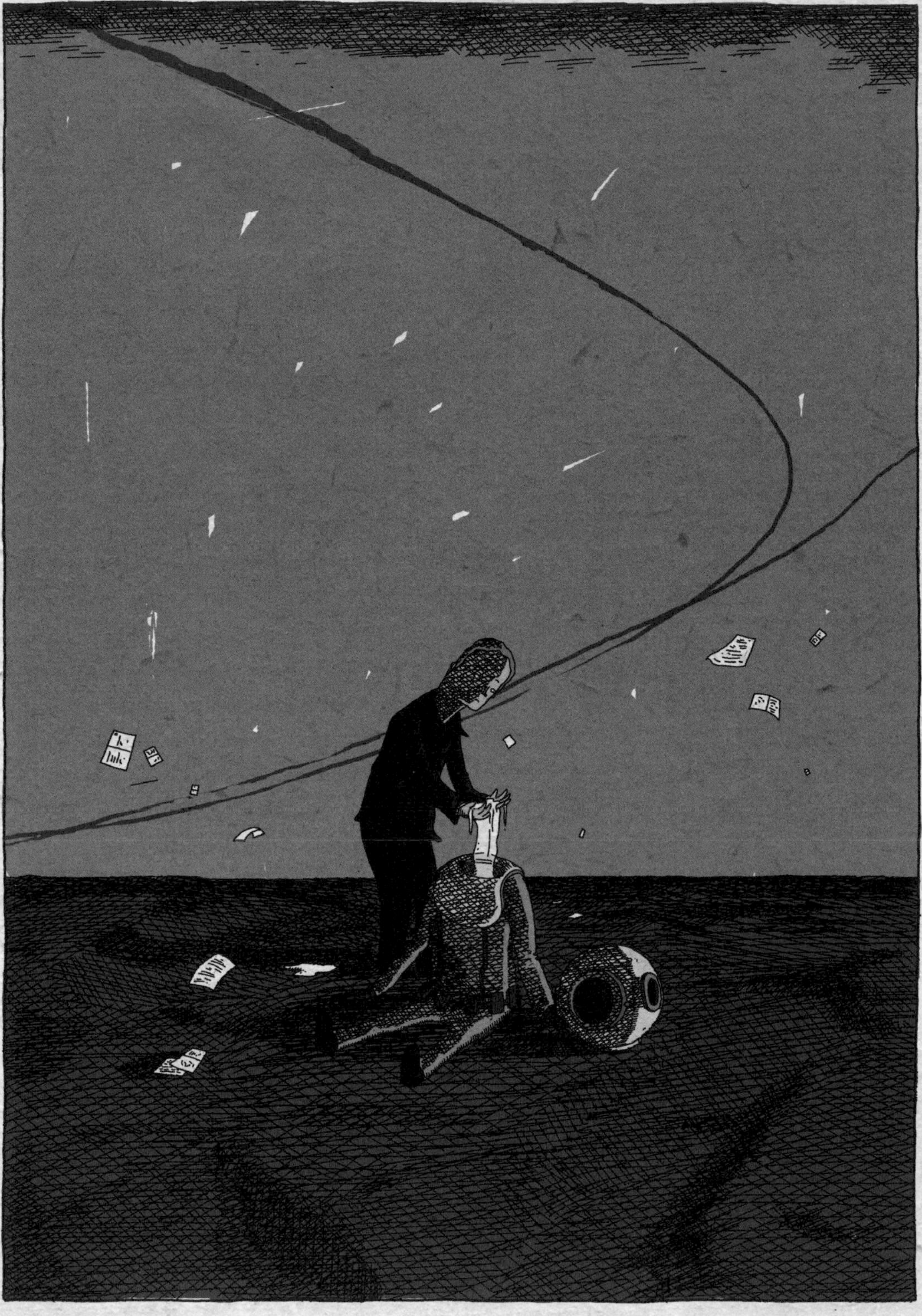

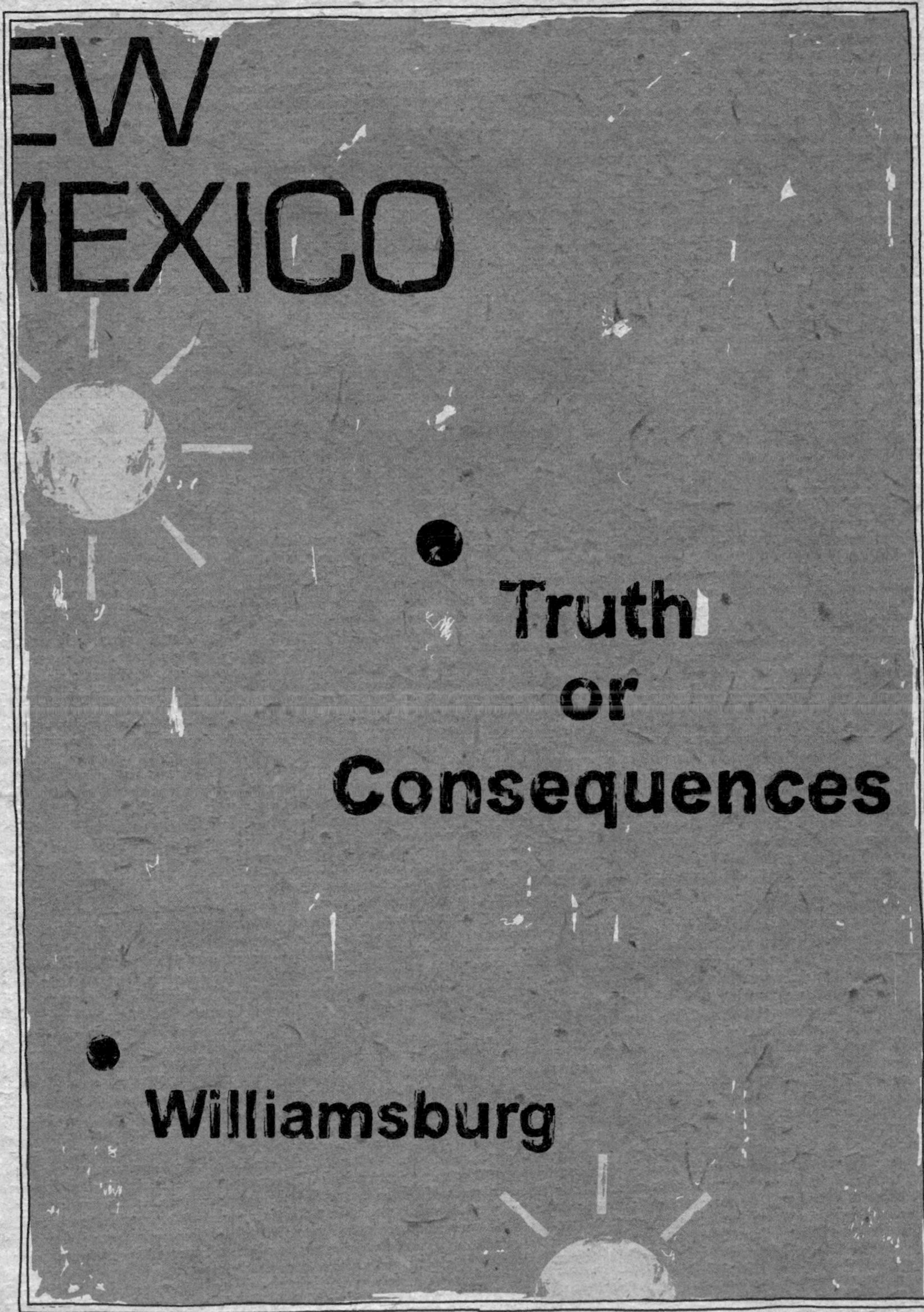
EW
MEXICO
Truth
or
Consequences
Williamsburg

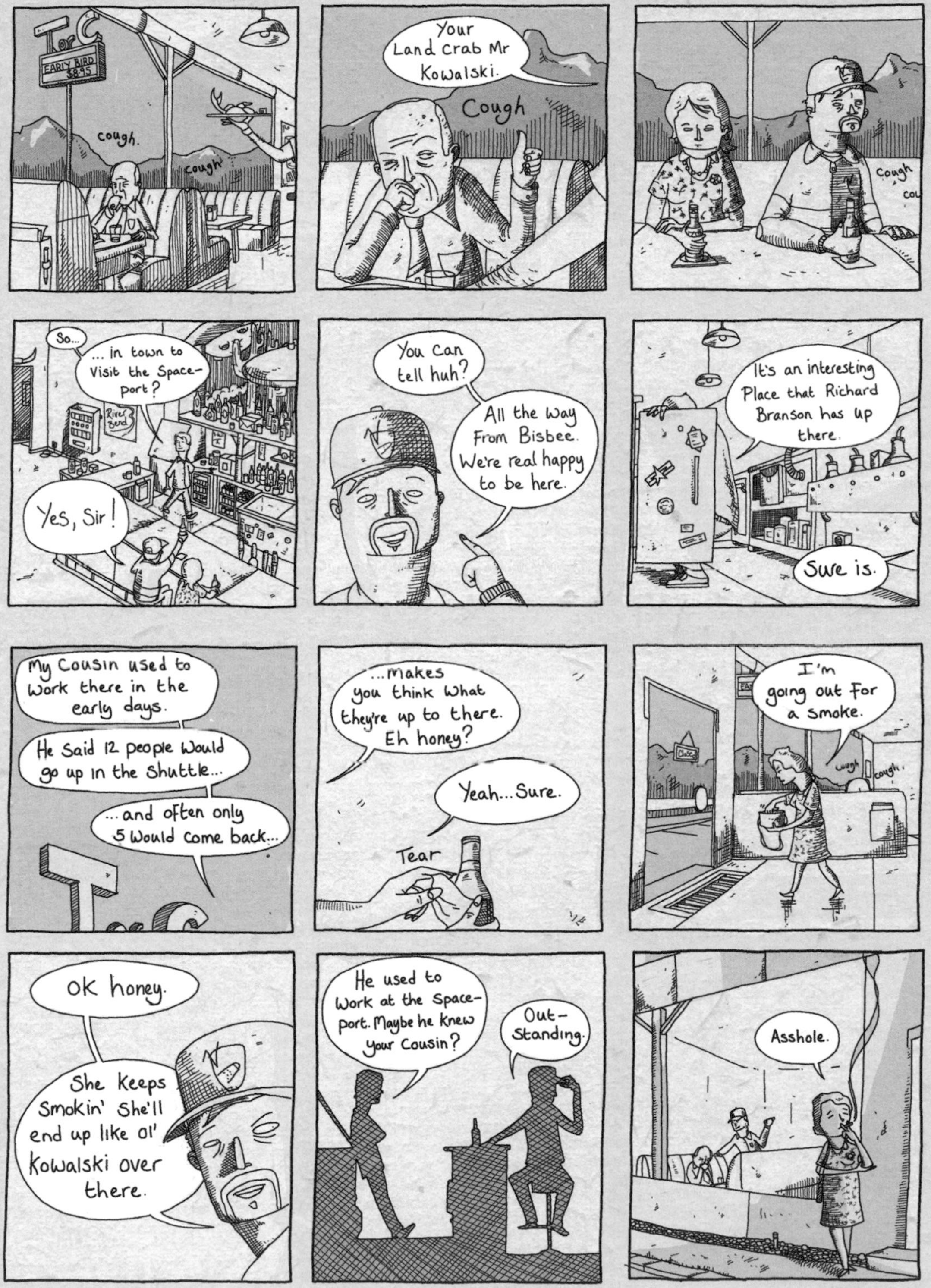

EARLY BIRD $8.95
cough.
cough
Your Land Crab Mr Kowalski.
Cough
Cough
So...
... in town to Visit the Space-port?
River Bend
Yes, Sir!
You can tell huh?
All the Way From Bisbee. We're real happy to be here.
It's an interesting Place that Richard Branson has up there.
Sure is.
My Cousin used to Work there in the early days.
He Said 12 people Would go up in the Shuttle...
...and often only 5 Would come back...
...makes you think What they're up to there. Eh honey?
Yeah...Sure.
Tear
I'm going out For a smoke.
cough
cough.
OK honey.
She Keeps Smokin' She'll end up like Ol' Kowalski over there.
He used to Work at the Space-port. Maybe he knew your Cousin?
Out-Standing.
Asshole.

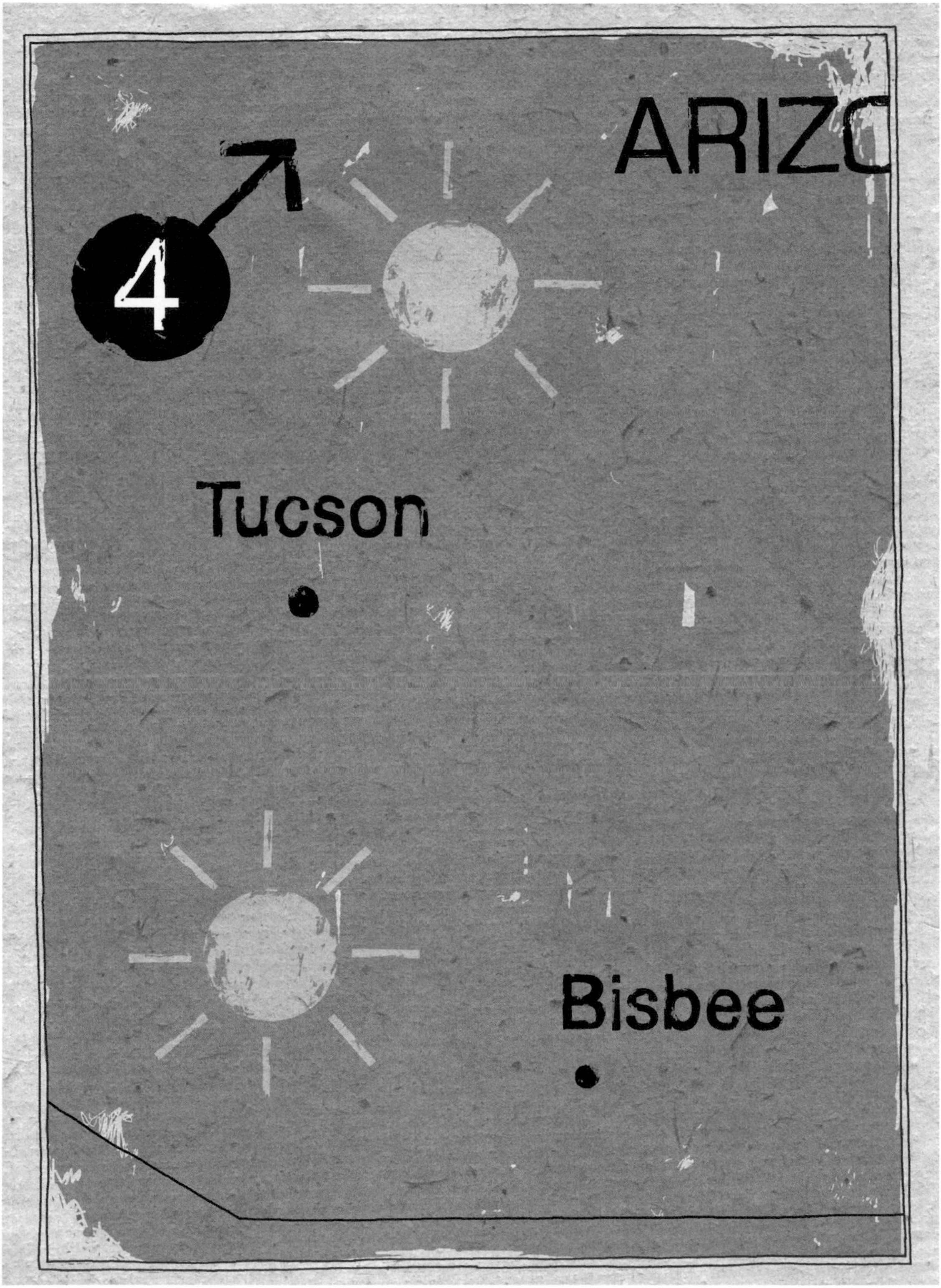
4
ARIZO
Tucson
Bisbee

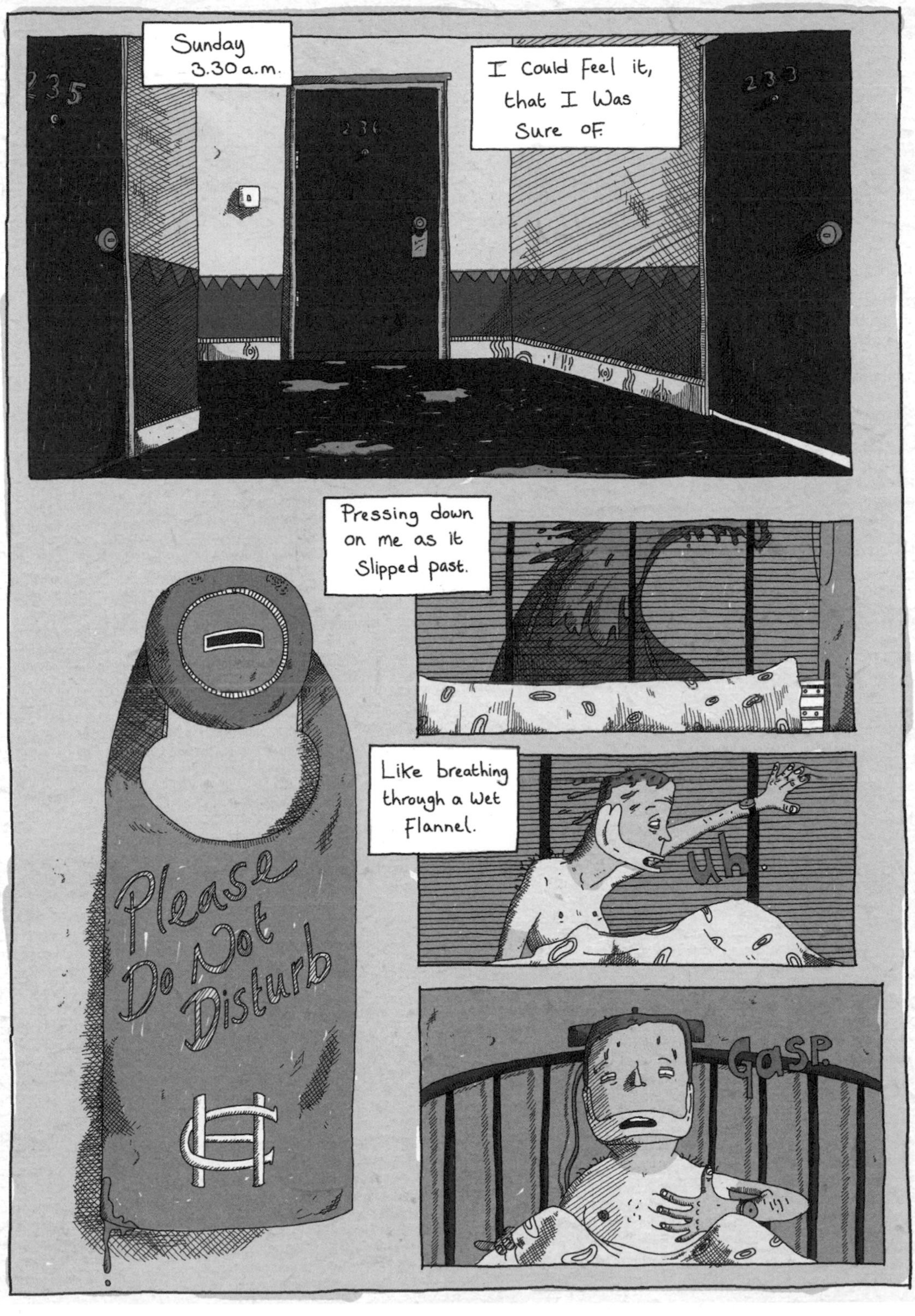

Sunday 3.30 a.m.
235
236
233
I Could Feel it, that I Was Sure of.
Pressing down on me as it Slipped past.
Please Do Not Disturb
Like breathing through a Wet Flannel.
uh.
GaSP.

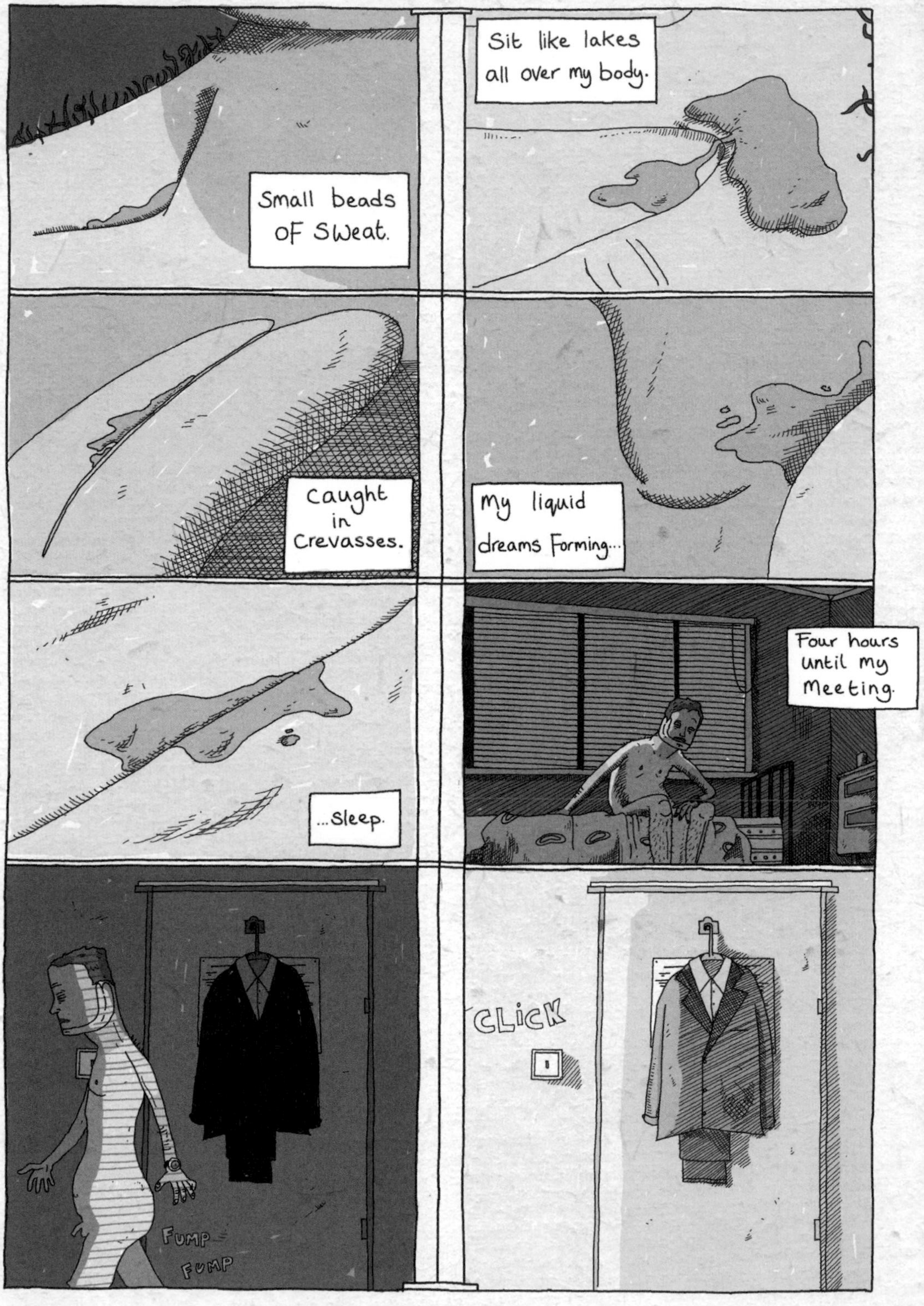
Small beads of sweat.
Sit like lakes all over my body.
Caught in crevasses.
My liquid dreams forming...
...sleep.
Four hours until my meeting.
FUMP
FUMP
CLICK

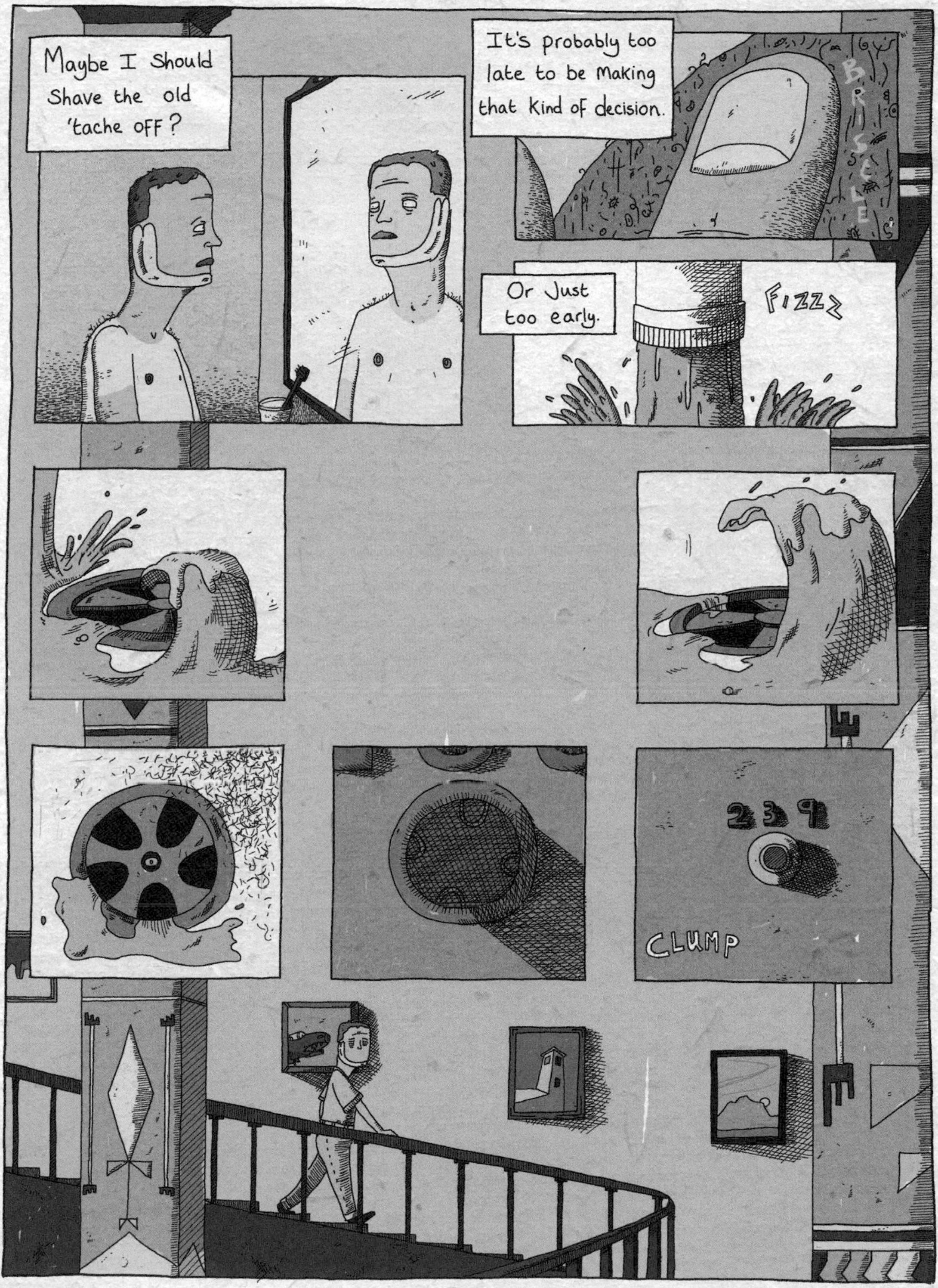
Maybe I should shave the old 'tache off?
It's probably too late to be making that kind of decision.
BRISTLE
Or just too early.
FIZZZ
239
CLUMP

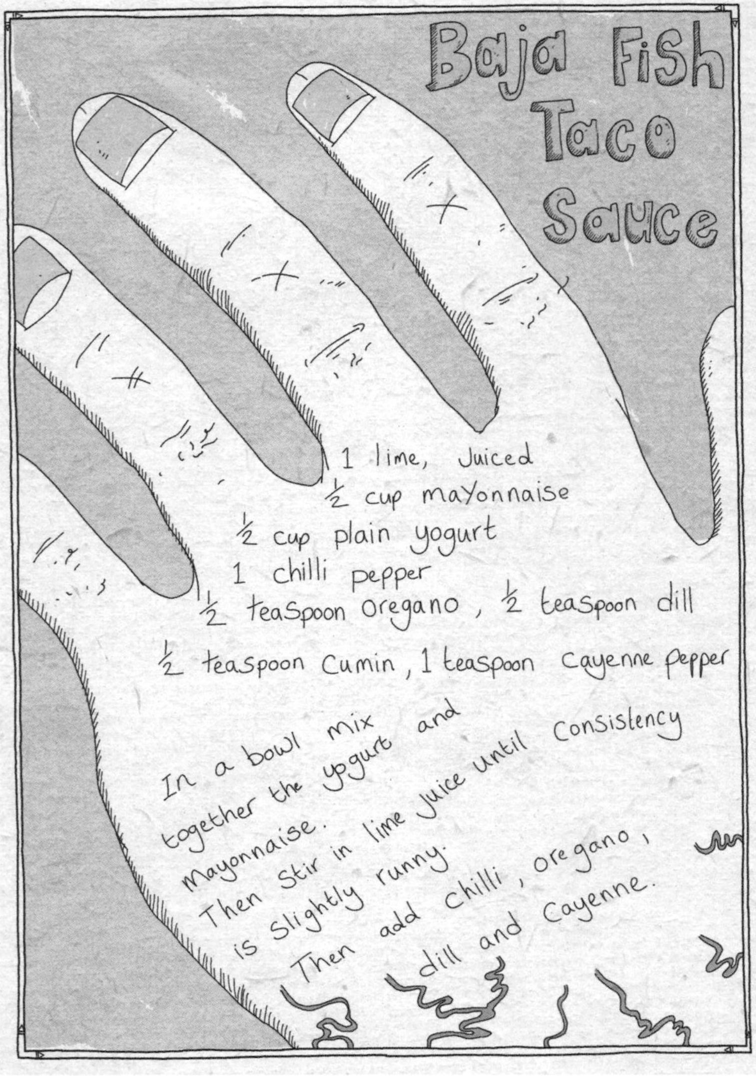

Baja Fish Taco Sauce
1 lime, Juiced
½ cup mayonnaise
½ cup plain yogurt
1 chilli pepper
½ teaspoon oregano, ½ teaspoon dill
½ teaspoon Cumin, 1 teaspoon cayenne pepper
In a bowl mix together the yogurt and mayonnaise. Then Stir in lime Juice until Consistency is Slightly runny. Then add chilli, oregano, dill and Cayenne.

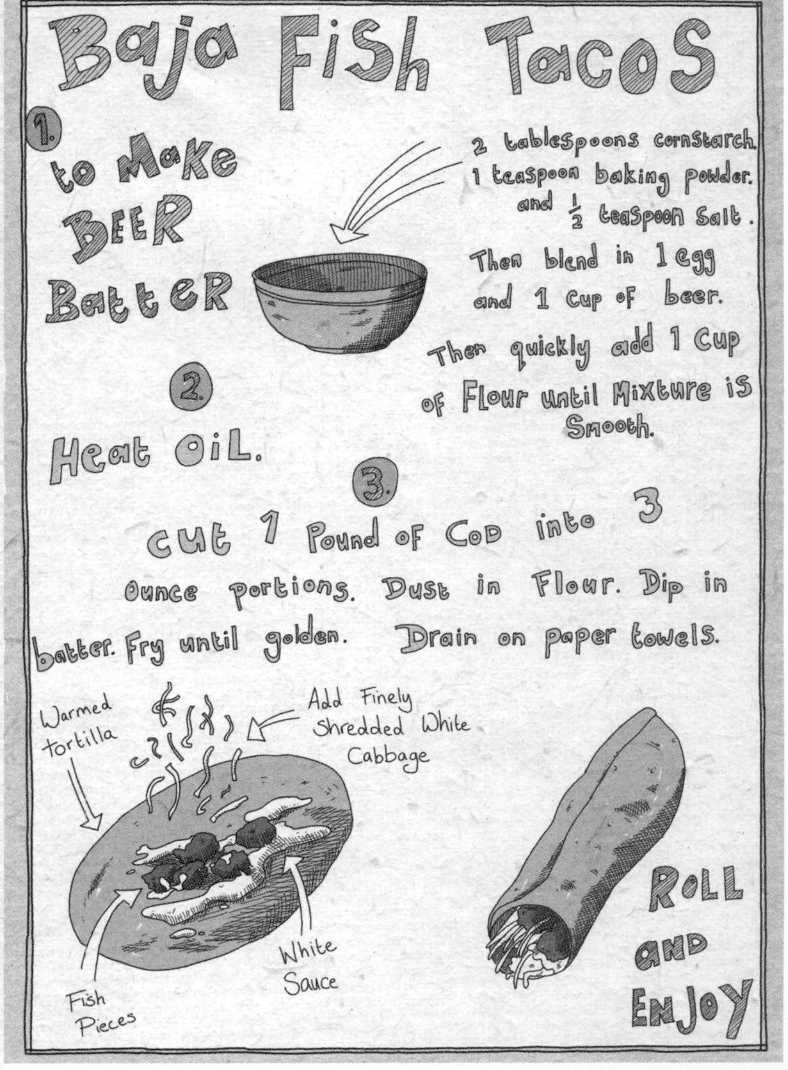

Baja Fish Tacos
1. to Make BEER Batter
2 tablespoons cornstarch, 1 teaspoon baking powder. and ½ teaspoon Salt.
Then blend in 1 egg and 1 cup of beer.
Then quickly add 1 Cup of Flour until Mixture is Smooth.
2. Heat oil.
3. cut 1 Pound of COD into 3 Ounce portions. Dust in Flour. Dip in batter. Fry until golden. Drain on paper towels.
Warmed tortilla
Add Finely Shredded White Cabbage
Fish Pieces
White Sauce
ROLL AND ENJOY

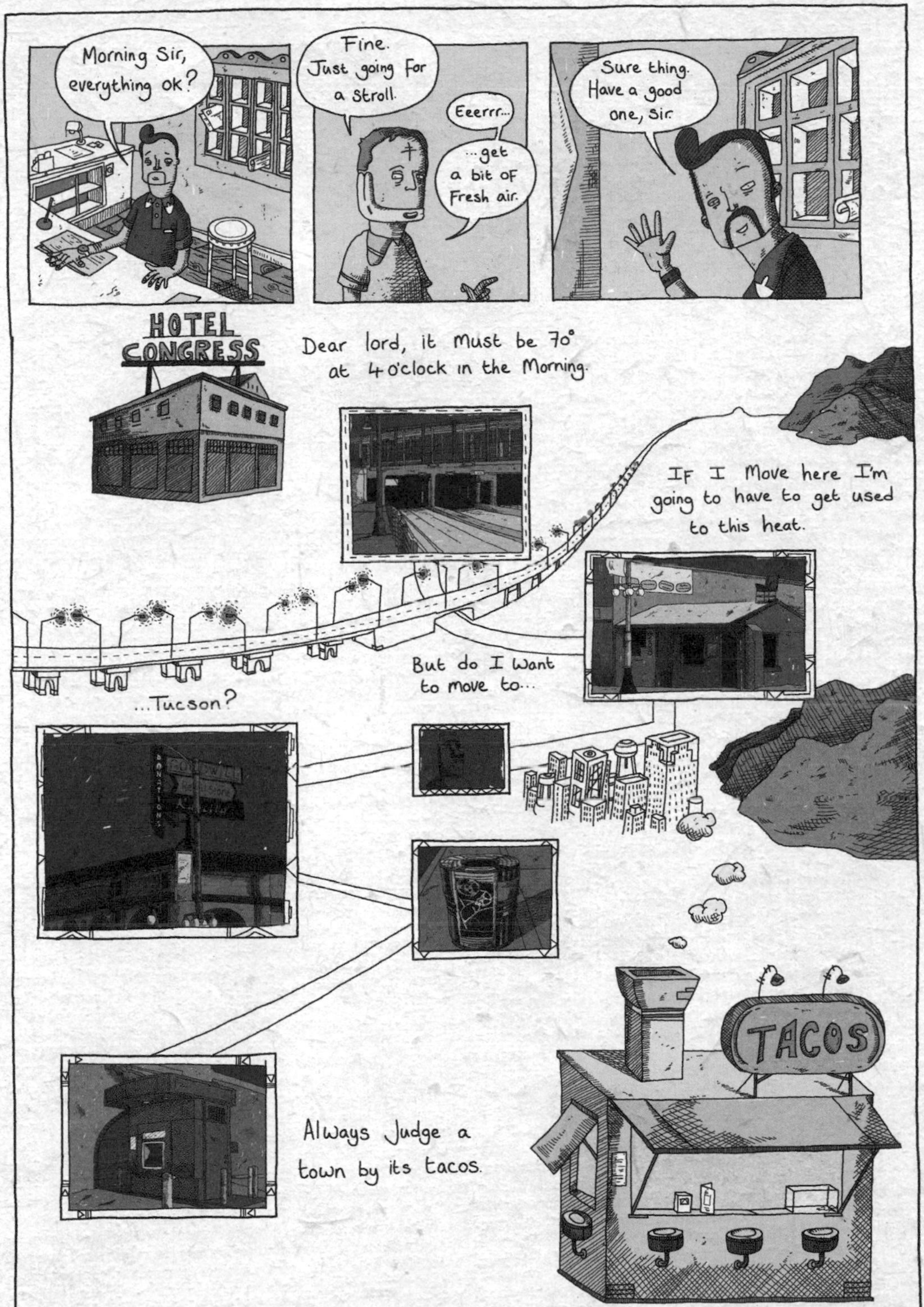
Morning Sir, everything ok?
Fine. Just going for a stroll.
Eeerrr...
...get a bit of fresh air.
Sure thing. Have a good one, Sir.
HOTEL CONGRESS
Dear lord, it must be 70° at 4 o'clock in the morning.
If I move here I'm going to have to get used to this heat.
But do I want to move to...
...Tucson?
Always judge a town by its tacos.
TACOS

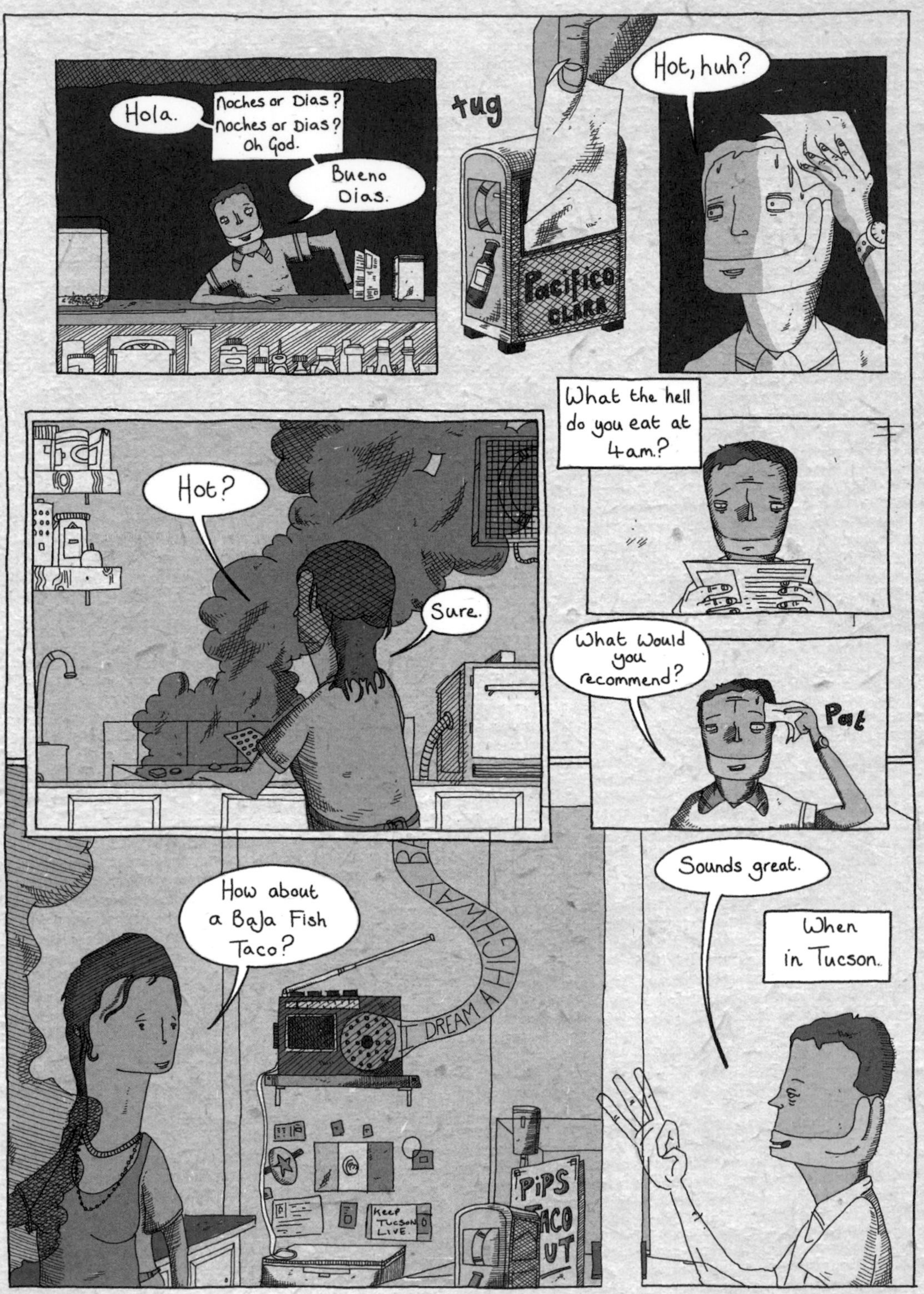

Hola.
Noches or Dias? Noches or Dias? Oh God.
Bueno Dias.
tug
Pacifico CLARA
Hot, huh?
What the hell do you eat at 4am.?
Hot?
Sure.
What Would you recommend?
Pat
How about a Baja Fish Taco?
I DREAM A HIGHWAY BA
KEEP TUCSON LIVE.
PIPS TACO OUT
Sounds great.
When in Tucson.

gurgle
You're not local, Señor?
tap
tap
No, I guess not.
HISS
I look like an out-of-towner, huh?
I tend to know my clients at this time of night. And of course we're near The Congress.
Of course.

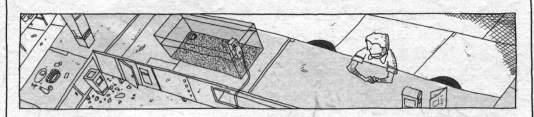

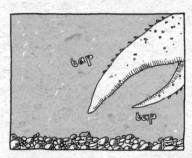

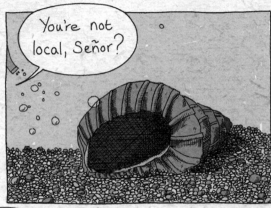

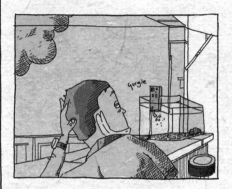

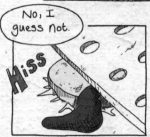

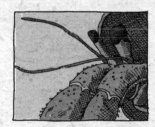

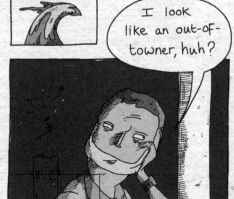

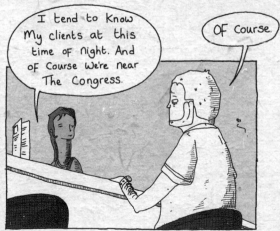

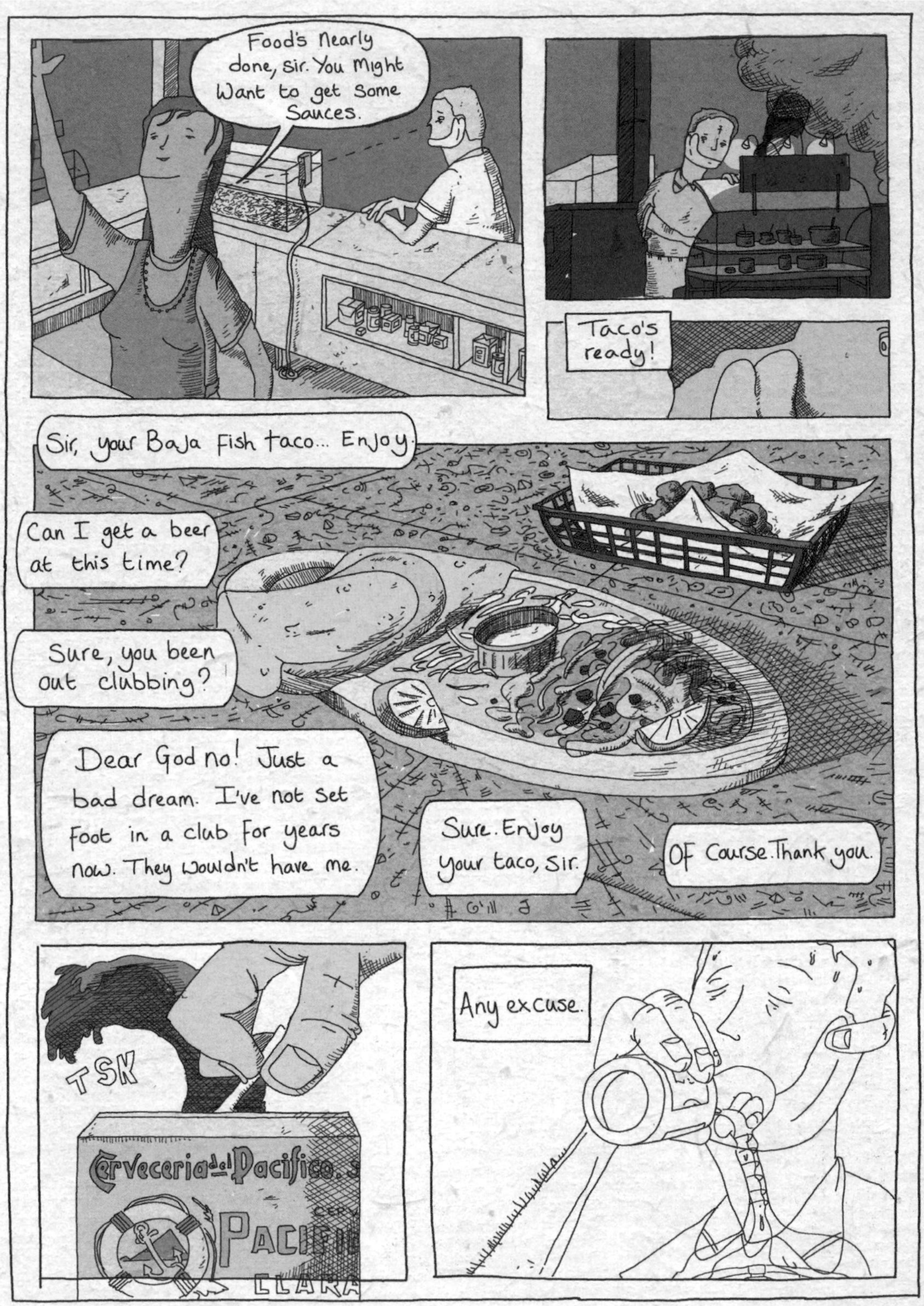
Food's nearly done, sir. You might want to get some sauces.
Taco's ready!
Sir, your Baja fish taco... Enjoy.
Can I get a beer at this time?
Sure, you been out clubbing?
Dear God no! Just a bad dream. I've not set foot in a club for years now. They wouldn't have me.
Sure. Enjoy your taco, sir.
Of course. Thank you.
TSK
Cerveceria del Pacifico
PACIFIC
CLARA
Any excuse.

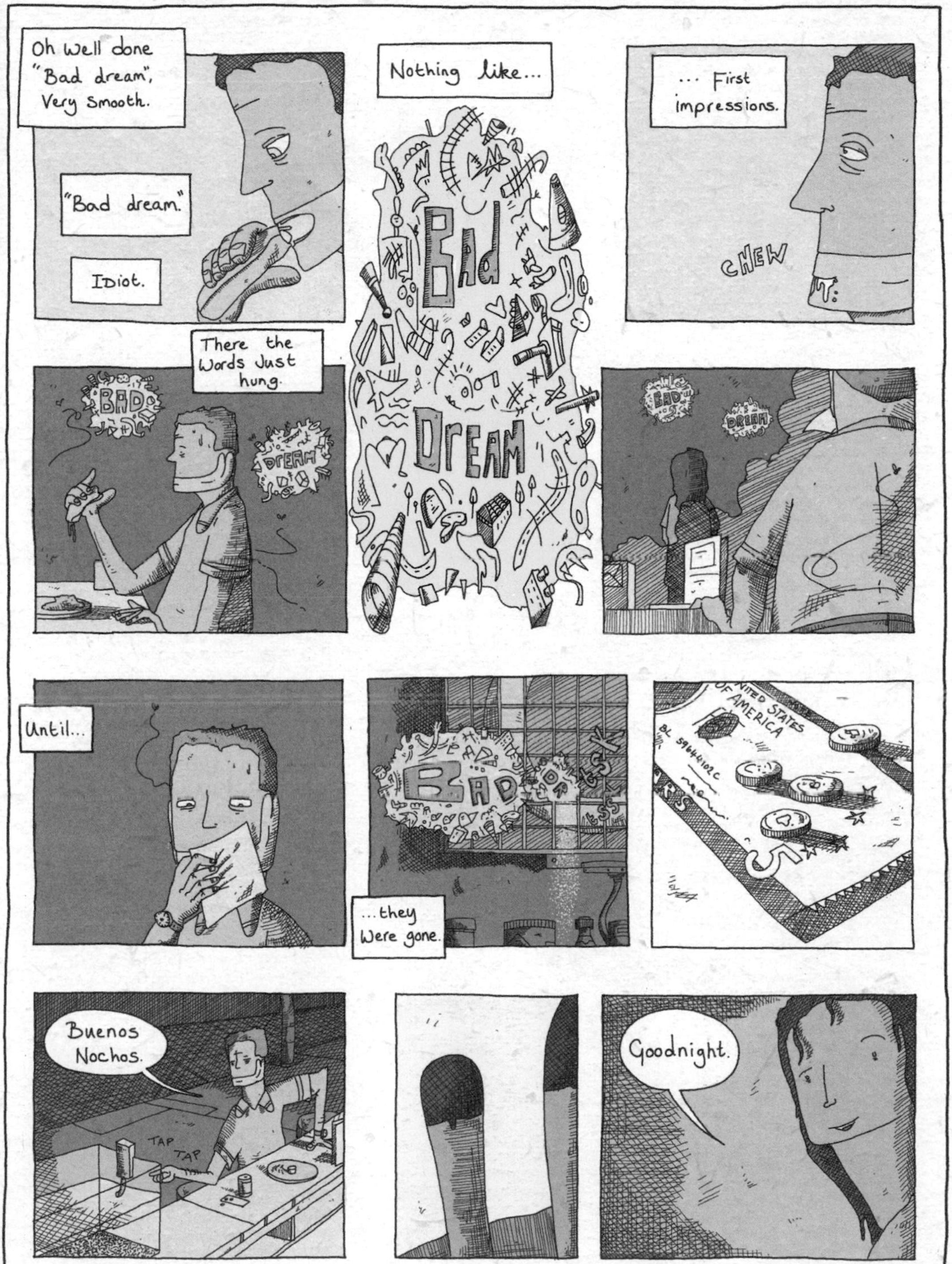

Oh well done "Bad dream", Very Smooth.
"Bad dream."
Idiot.
Nothing like...
Bad
Dream
... First impressions.
CHEW
There the Words Just hung.
BAD
DREAM
BAD
DREAM
Until...
BAD
...they Were gone.
UNITED STATES OF AMERICA
Buenos Nochos.
TAP TAP
Goodnight.

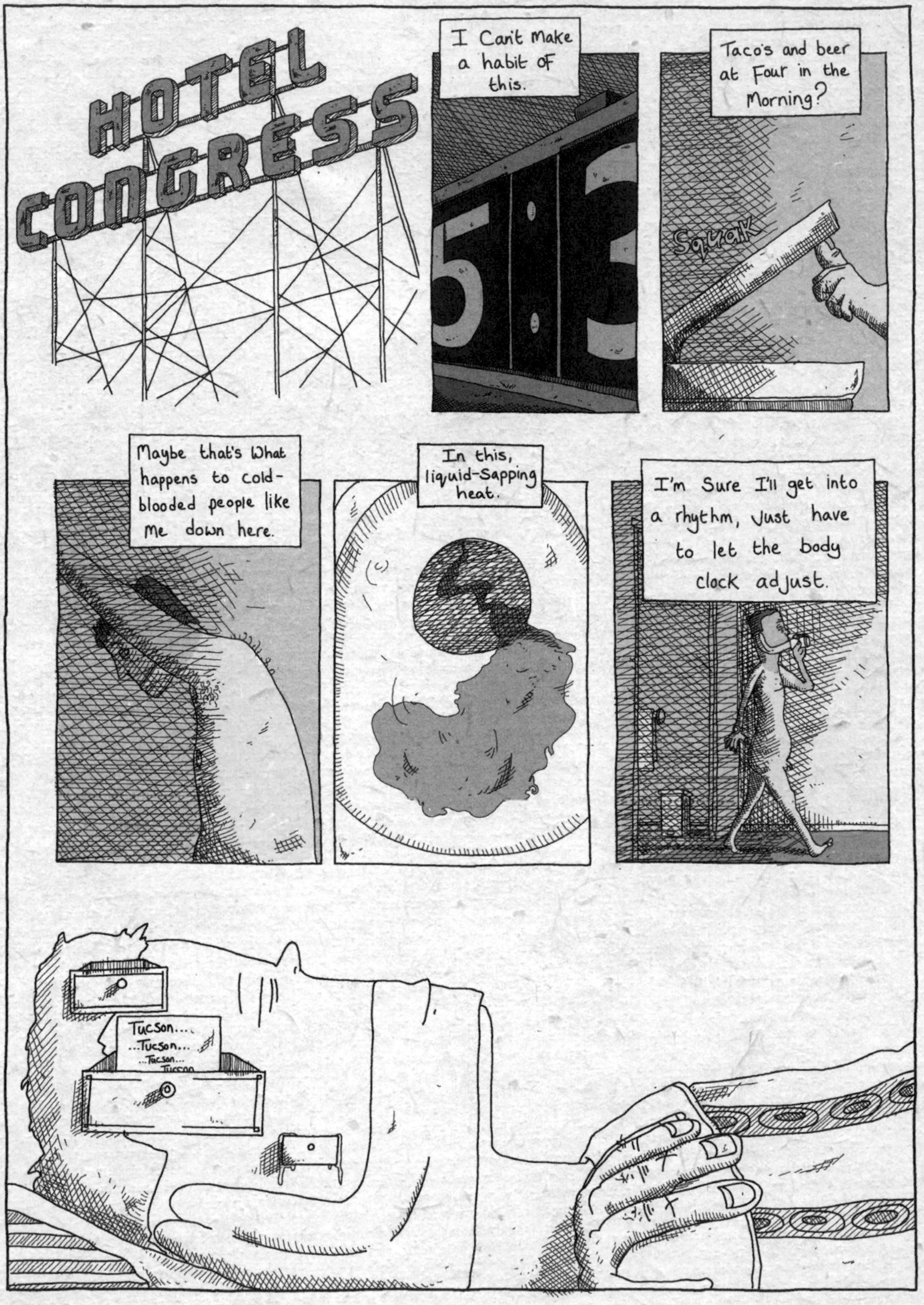
HOTEL CONGRESS
I Can't make a habit of this.
5:3
Taco's and beer at Four in the Morning?
Squak
Maybe that's What happens to cold-blooded people like me down here.
In this, liquid-Sapping heat.
I'm Sure I'll get into a rhythm, Just have to let the body clock adjust.
Tucson...
...Tucson...
...Tucson...

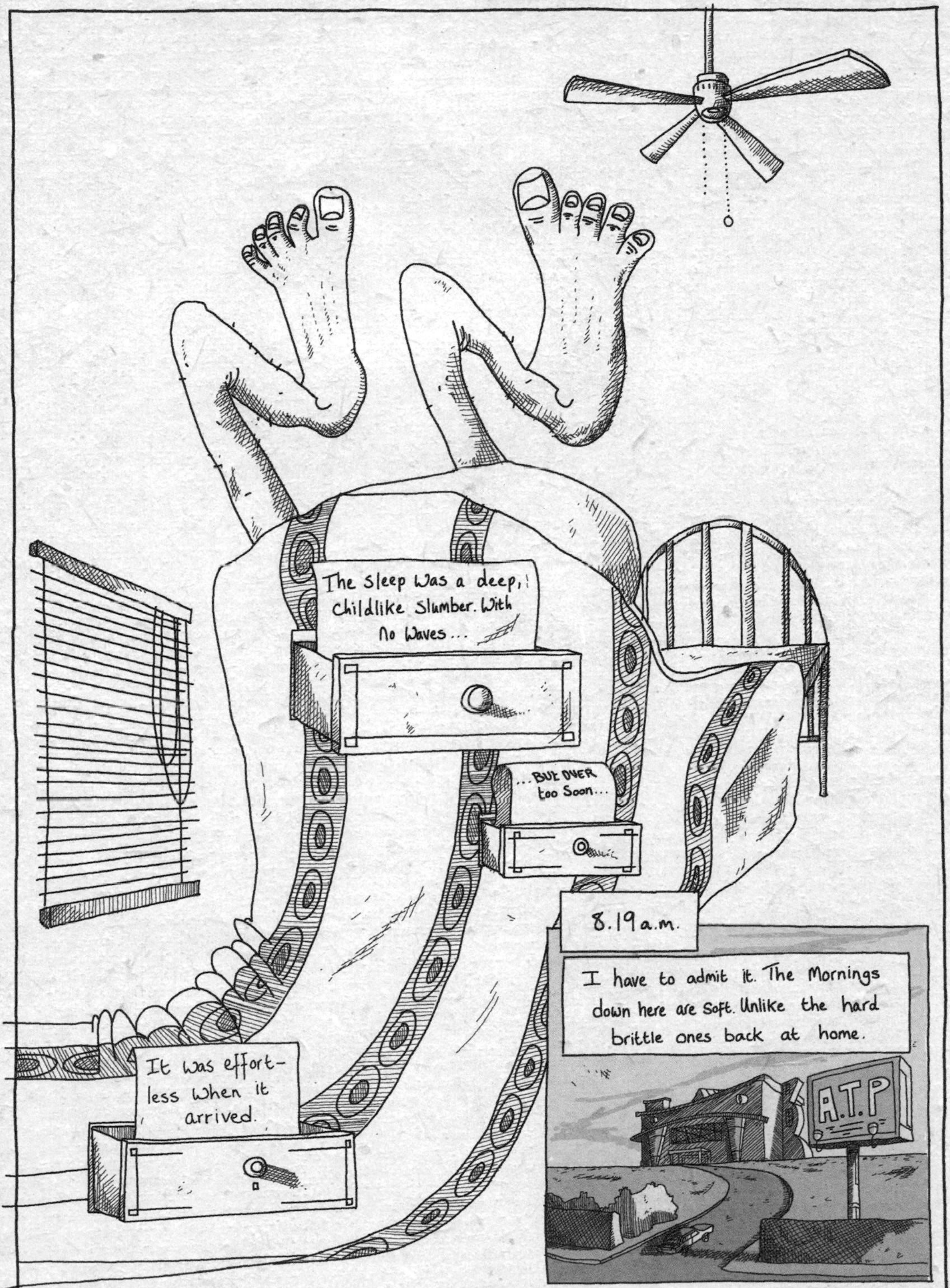
The sleep was a deep, childlike slumber. With no waves...
...BUT OVER too soon...
It was effortless when it arrived.
8.19 a.m.
I have to admit it. The mornings down here are soft. Unlike the hard brittle ones back at home.
A.T.P

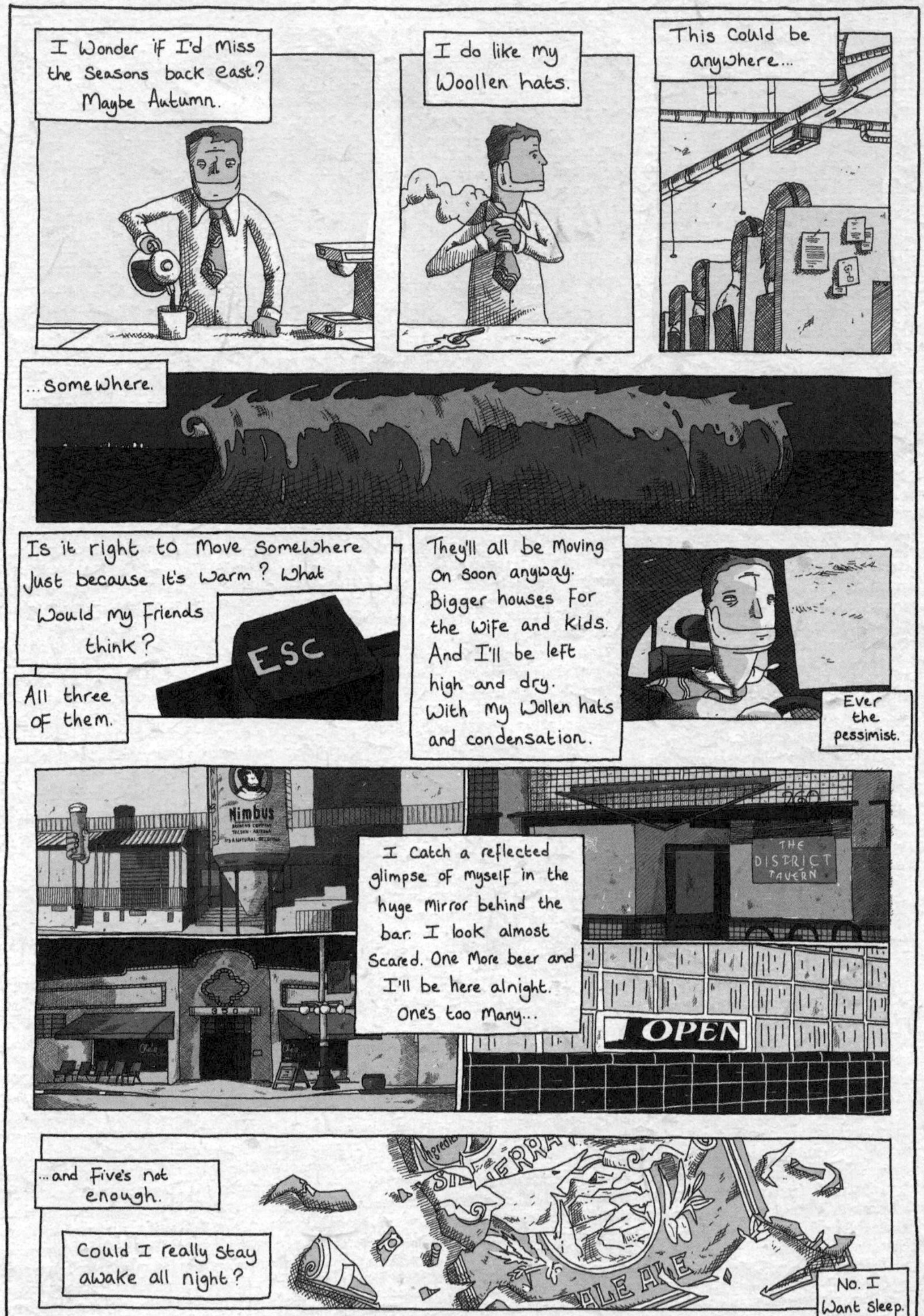
I Wonder if I'd Miss the Seasons back east? Maybe Autumn.
I do like my Woollen hats.
This Could be anywhere...
...somewhere.
Is it right to Move somewhere Just because it's warm? What Would my Friends think?
ESC
All three of them.
They'll all be moving on soon anyway. Bigger houses for the wife and kids. And I'll be left high and dry. With my Wollen hats and condensation.
Ever the pessimist.
Nimbus
THE DISTRICT TAVERN
I Catch a reflected glimpse of myself in the huge mirror behind the bar. I look almost Scared. One More beer and I'll be here alnight. One's too Many...
OPEN
...and Five's not enough.
Could I really stay awake all night?
ALE ALE
No. I Want sleep.

But I know it's coming.

And with a blink of an eye, I'm also gone.

Tuesday 3.46 a.m.

Jesus!

I couldn't believe that small ball of muscle in my chest could keep twitching for much longer. When it did stop would I know? Would I feel it?

I knew I needed to distract the other muscle that had conjured up the images. With the hotel having an admirable no TVs in the room policy.

I was already on my way.

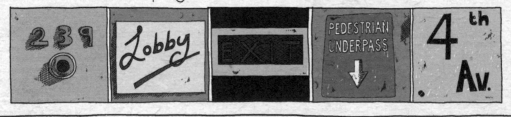

239   Lobby   EXIT   PEDESTRIAN UNDERPASS   4th Av.

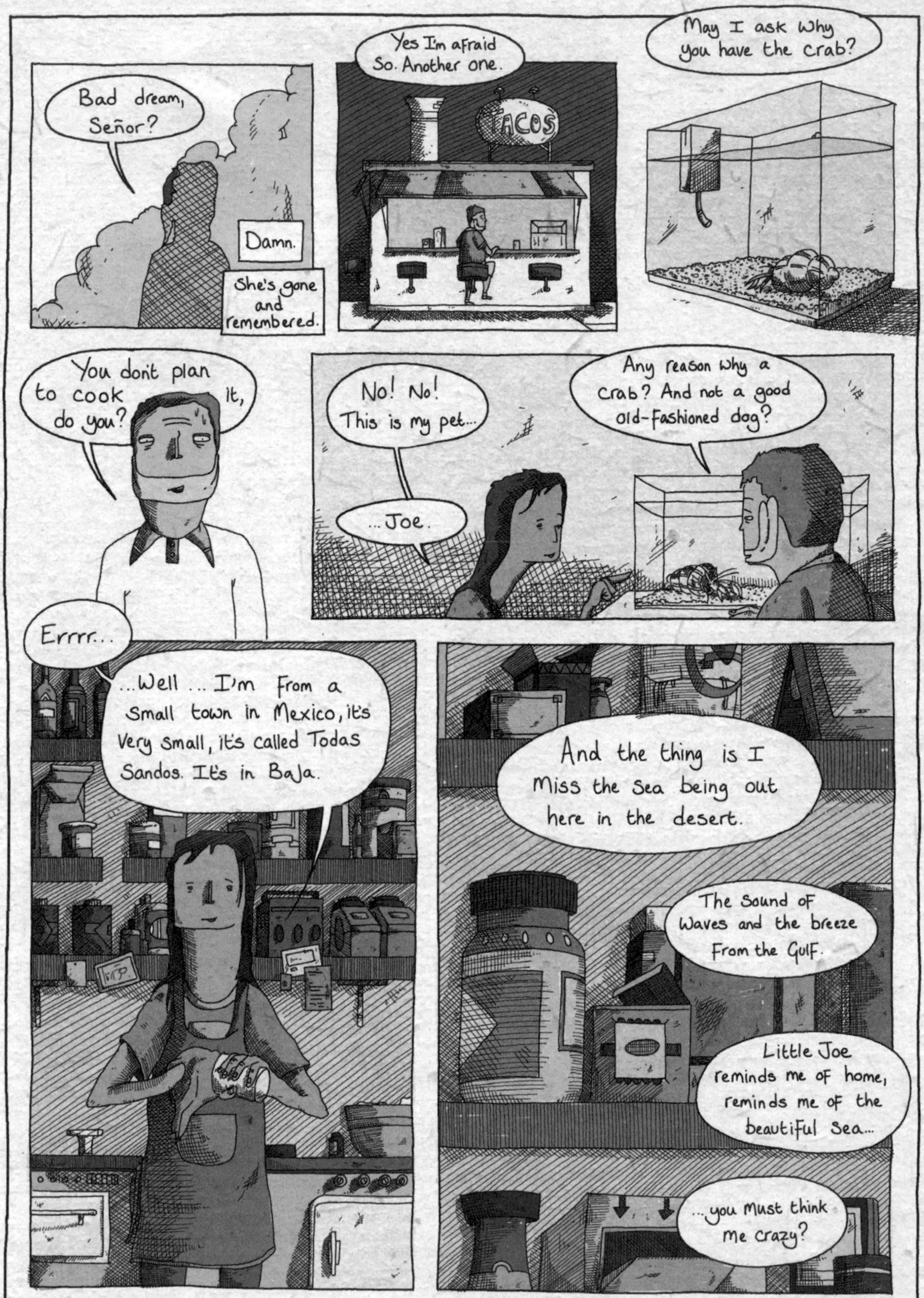
Bad dream, Señor?
Damn.
She's gone and remembered.
Yes I'm afraid so. Another one.
TACOS
May I ask why you have the crab?
You don't plan to cook it, do you?
No! No! This is my pet...
...Joe.
Any reason why a crab? And not a good old-fashioned dog?
Errrr...
...Well ... I'm from a small town in Mexico, it's very small, it's called Todas Sandos. It's in Baja.
And the thing is I miss the sea being out here in the desert.
The sound of waves and the breeze from the Gulf.
Little Joe reminds me of home, reminds me of the beautiful sea...
...you must think me crazy?

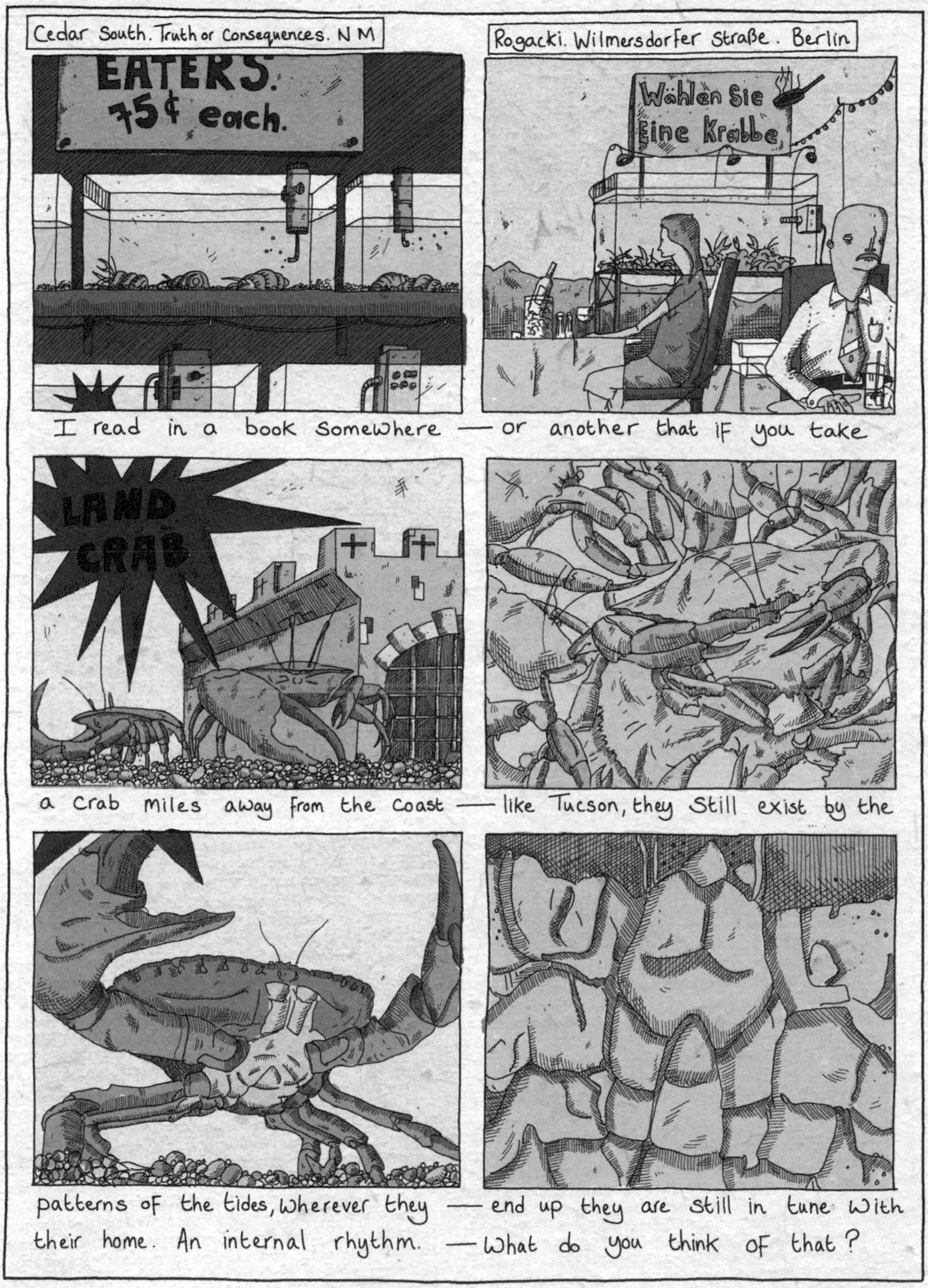
Cedar South. Truth or Consequences. N M
EATERS. 75¢ each.
Rogacki. Wilmersdorfer Straße. Berlin
Wählen Sie Eine Krabbe
I read in a book somewhere — or another that if you take
LAND CRAB
a crab miles away from the coast — like Tucson, they still exist by the
patterns of the tides, wherever they — end up they are still in tune with their home. An internal rhythm. — What do you think of that?

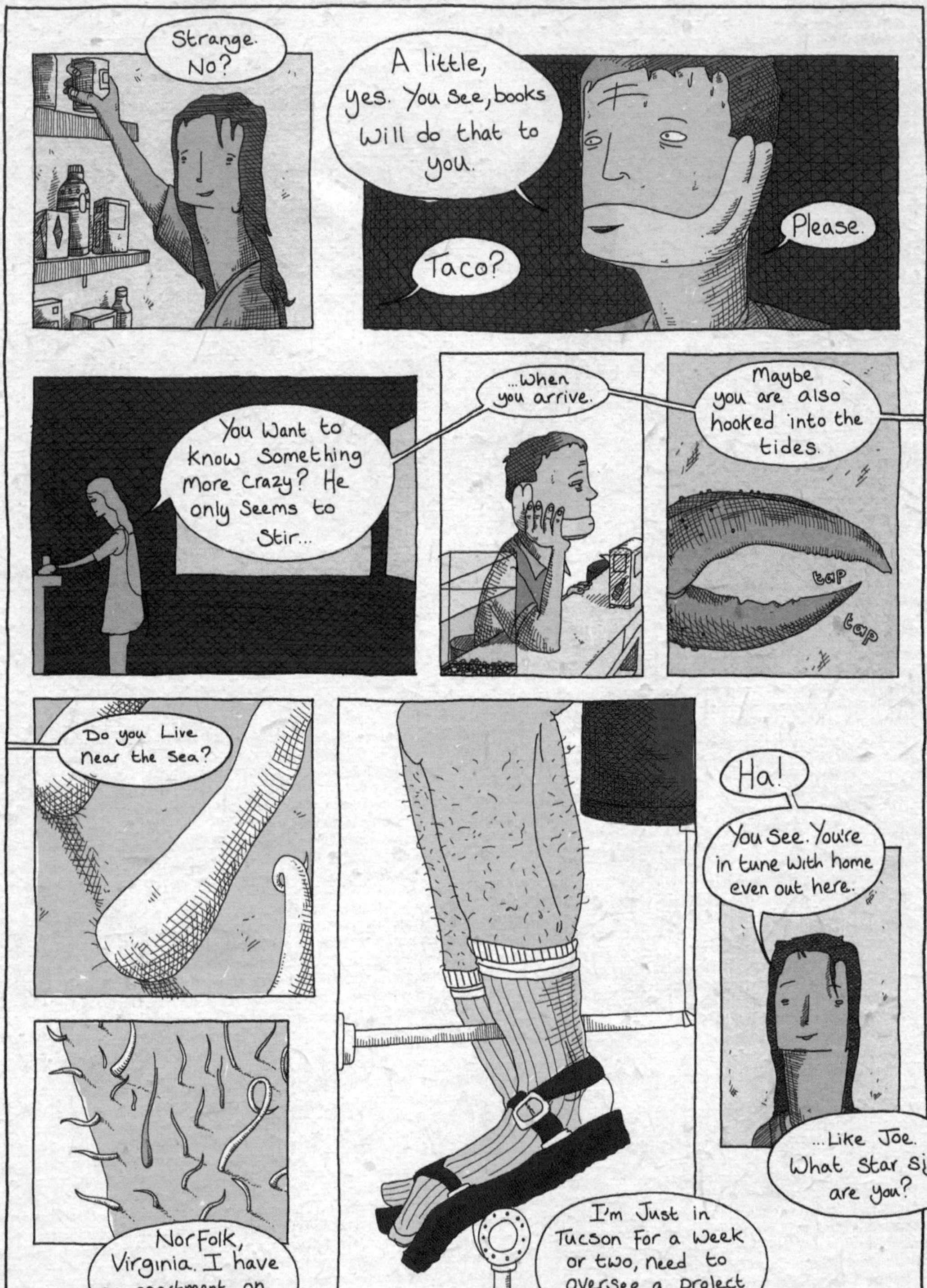
Strange. No?
A little, yes. You see, books will do that to you.
Taco?
Please.
You want to know something more crazy? He only seems to stir...
...when you arrive.
Maybe you are also hooked into the tides.
tap
tap
Do you live near the sea?
Norfolk, Virginia. I have an apartment on the shore.
I'm just in Tucson for a week or two, need to oversee a project just out of town.
Ha!
You see. You're in tune with home even out here.
...Like Joe. What star sign are you?

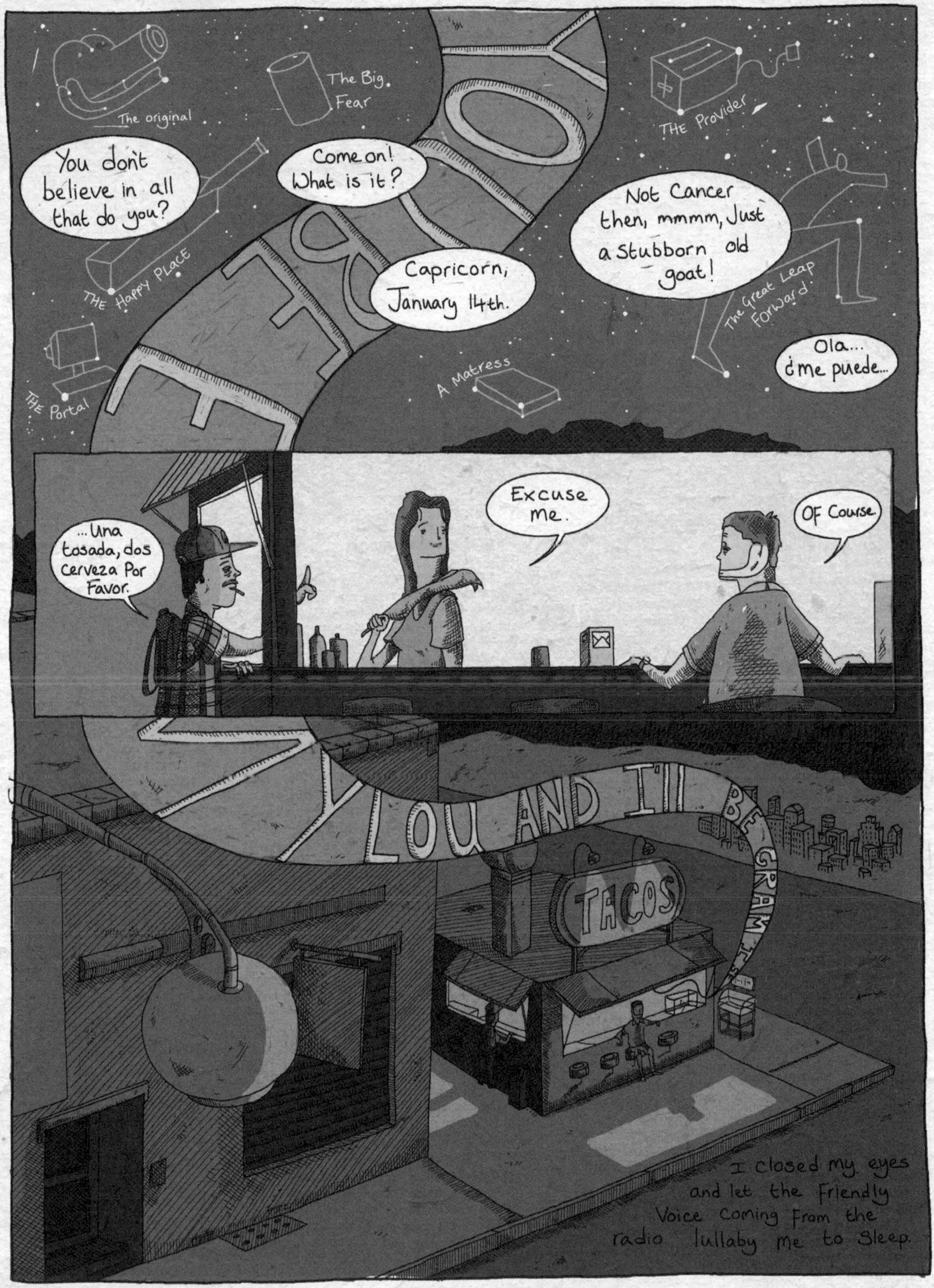
The original
The Big Fear
THE Provider
You don't believe in all that do you?
Come on! What is it?
THE Happy PLACE
Capricorn, January 14th.
Not Cancer then, mmmm, Just a Stubborn old goat!
The Great Leap Forward
THE Portal
A Matress
Ola... ¿me puede...
...Una tosada, dos cerveza Por Favor.
Excuse me.
OF Course.
TACOS
I closed my eyes and let the Friendly Voice coming from the radio lullaby me to Sleep.

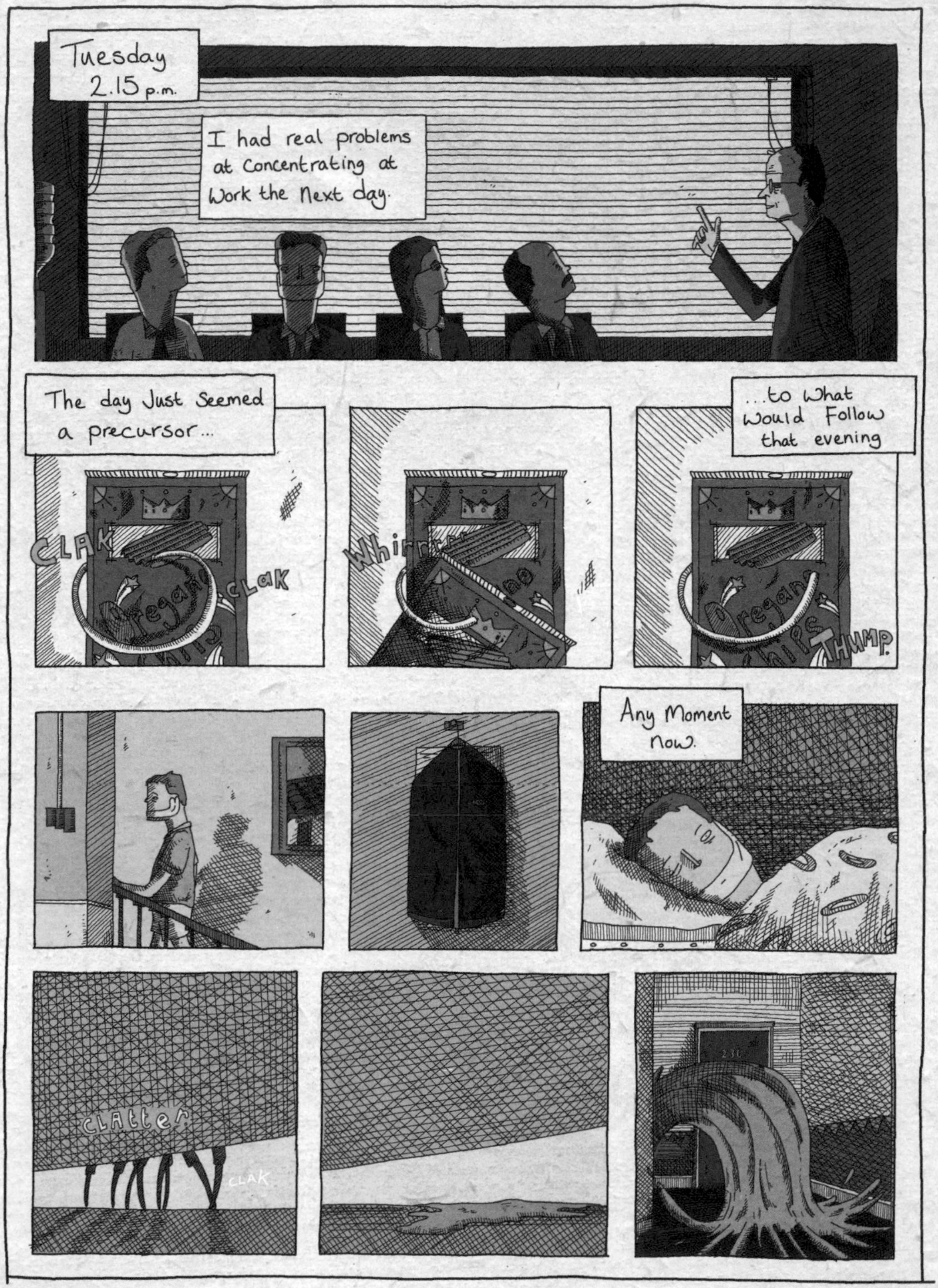
Tuesday
2.15 p.m.
I had real problems at concentrating at work the next day.
The day just seemed a precursor...
CLAK
CLAK
Oregano
Whirrrr
...to what would follow that evening
Oregano Chips
THUMP.
Any moment now.
clatter
CLAK
231

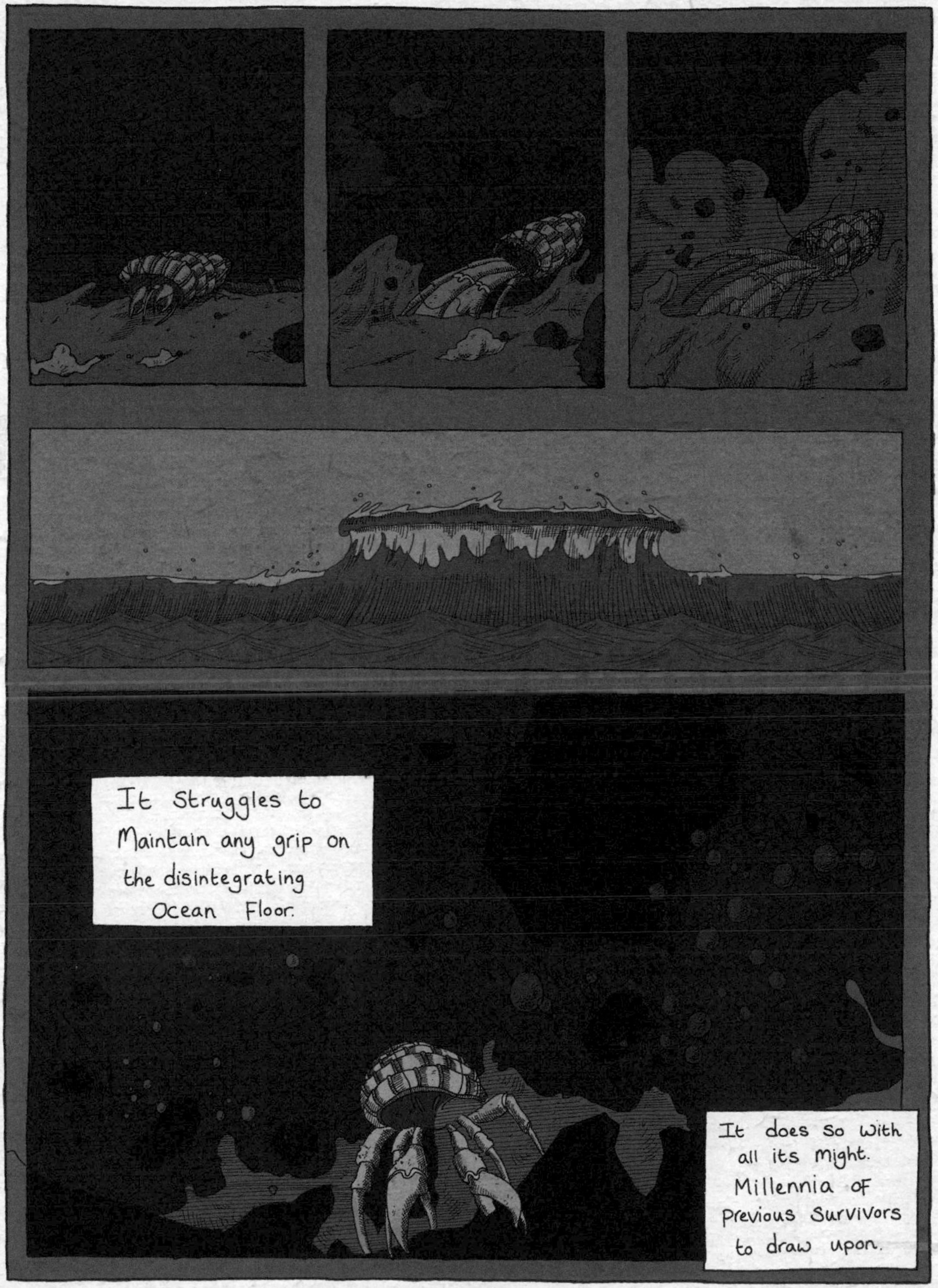
It Struggles to Maintain any grip on the disintegrating Ocean Floor.
It does so with all its might. Millennia of Previous Survivors to draw upon.

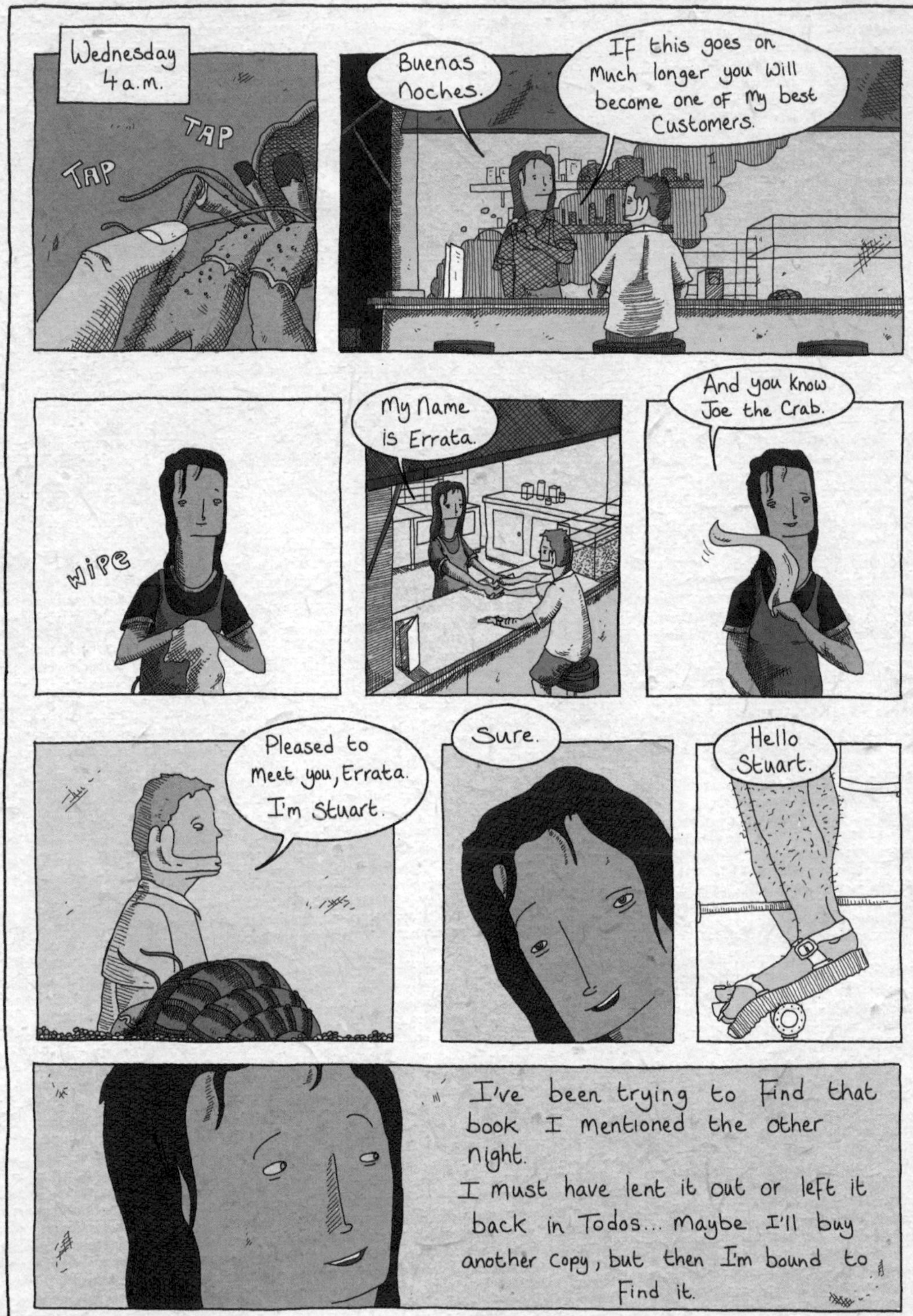
Wednesday 4 a.m.
TAP
TAP
Buenas Noches.
If this goes on much longer you will become one of my best customers.
wipe
My name is Errata.
And you know Joe the Crab.
Pleased to meet you, Errata. I'm Stuart.
Sure.
Hello Stuart.
I've been trying to find that book I mentioned the other night.
I must have lent it out or left it back in Todos... maybe I'll buy another copy, but then I'm bound to find it.

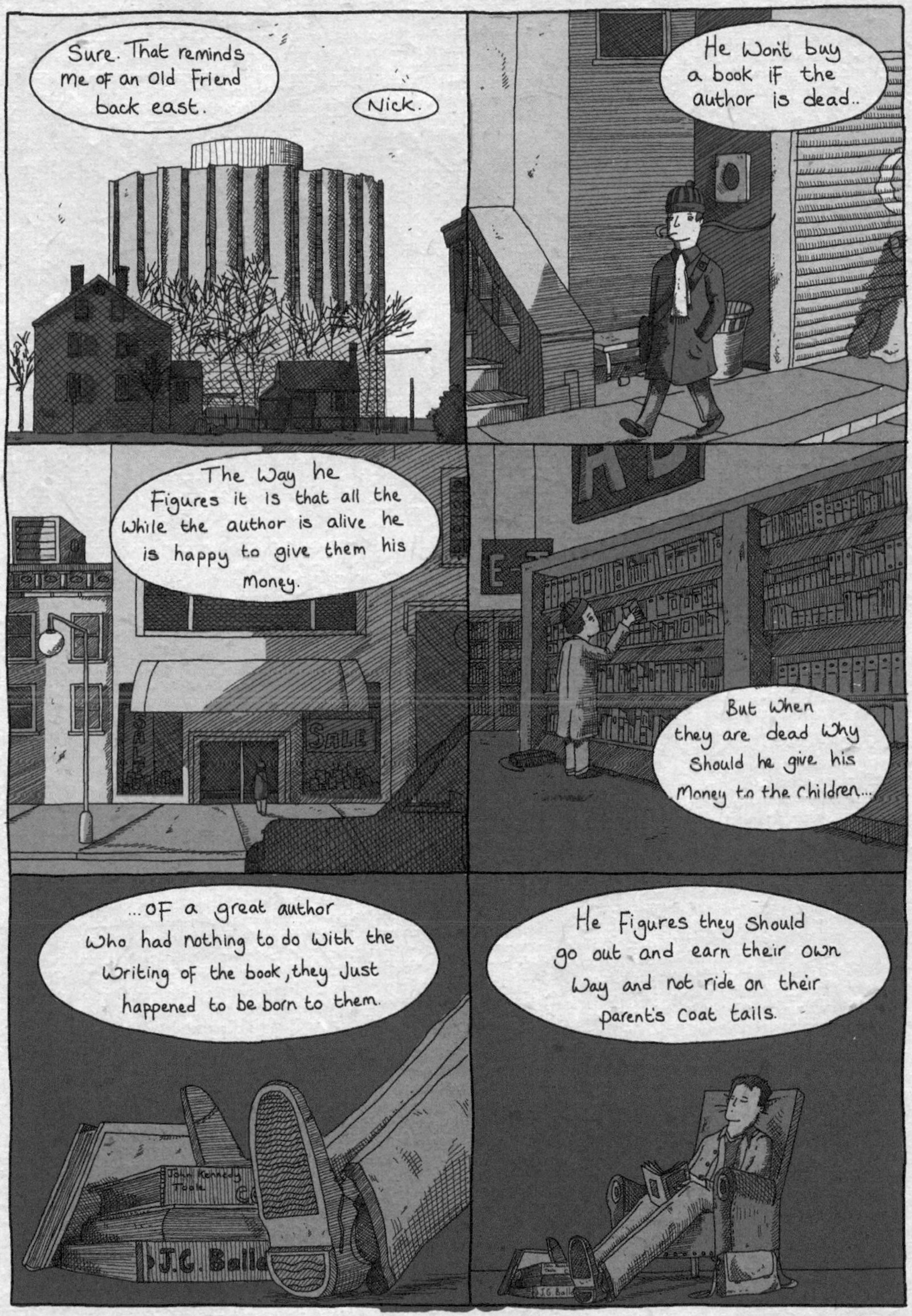

Sure. That reminds me of an Old Friend back east.
Nick.
He Won't buy a book if the author is dead..
The Way he Figures it is that all the While the author is alive he is happy to give them his Money.
But When they are dead Why Should he give his Money to the children...
...OF a great author Who had nothing to do with the Writing of the book, they Just happened to be born to them.
He Figures they should go out and earn their own Way and not ride on their parent's Coat tails.
John Kennedy Toole
J.G. Balla

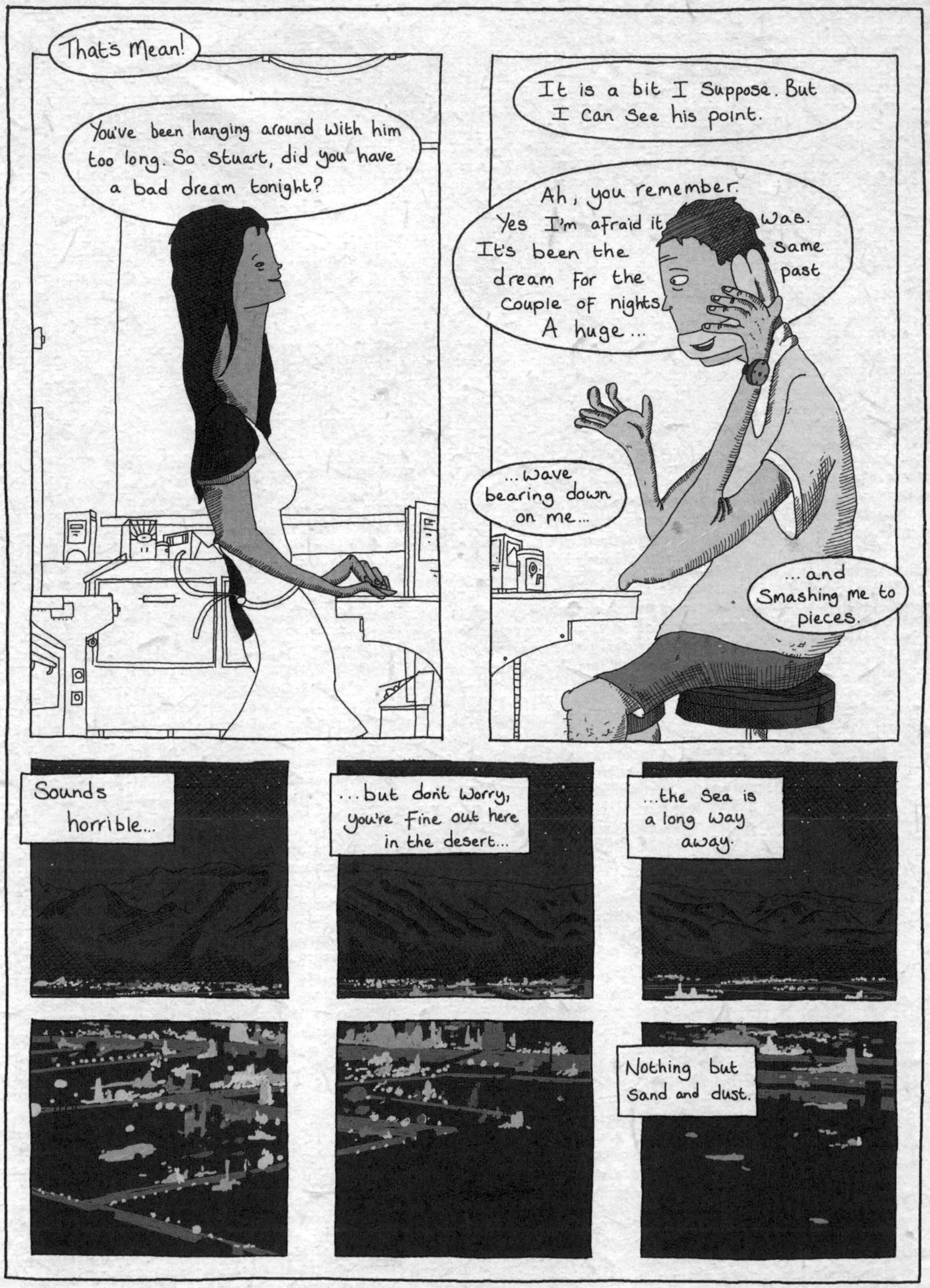
That's Mean!
You've been hanging around with him too long. So Stuart, did you have a bad dream tonight?
It is a bit I Suppose. But I can see his point.
Ah, you remember. Yes I'm afraid it was. It's been the same dream for the past couple of nights. A huge...
...wave bearing down on me...
...and Smashing me to pieces.
Sounds horrible...
...but don't worry, you're fine out here in the desert...
...the Sea is a long way away.
Nothing but Sand and dust.

What is it? We are 80% Water.

No! Much more than that. Nearly 90%. Now I read that in a book...

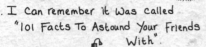

...I can remember it was called "101 Facts To Astound Your Friends With".

Well, consider me astounded!

Again my sentence hung in the air.

Was that too forward? A little misjudged? Or was it just plain old foot-in-mouth clumsy?

TSSK

Can I get a taco?

BUZZ

Sure.

TSSSkk

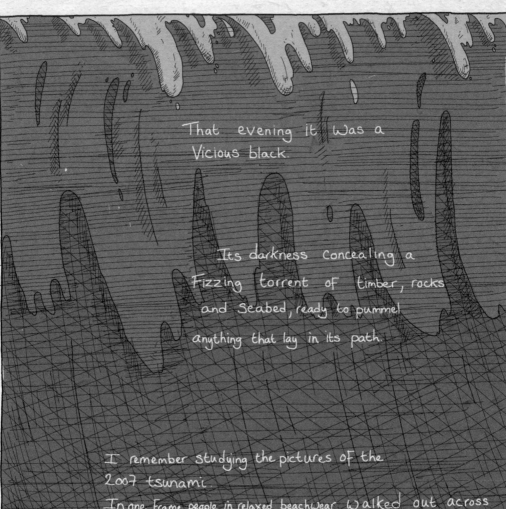

That evening it was a
vicious black.

Its darkness concealing a
fizzing torrent of timber, rocks
and seabed, ready to pummel
anything that lay in its path.

I remember studying the pictures of the
2007 tsunami.
In one frame people in relaxed beachwear walked out across
the newly exposed seabed thinking they had
got more than the brochure had mentioned, they
seemed drawn towards the oddity, unable to
comprehend. Then the white line on the horizon
gets bigger. In the next frame they are running
knees high in the air as they scrambled through the water
aware of their folly. All captured on film for the world to
stare at over their breakfast.

Tonight I sat and watched it
until it blocked out all light.

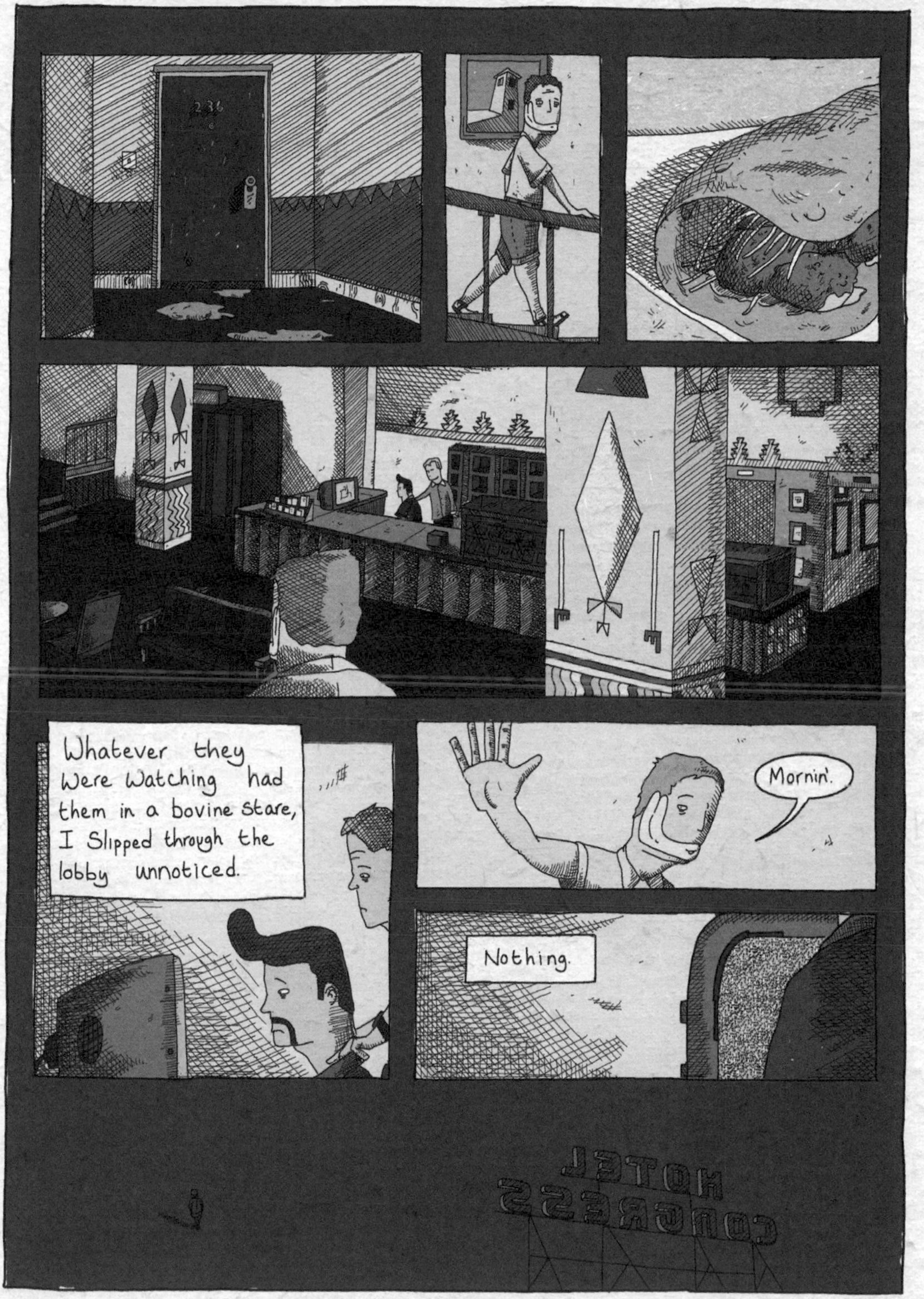
Whatever they were watching had them in a bovine stare, I slipped through the lobby unnoticed.
Mornin'.
Nothing.
HOTEL CONGRESS

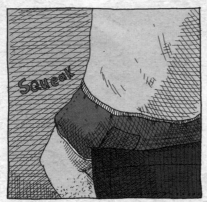

Squeak

go back to the ne...
...date an For room

Stuart.

It's your dream.

Scrape

It's happened..

Listen, come in. The hatch is over there.

Scrape

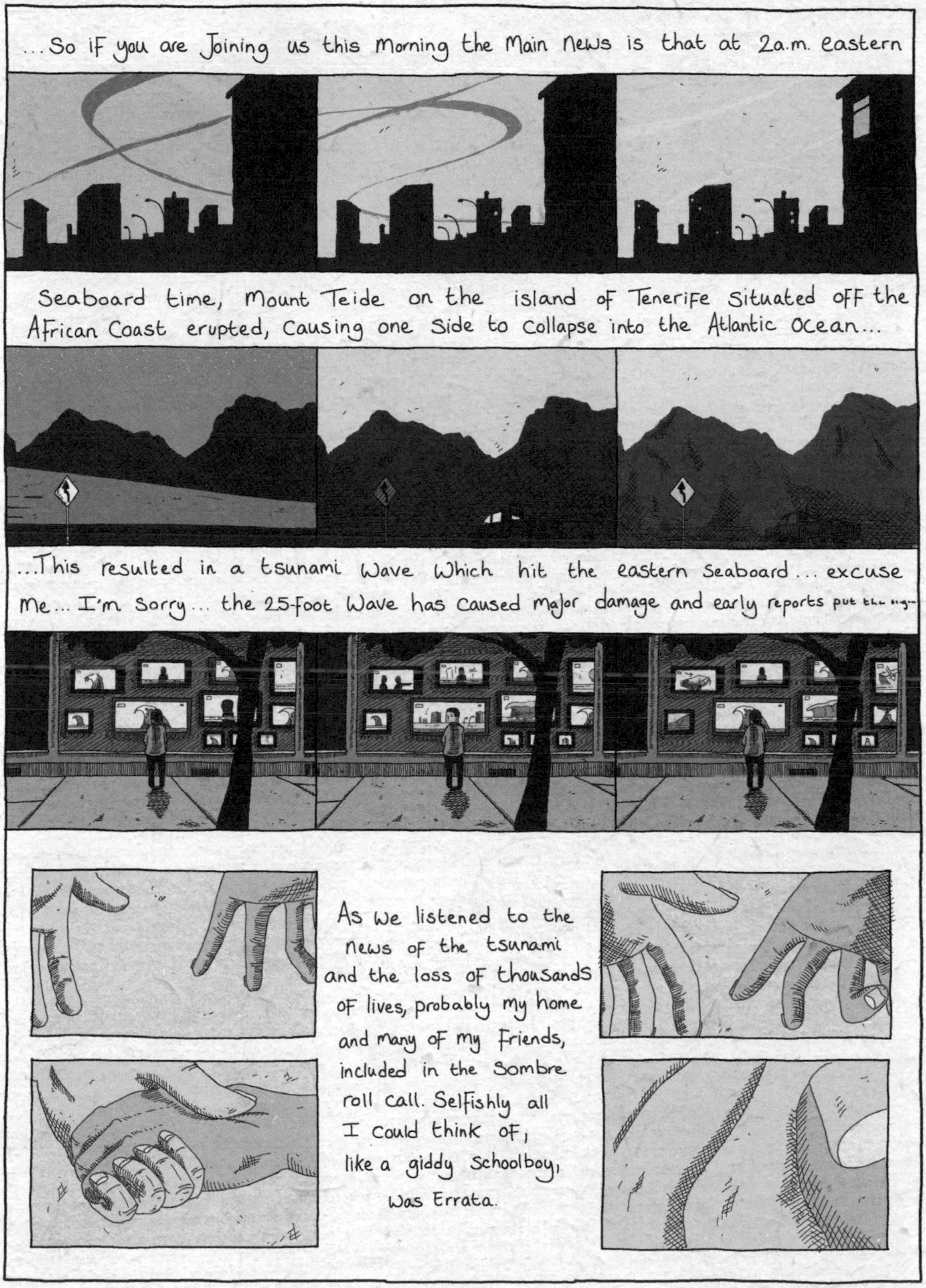
...So if you are Joining us this Morning the Main News is that at 2a.m. eastern
Seaboard time, Mount Teide on the island of Tenerife situated off the African Coast erupted, Causing one side to collapse into the Atlantic Ocean...
...This resulted in a tsunami Wave Which hit the eastern Seaboard... excuse me... I'm Sorry... the 25-foot Wave has Caused major damage and early reports put
As we listened to the news of the tsunami and the loss of thousands of lives, probably my home and many of my friends, included in the Sombre roll call. Selfishly all I could think of, like a giddy Schoolboy, Was Errata.

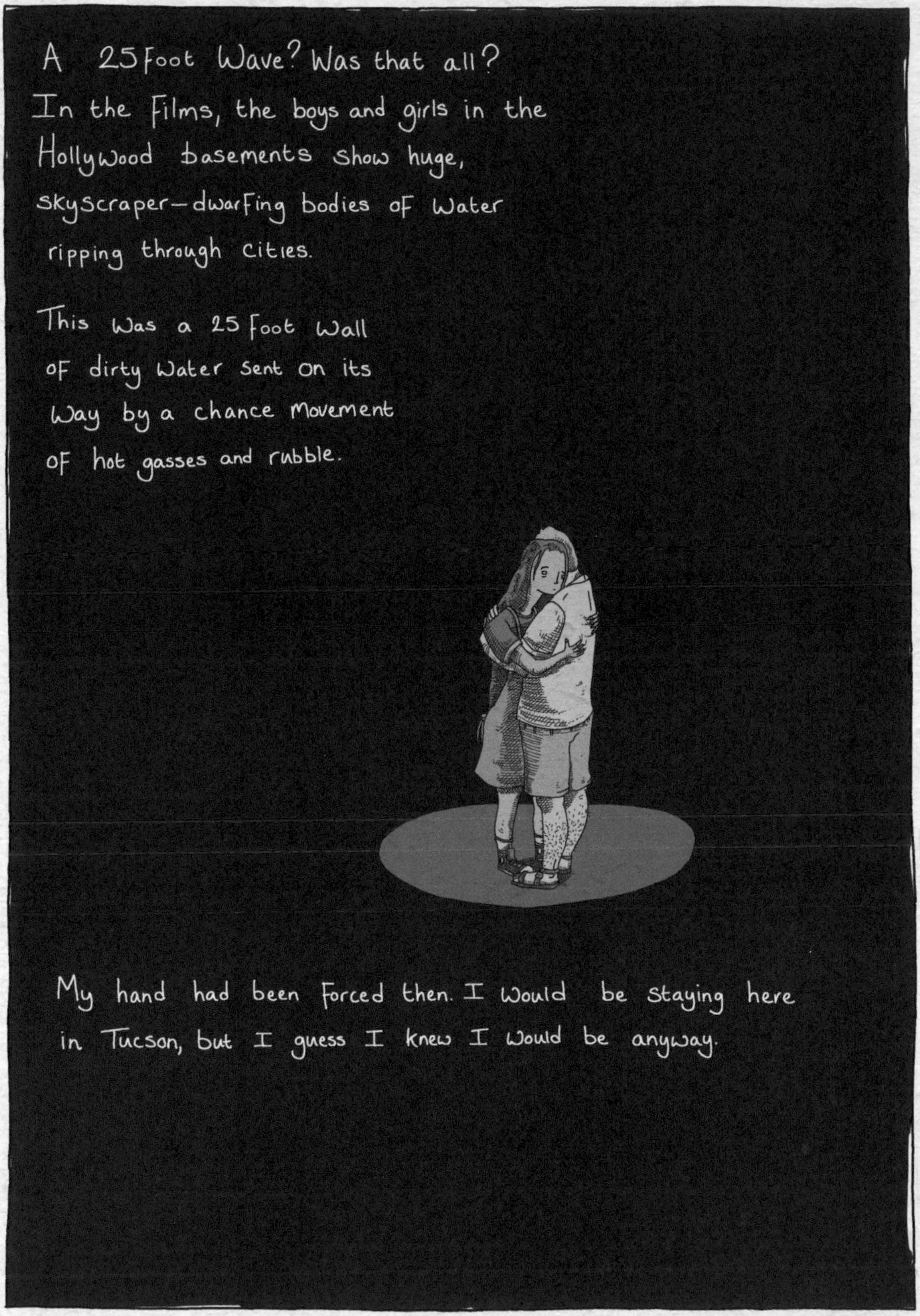
A 25 foot Wave? Was that all?
In the films, the boys and girls in the Hollywood basements show huge, skyscraper-dwarfing bodies of water ripping through cities.
This was a 25 foot wall of dirty water sent on its way by a chance movement of hot gasses and rubble.
My hand had been forced then. I would be staying here in Tucson, but I guess I knew I would be anyway.

I haven't had a bad dream for some five years now.

I now sleep deeply in the Tucson Suburbs.

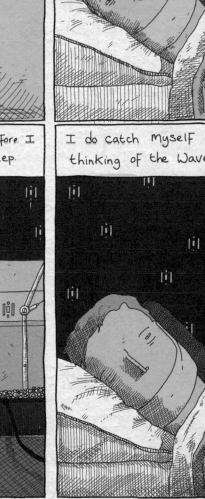

With Errata next to me.

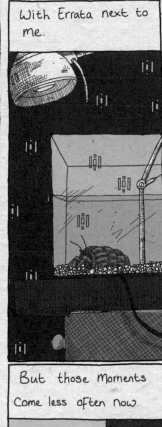

Sometimes just before I drift off to sleep.

I do catch myself thinking of the Wave.

But those moments come less often now.

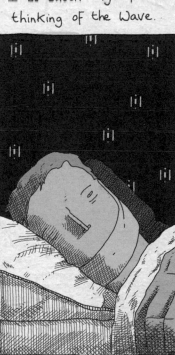

Denge
eness
Winner of the
Observer/Jonathan Cape/Comica
Graphic Short Story Prize

SAND DUNES & SONIC BOOMS

Dymchurch.

Pett Marsh.

Denge. East Sussex.

Are they American Dad?

Turn around please Julian.

Back in the 1970s My dad would take me on tours of World War II plane crash sites that littered the South Coast.

Pat
Pat

Whether by luck or planning we happened on a tour of the 'Sound Mirrors' of Denge. He could be jammy like that.

RAT A TAT TAT

The Sound Mirrors Were designed to hear approaching enemy aircraft over the English channel.
The Sound Waves being concentrated into one of the three 'Mirrors', all built in Britains only desert.
With the invention of radar they become obsolete, Mere spectators of the 'Battle of Britian' that raged overhead.

RAT A TAT

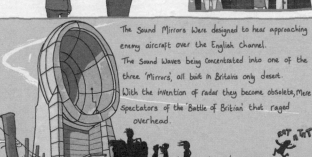

Rye Harbour.

Camber Sands.

Winchelsea Beach.

Fairlight.

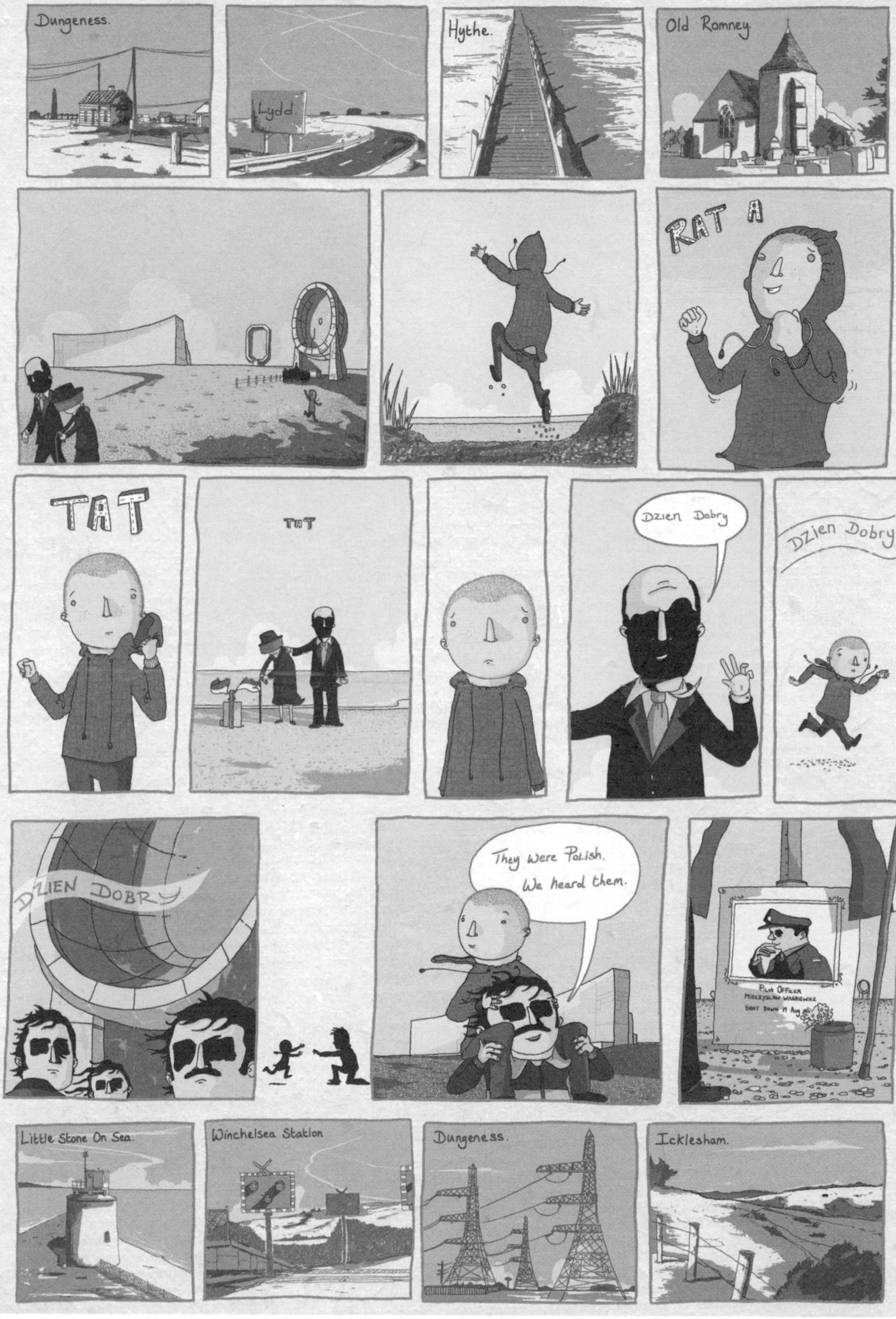

Dungeness.
Lydd.
Hythe.
Old Romney.
RAT A
TAT
TAT
Dzien Dobry
Dzien Dobry
DZIEN DOBRY
They were Polish. We heard them.
Pilot Officer
Little Stone On Sea.
Winchelsea Station
Dungeness.
Icklesham.

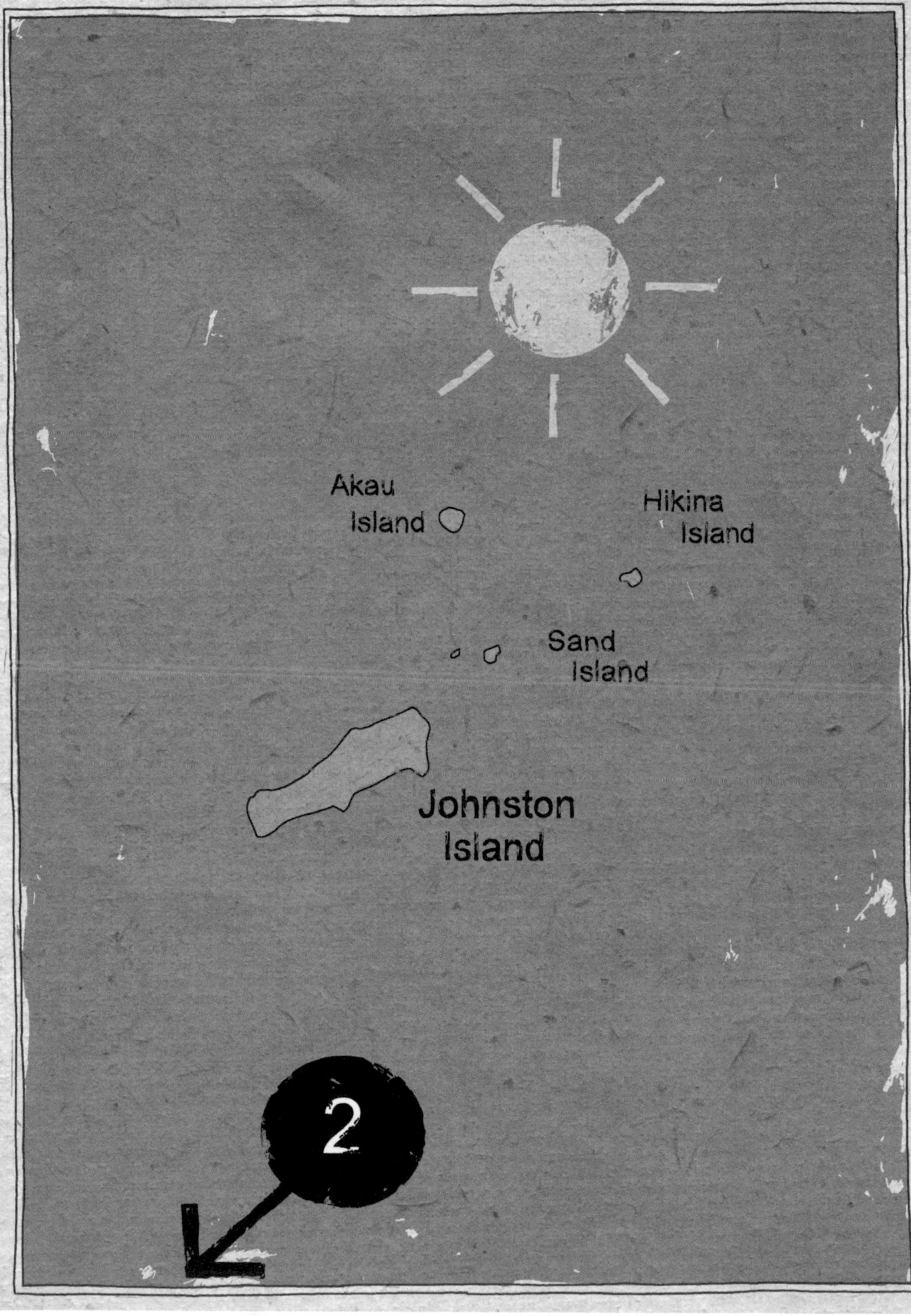
Akau
Island
Hikina
Island
Sand
Island
Johnston
Island
2

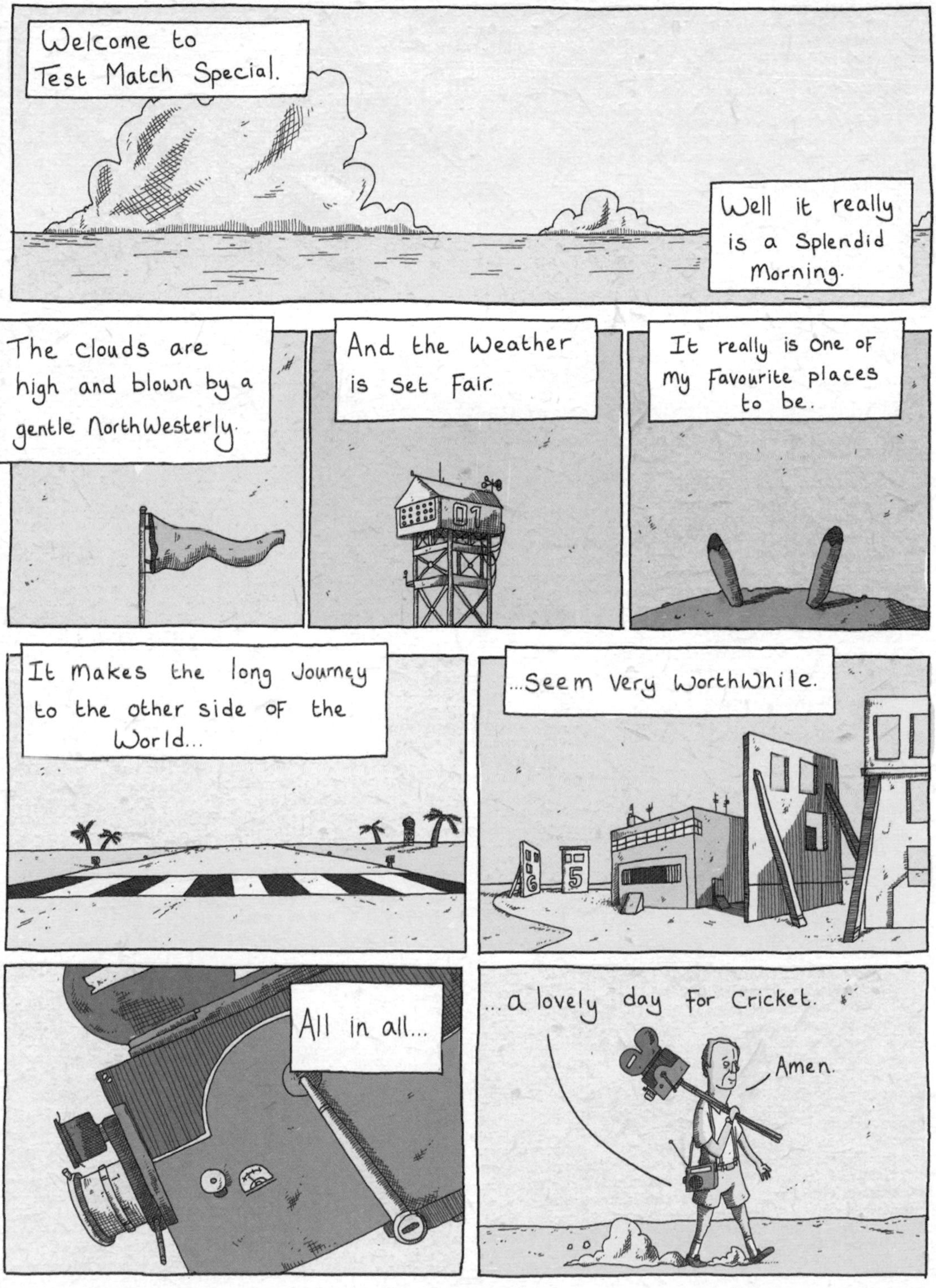
Welcome to Test Match Special.
Well it really is a Splendid Morning.
The clouds are high and blown by a gentle NorthWesterly.
And the Weather is set Fair.
01
It really is one of my Favourite places to be.
It makes the long Journey to the other side of the World...
...Seem Very WorthWhile.
6
5
All in all...
...a lovely day for Cricket.
Amen.

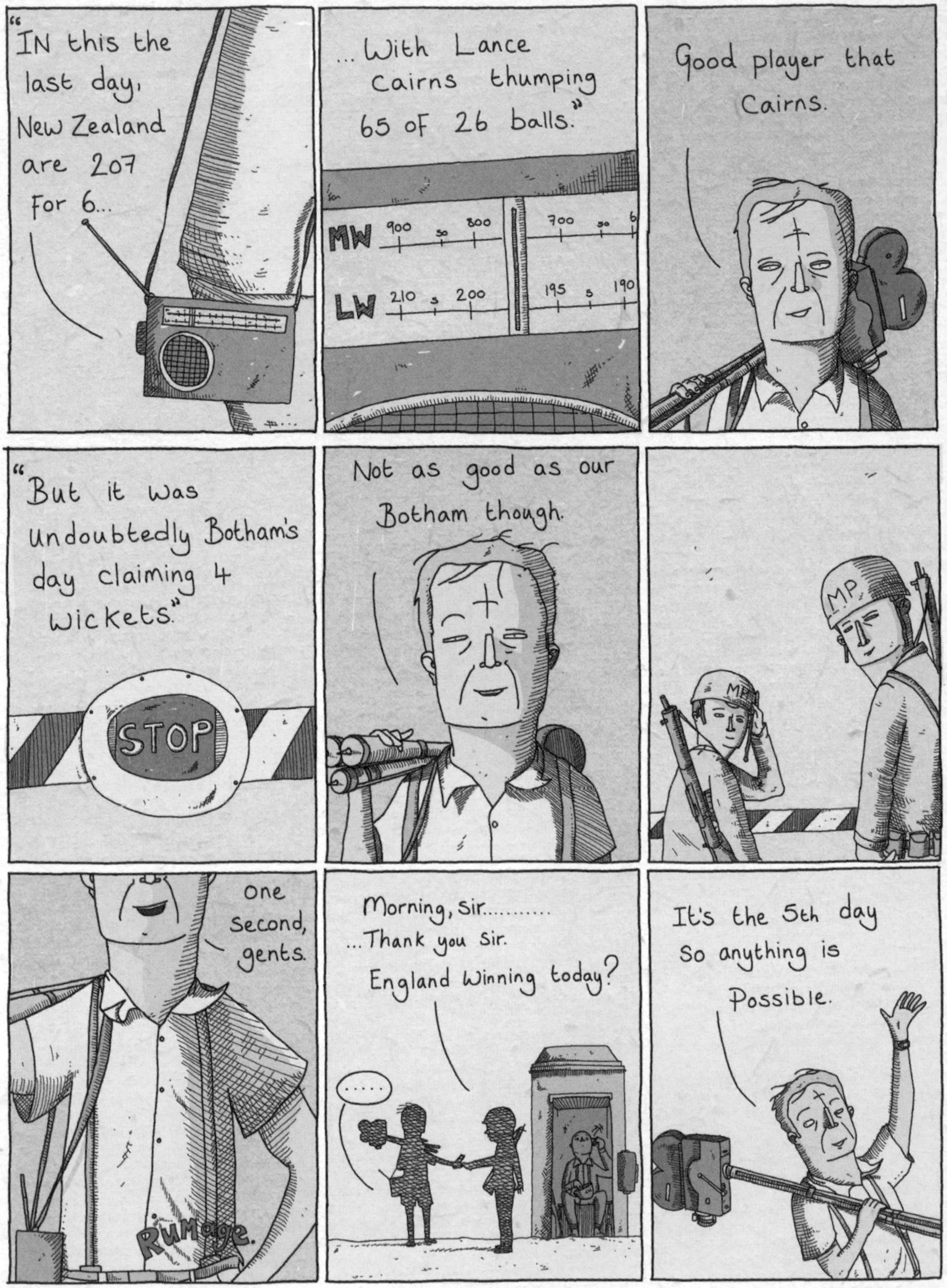
"IN this the last day, New Zealand are 207 For 6...
...With Lance Cairns thumping 65 of 26 balls."
MW
900
50
800
700
50
LW
210
5
200
195
5
190
Good player that Cairns.
"But it was undoubtedly Botham's day claiming 4 wickets."
STOP
Not as good as our Botham though.
MP
MP
One second, gents.
RUMAGE
Morning, sir..........
...Thank you sir.
England winning today?
.....
It's the 5th day so anything is possible.

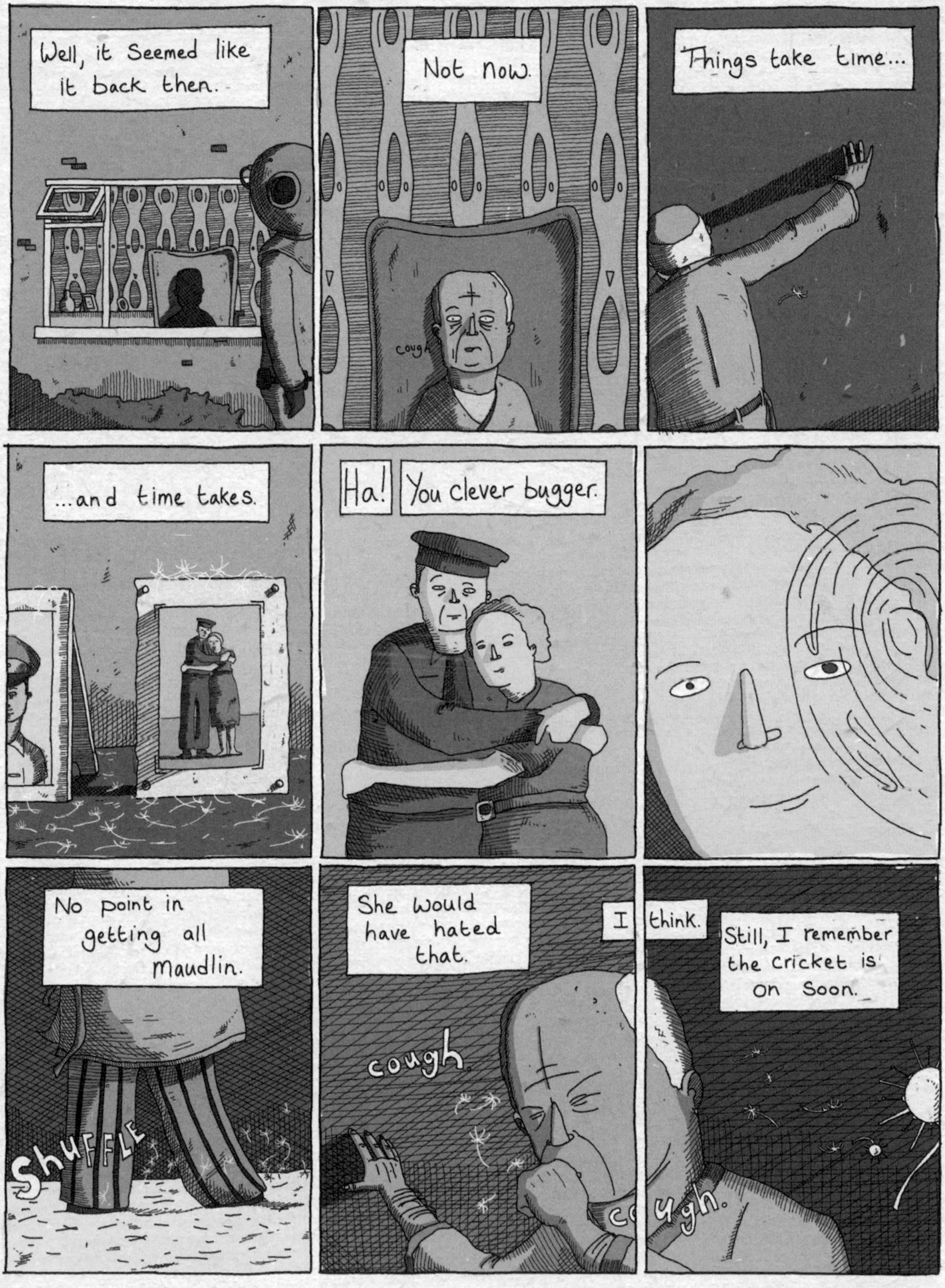
Well, it Seemed like it back then.
Not now.
cough
Things take time...
...and time takes.
Ha!
You clever bugger.
No point in getting all maudlin.
SHUFFLE
She would have hated that.
cough.
I
think.
Still, I remember the cricket is on Soon.
cough.

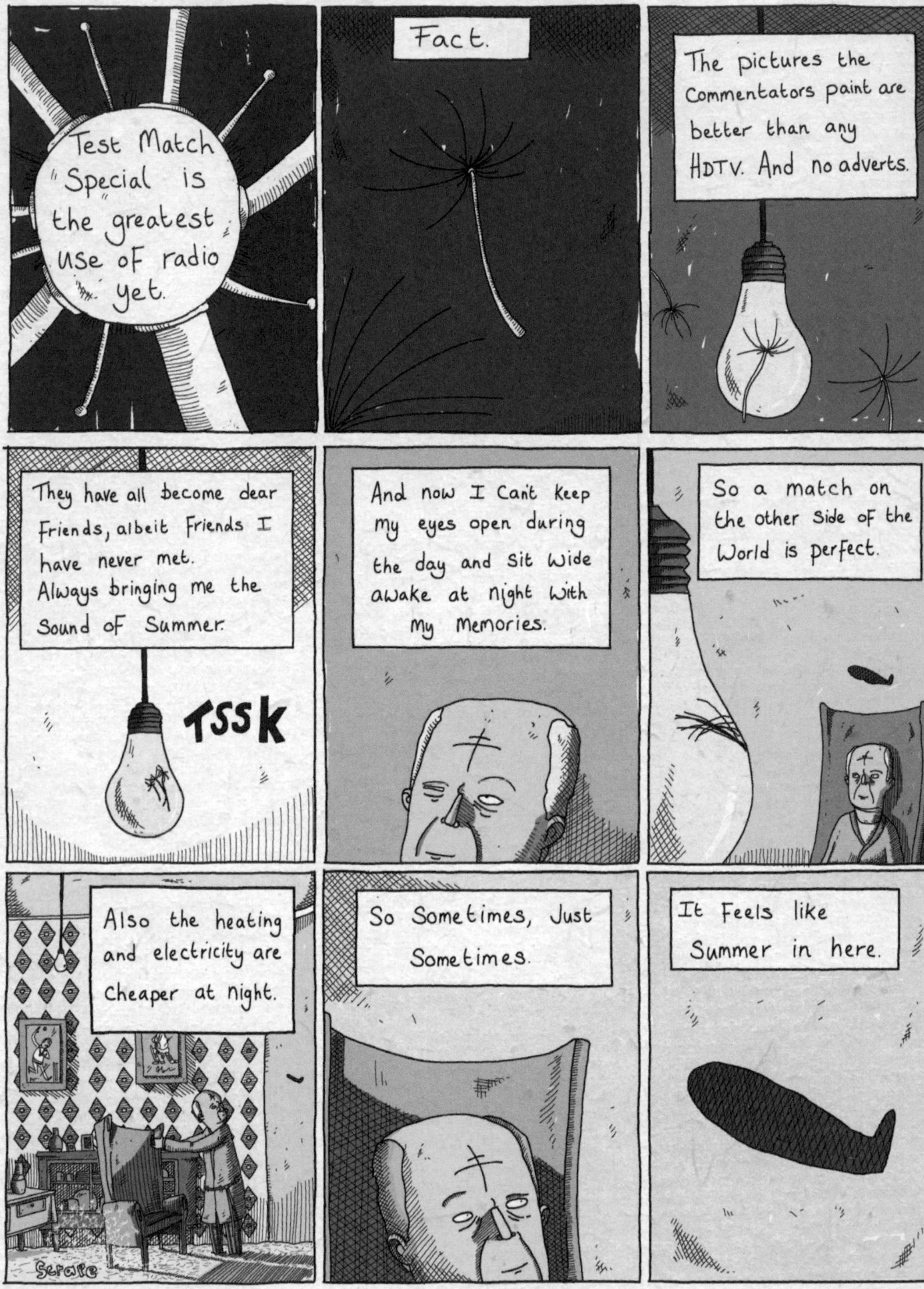
"Test Match Special" is the greatest use of radio yet.
Fact.
The pictures the Commentators paint are better than any HDTV. And no adverts.
They have all become dear Friends, albeit Friends I have never met. Always bringing me the Sound of Summer.
TSSK
And now I Can't keep my eyes open during the day and sit wide awake at night with my memories.
So a match on the other side of the World is perfect.
Also the heating and electricity are cheaper at night.
So Sometimes, Just Sometimes.
It Feels like Summer in here.
Serafe

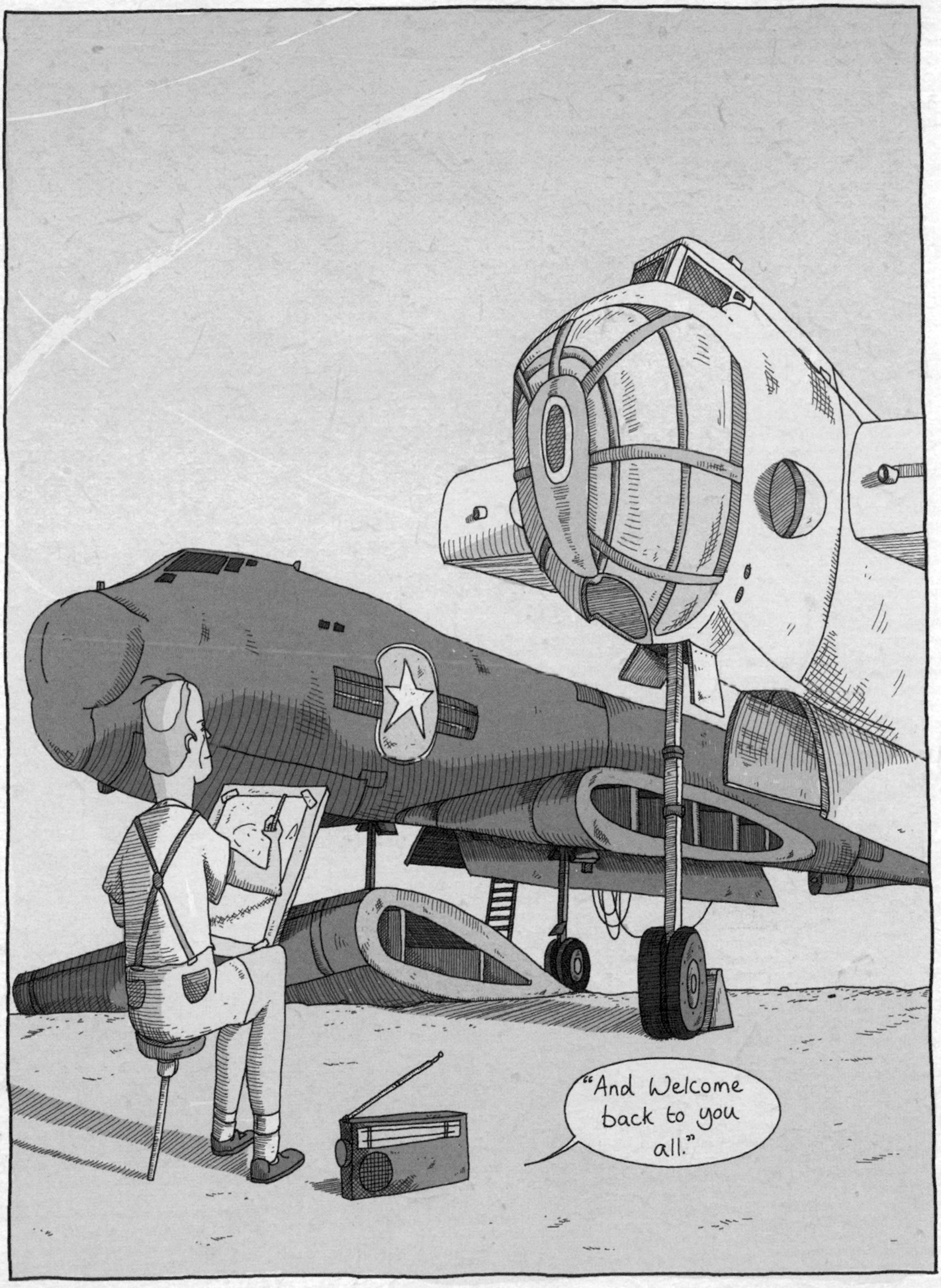
"And Welcome back to you all."

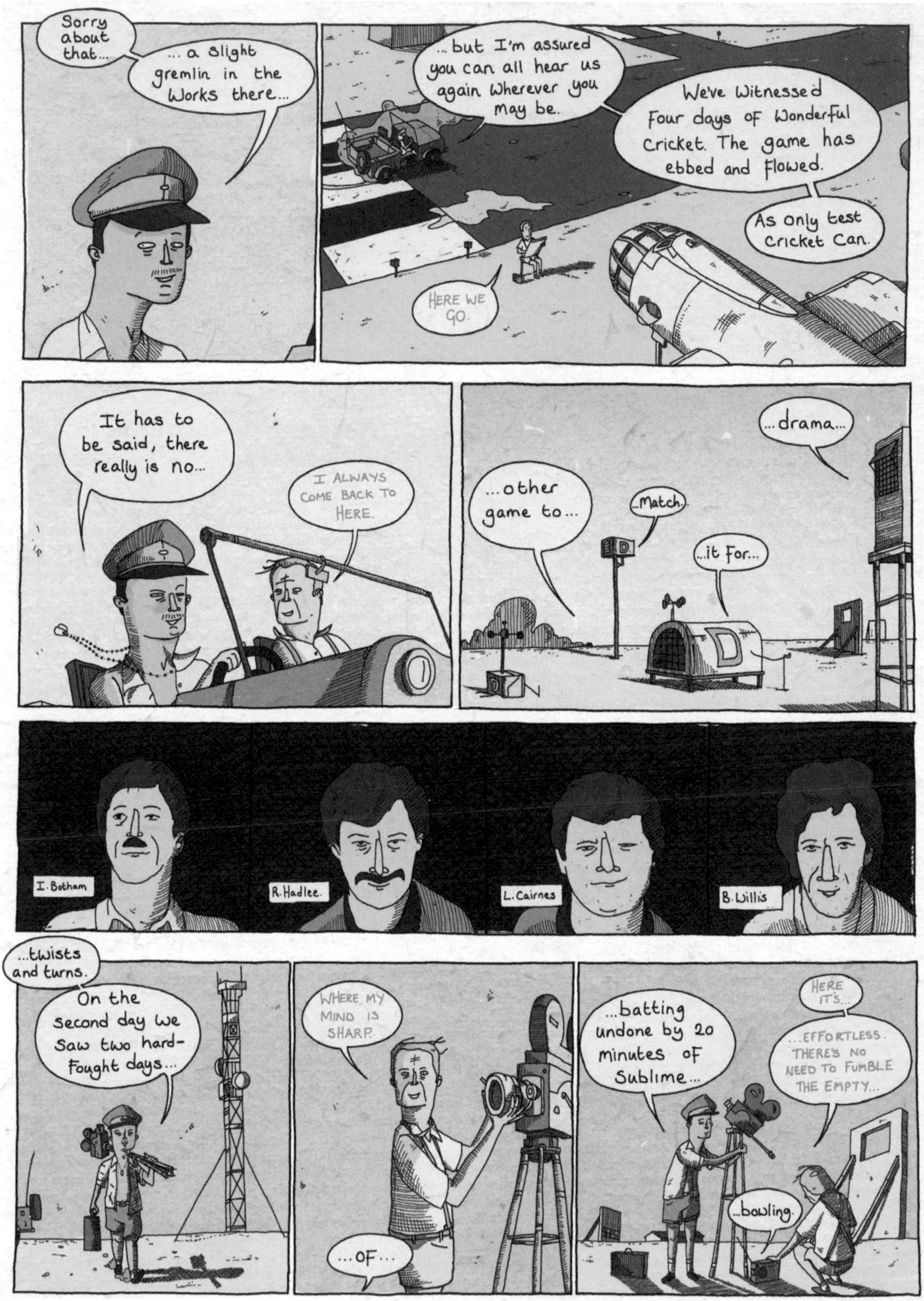
Sorry about that...
... a slight gremlin in the Works there...
... but I'm assured you can all hear us again Wherever you may be.
We've Witnessed Four days of Wonderful Cricket. The game has ebbed and Flowed.
As only test cricket Can.
HERE WE GO.
It has to be said, there really is no...
I ALWAYS COME BACK TO HERE.
...other game to...
...Match.
...it For...
...drama...
I. Botham
R. Hadlee.
L. Cairnes
B. Willis
...twists and turns.
On the second day we saw two hard-Fought days...
WHERE MY MIND IS SHARP.
...OF...
...batting undone by 20 minutes of Sublime...
HERE IT'S...
...EFFORTLESS. THERE'S NO NEED TO FUMBLE THE EMPTY...
...bowling.

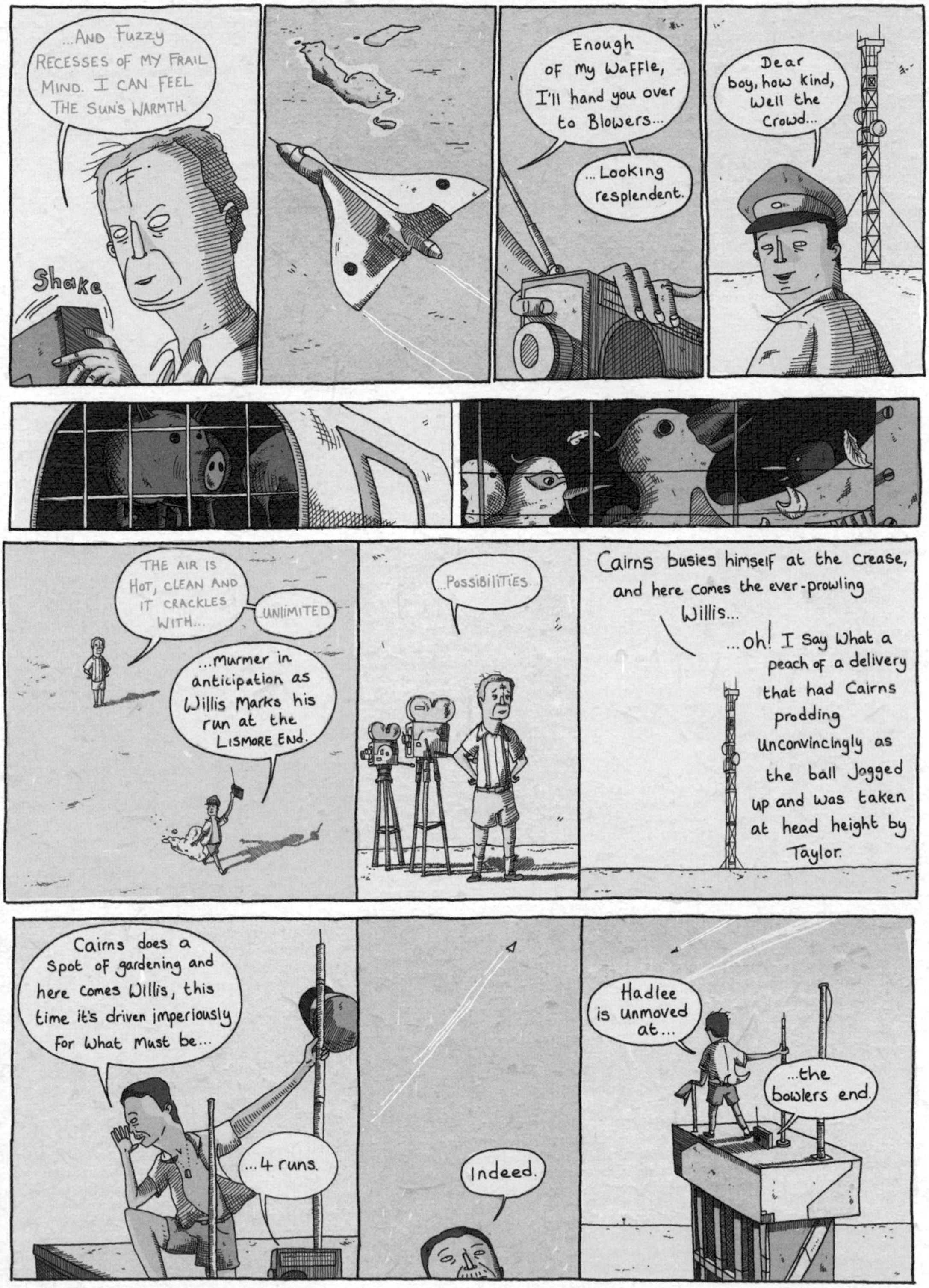
...AND FUZZY RECESSES OF MY FRAIL MIND. I CAN FEEL THE SUN'S WARMTH.
Shake
Enough of my Waffle, I'll hand you over to Blowers...
...Looking resplendent.
Dear boy, how kind, Well the Crowd...
THE AIR IS HOT, CLEAN AND IT CRACKLES WITH...
...murmer in anticipation as Willis Marks his run at the LISMORE END.
...UNLIMITED
...POSSIBILITIES...
Cairns busies himself at the crease, and here comes the ever-prowling Willis...
...oh! I say What a peach of a delivery that had Cairns prodding Unconvincingly as the ball Jogged up and was taken at head height by Taylor.
Cairns does a Spot of gardening and here comes Willis, this time it's driven imperiously For What must be...
...4 runs.
Indeed.
Hadlee is unmoved at...
...the bowlers end.

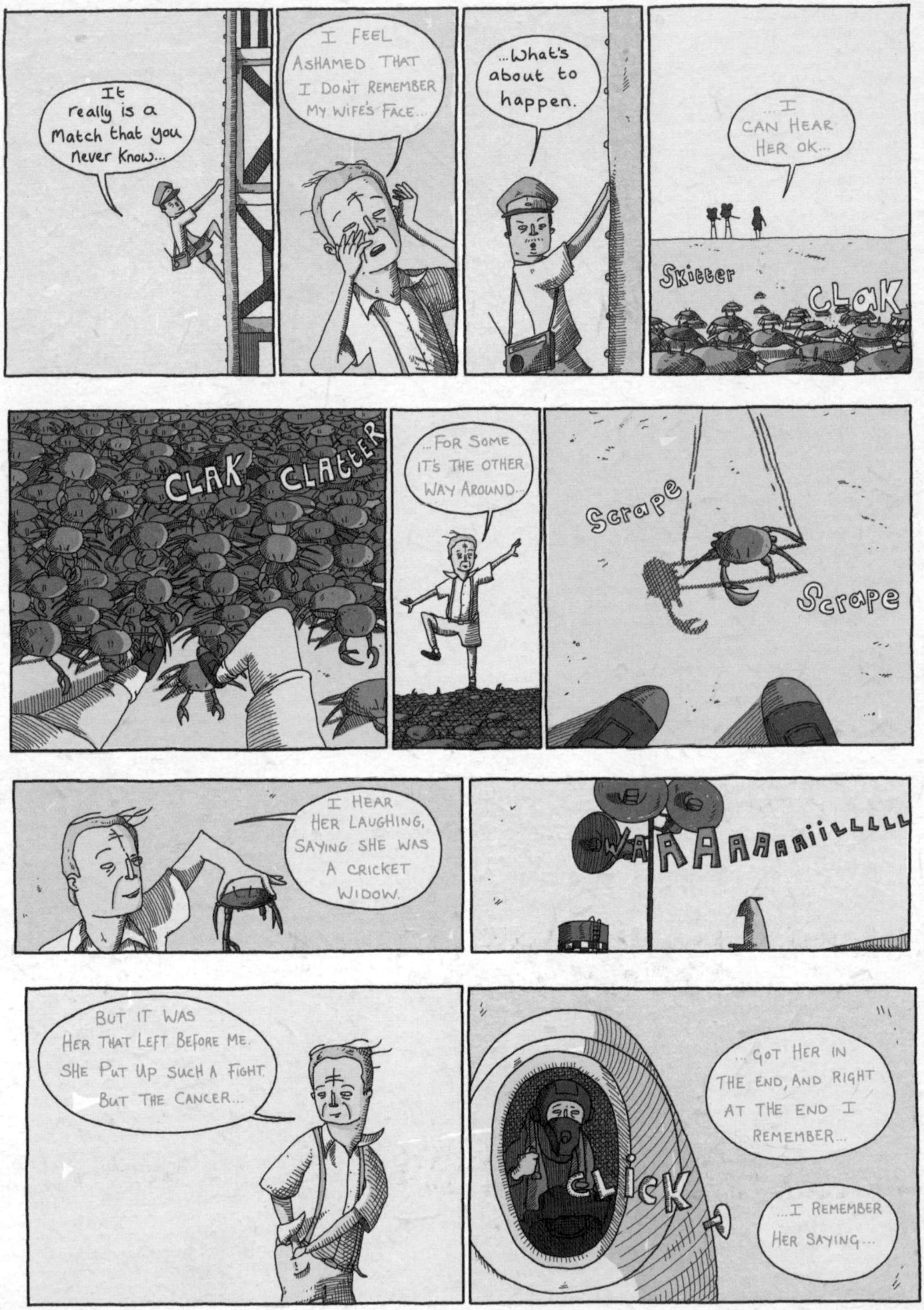
It really is a Match that you never Know...
I FEEL ASHAMED THAT I DON'T REMEMBER MY WIFE'S FACE...
...What's about to happen.
...I CAN HEAR HER OK...
Skitter
CLAK
CLAK
CLAtteR
...FOR SOME IT'S THE OTHER WAY AROUND...
Scrape
Scrape
I HEAR HER LAUGHING, SAYING SHE WAS A CRICKET WIDOW.
WAAAAAARiiLLLLL
BUT IT WAS HER THAT LEFT BEFORE ME. SHE PUT UP SUCH A FIGHT. BUT THE CANCER...
...GOT HER IN THE END, AND RIGHT AT THE END I REMEMBER...
CLICK
...I REMEMBER HER SAYING...

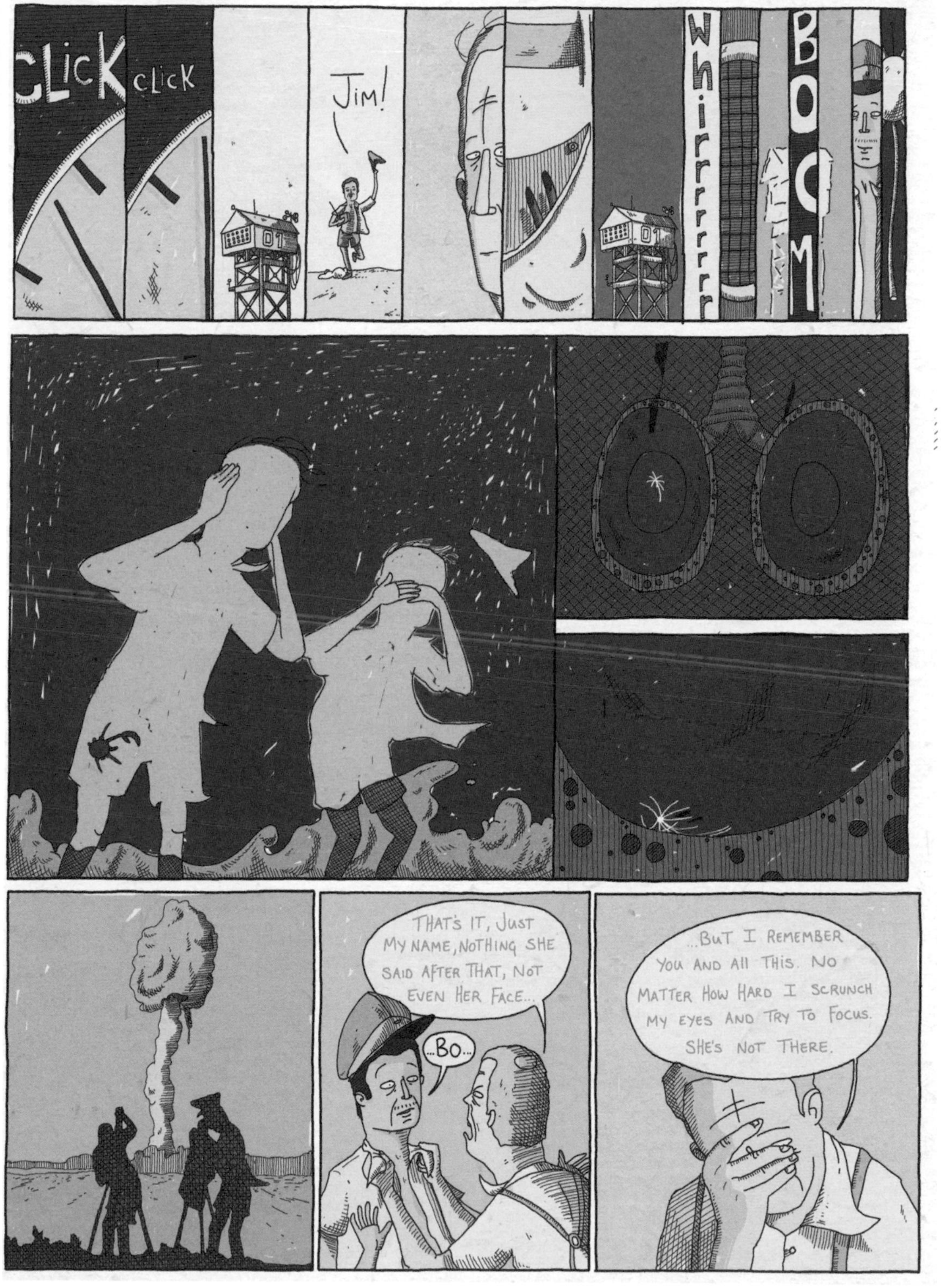
CLICK
CLICK
JIM!
Whirrrrrr
BOOM
THAT'S IT, JUST MY NAME, NOTHING SHE SAID AFTER THAT, NOT EVEN HER FACE...
...BO...
...BUT I REMEMBER YOU AND ALL THIS. NO MATTER HOW HARD I SCRUNCH MY EYES AND TRY TO FOCUS. SHE'S NOT THERE.

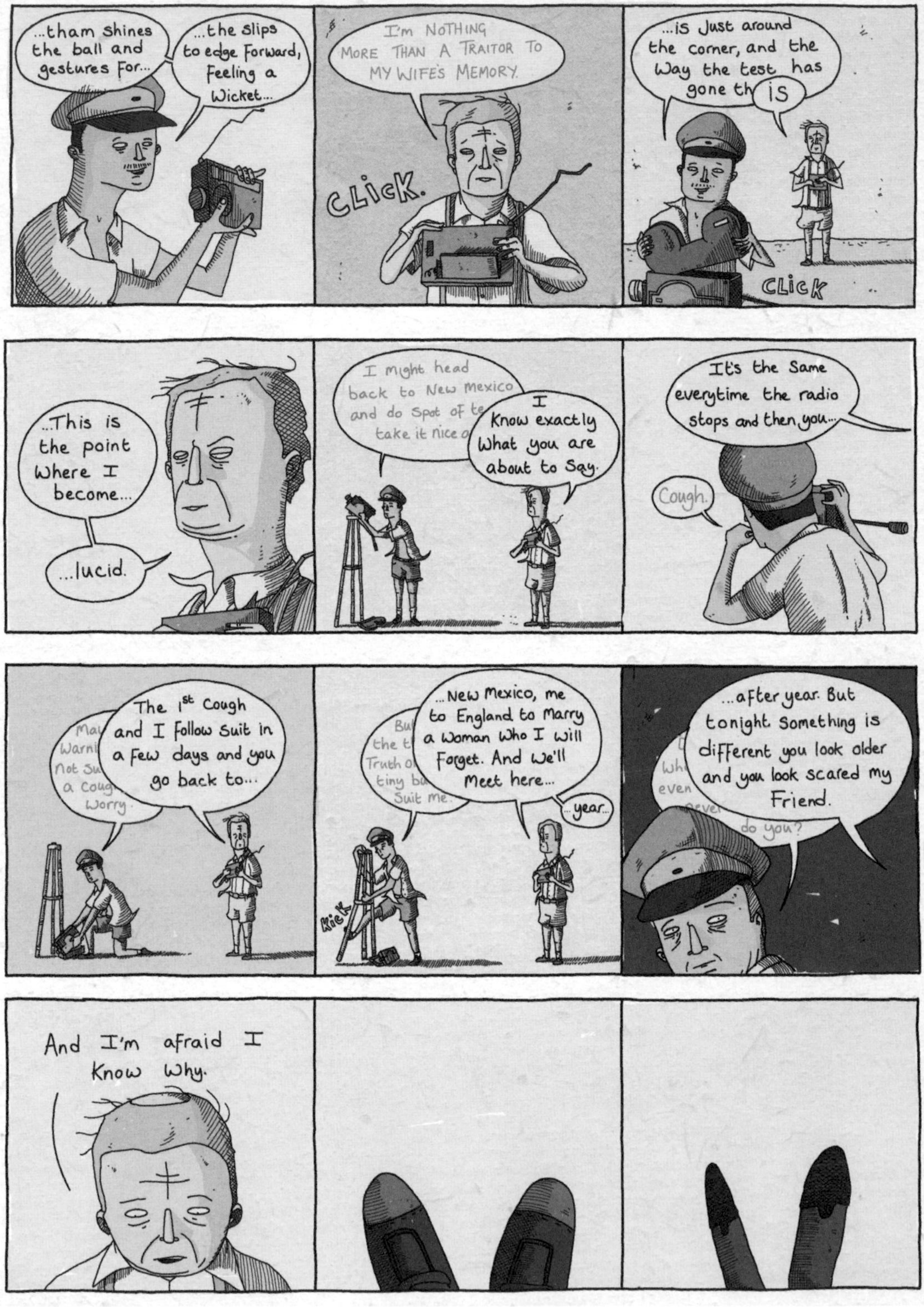
...tham shines the ball and gestures For...
...the slips to edge Forward, Feeling a Wicket...
I'm NOTHING MORE THAN A TRAITOR TO MY WIFE'S MEMORY.
CLICK.
...is Just around the corner, and the Way the test has gone th
IS
CLICK
...This is the point Where I become...
...lucid.
I might head back to New mexico and do Spot of te
take it nice o
I Know exactly What you are about to Say.
It's the Same everytime the radio stops and then you...
Cough.
The 1st Cough and I follow suit in a Few days and you go back to...
...New mexico, me to England to Marry a Woman Who I will Forget. And We'll Meet here...
...year...
Suit me.
Kick
...after year. But tonight Something is different you look older and you look scared my Friend.
do you?
And I'm afraid I Know Why.

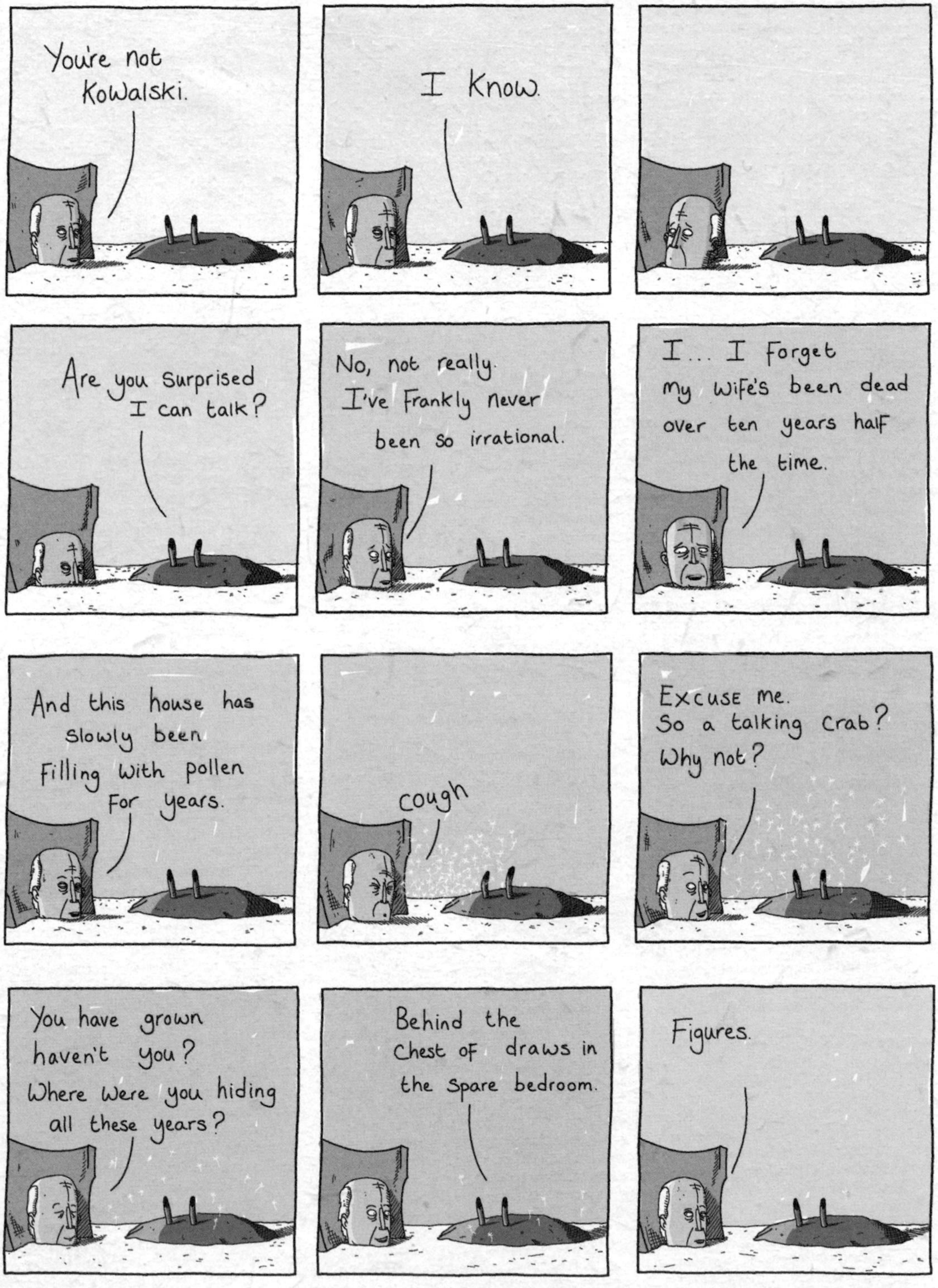
You're not Kowalski.
I Know.
Are you surprised I can talk?
No, not really. I've Frankly never been so irrational.
I... I Forget my wife's been dead over ten years half the time.
And this house has slowly been Filling with pollen For years.
cough
Excuse me. So a talking crab? Why not?
You have grown haven't you? Where were you hiding all these years?
Behind the chest of draws in the spare bedroom.
Figures.

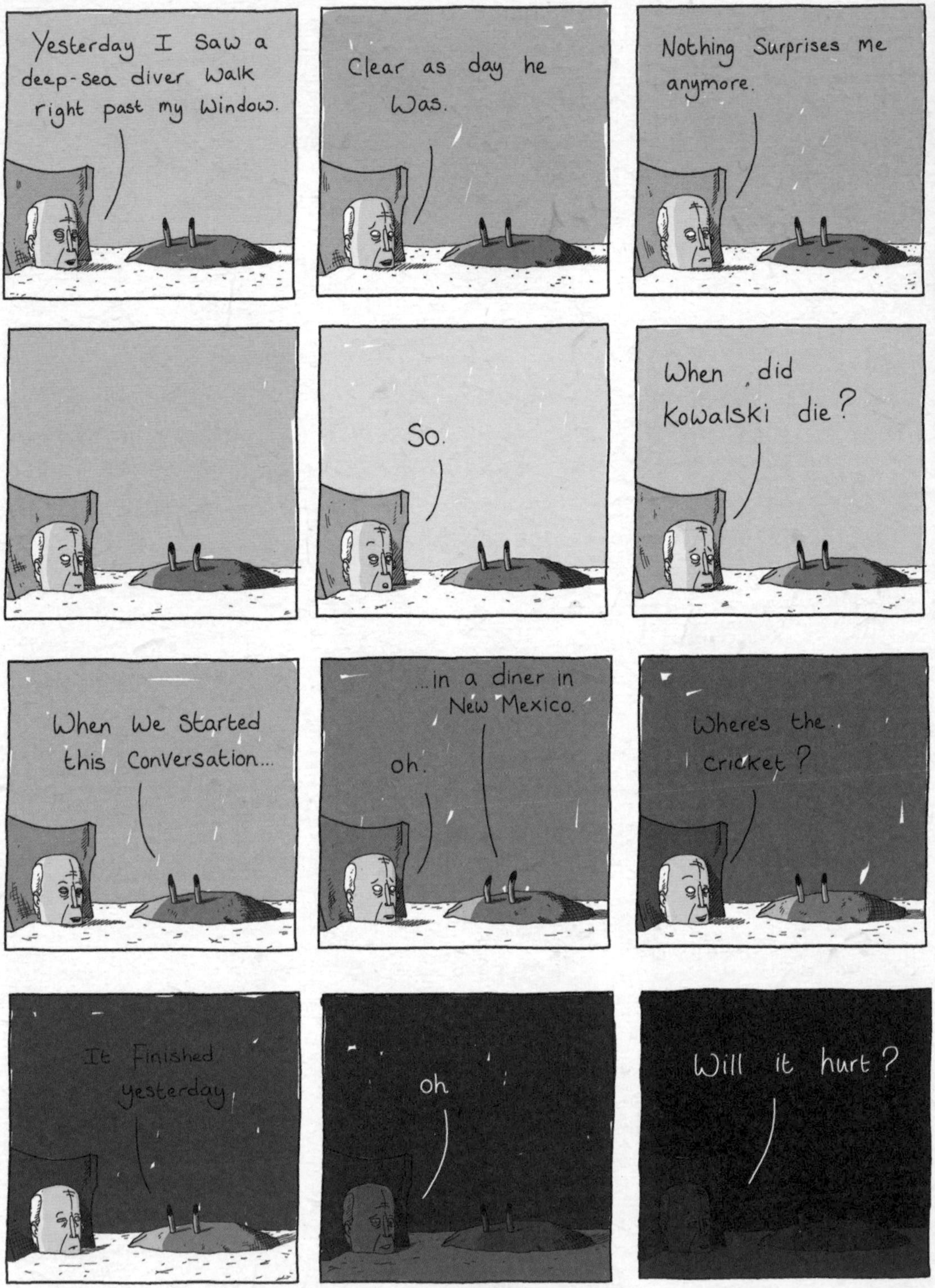
Yesterday I saw a deep-sea diver walk right past my window.
Clear as day he was.
Nothing surprises me anymore.
So.
When did Kowalski die?
When we started this conversation...
oh.
...in a diner in New Mexico.
Where's the cricket?
It finished yesterday.
oh
Will it hurt?

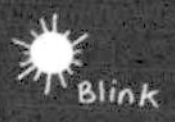
Blink

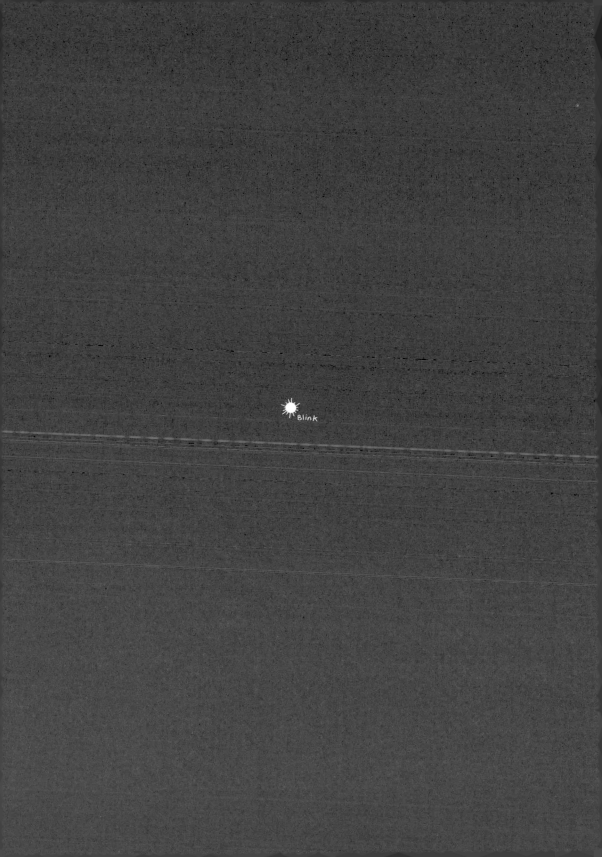

Published BY
Jonathan CaPe.

2 4 6 8 1 0 9 7 5 3 1

copyright ©
JuLian Hanshaw 2011

I Dream A
Highway

© Gillian Welch

First published in Great Britain in 2012 by
Jonathan CaPe
Random House, 20 Vauxhall Bridge Road
London. SW1V 2SA.
ISBN 9780224096447

The Random House Group limited makes every effort to ensure that the papers used in its books are Made From trees that have been legally Sourced from Well managed and credibly certified forests. our paper procurements policy can be found at WWW.randomhouse.co.uk/paper.htm

Printed and bound in China by C and C offset printing Co Ltd

www.rbooks.co.uk
Addresses for companies Lithin the Random House Group limited Can be found at www.randomhouse.co.uk/offices.htm

THE RANDOM HOUSE Group Limited reg no. 954009

A CIP Catalogue record For this book is available from the British Library.

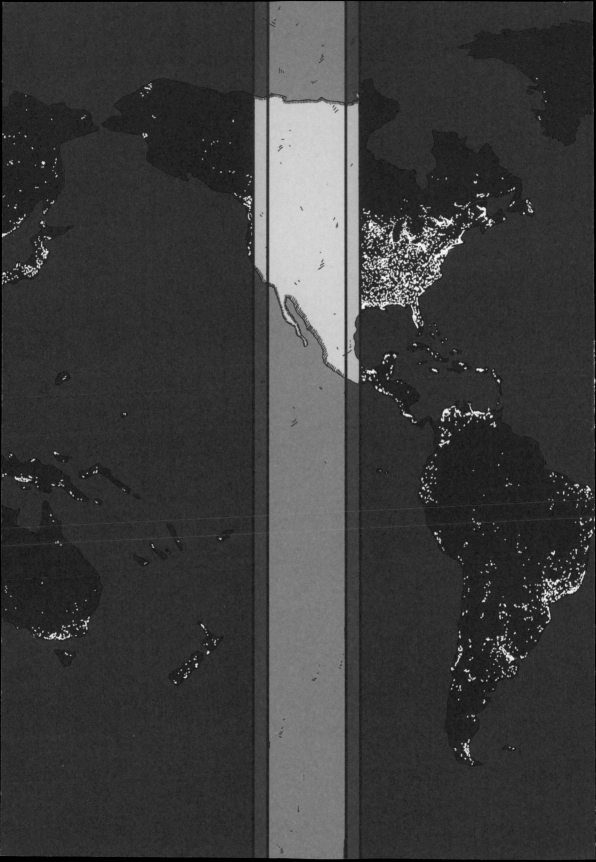